The Twelve Quickies of Christmas
Volume 1

Rachel Bo   R. Casteel

Lora Leigh   Kate Douglas

Shiloh Walker   Ashleigh Raine

ELLORA'S CAVE
ROMANTICA PUBLISHING

Angel in Moonlight

By Ashleigh Raine

Being a Polgaran Pleasure goddess isn't all it's cracked up to be. Sex isn't exactly boring, but it is just sex, limited emotion involved. Lita craves the intrigue of strong human emotions. Her wish is granted, to spend a year among humans, learning and experiencing their emotions. Then destiny throws her for quite a loop when she's pulled into Ben's arms and discovers just how wonderful love is. But the clock is ticking. If she stays, she'll lose everything, but if she leaves Ben, she'll lose even more.

Men of August: August Heat

By Lora Leigh

Join the August Family for Christmas. It's been a little more than a year since Cade, Brock and Sam wrestled their lives back from the woman determined to destroy them. Join them in this first August family Christmas celebration, August Heat, and see if their wives have been naughty or nice, or if the brothers must show them once again how proper August wives should act.

The Toymaker

By R. Casteel

Samantha, widowed with two small children on the Missouri frontier, struggles to survive through the harsh winter. When she gives the small toymaker named Claudius shelter from a storm, little miracles begin to happen. But are they enough to restore love, and her belief in the Magic of Christmas.

Make Me Believe

By Shiloh Walker

Chelly is going nuts…she thinks. And she's fighting for the right to keep her little boy. Right before Christmas, her ex announces he is going to sue for custody of their child. Because she is losing her mind. She is talking to a man who doesn't exist. A tall, sexy creature with wicked blue eyes and magic in his hands. And he can't possibly exist.

After all, elves aren't real.

Just A Little Magic

By Kate Douglas

Beth Adams expected a proposal of marriage on Christmas Eve. What she gets is a wanna-be Santa Claus who's just gotten pink-slipped. Dominic Claus isn't merely good looking, he's perfect…he's just not Santa material. Beth could care less, especially once she discovers that Dom is a lot more than a good looking guy in a Santa suit—he's the lover of her dreams, toys included. Unfortunately, he actually thinks he's an elf. Differences aside, Beth discovers that all it takes is Just a Little Magic to find true love.

Ringing in the Season

By Rachel Bo

Christmas is only two days away, and Traci Campbell has never felt more miserable. Her seventeen-year marriage seems on the verge of failure. Rick makes no time for the kids, for her…they haven't made love in four months. She can't stand the thought of losing Rick, but her heartfelt appeal a month ago appears to have meant nothing to him.

But a determined husband can make a lot happen in a few short weeks, and a very unusual treasure hunt leads Traci on an erotic journey down memory lane. Can love, determination, and five tiny golden rings save a marriage?

An Ellora's Cave Romantica Publication

www.ellorascave.com

The Twelve Quickies of Christmas Volume 1

ISBN 1419950711, 9781419950711
ALL RIGHTS RESERVED.
Angel in Moonlight Copyright © 2003 Ashleigh Raine.
August Heat Copyright © 2003 Lora Leigh.
Make Me Believe Copyright © 2003 Shiloh Walker.
Just a Little Magic Copyright © 2003 Kate Douglas.
Ringing in the Season Copyright © 2003 Rachel Bo.
The Toymaker Copyright © 2003 R. Casteel.
Cover art by Syneca.

This book printed in the U.S.A. by Jasmine–Jade Enterprises,
LLC.

Trade paperback Publication November 2004

THE TWELVE QUICKIES OF CHRISTMAS
VOLUME 1

ANGEL IN MOONLIGHT
Ashleigh Raine

ജ

Dedication

&

To Honey and BeeBie, we'd never have made it this far
without you holding our hands...and our hearts...

To Gail, for opening her home.

To Bree, for crying happy tears.

To our Fake Reality group. For being there every day, for
the unending support and for always demanding more.
You keep us smilin'.

Chapter One

∽

The tall, majestically engraved doors opened, affording Lita entrance into the High Chamber. This was her first time within these walls and for some reason she'd thought it would be different. Lita had imagined the room as cold and devoid of color, but the warm lighting and murals of Polgaran life adorning the walls were actually somewhat welcoming.

She forced her feet to propel her forward, down the long stretch of open space, toward the tables where the Controllers presided. They sized her up, scrutinizing her so closely she could feel their heavy stares right through her skin to the very core of her body. For the first time in her life, she wished her clothing offered a bit more modesty. She took a deep breath, keeping her jitteriness at bay, forcing herself to remain cool and calm on the outside as protocol required. This was her only chance to ask for what her heart truly wanted so she willed her excitement not to screw this up.

Lita stepped onto the interrogation platform. Many lives had been judged on the very same white square of marble beneath her feet. Her nerves raged to explosive proportions. Imorga, High Controller, nodded toward the Herald. Lita immediately bowed her head and clasped her hands behind her back, showing the proper respect for the Controllers as the Herald began. "Lita, of the Damescine sect, high Platine quadrant, first time requesting audience of Controllers. Humbly petitioning permission for withdrawal from Polgara."

At the Herald's words, some of the Controllers burst into laughter. Lita cringed. She had known her petition would be considered unusual. Everyone wanted to come to Polgara; no one wanted to leave. Amid the fading chuckles, Lita heard clicking and sliding and snapping. It sounded like they were looking her up in the main directory, seeking something in her past that would explain her desires. But they wouldn't find it in their directories.

Lita remained in her stance of obeisance, waiting for the Controllers to give her permission to move. If it didn't come soon, her calm, collected exterior was going to be rattled away by her shaking, quaking interior.

"By my lead, Lita, you may naturalize. I would certainly benefit from seeing your eyes as you stand before me while petitioning such a large request."

Lita took a deep breath and lifted her head to meet the penetrating stares of those who held her fate in their hands. Her attention rested on Imorga as she continued.

"We will consider your petition if you would express your reasons for requesting departure from our fine world. You are aware that this may be your life's only chance to speak in our presence."

Lita nodded in reply as she tried to find the right words. "I seek knowledge of other worlds. I have the desire to learn how other beings live outside of our dimension, to further discern what brings others to Polgara."

She couldn't tell the Controllers the full reason she wanted to leave, because they would never understand. For twelve years, her companion, Stephan, had sought her out each time he'd come to Polgara. They had shared their bodies, their passions and their desires, but love was never involved until the last time he visited. But it wasn't love for Lita. Stephan had found his heart link and Lita had sensed the depth of the love Stephan would share with his woman. Although Lita was quite happy for him, the joy also made her hunger. Human emotions were so much stronger than Polgaran emotions and Lita wished to identify and experience them for herself.

Imorga shook her head. Lita's stomach clenched. Was she being so quickly dismissed? "Have we not respected and cared for you as Pleasurers require? Why would you seek to learn the darker, non-pleasurable side of existence? There is no place as perfect as Polgara."

"Yes, High Controller Imorga, I have been treated with great esteem as befitting my station. What I seek is to understand the differences between Polgara and other dimensions, to offer that regard to my future companions. I would like to visit a human dimension."

"You want to experience human emotions? In a human dimension? Have you no idea how cruel humans can be? I assure you a human existence is nowhere near the exaltation you afford it. Be it in day-to-day activity, emotion, or environment, a human existence can be quite chaotic and potentially dangerous." Imorga cast a glance down the table at her fellow Controllers and they nodded in agreement.

Lita's pulse raced. They were going to deny her. She had to convince them otherwise. Although far from rational, Lita knew she absolutely needed to experience more than a life of lust and pleasure on Polgara. "Please understand, I do not seek to leave forever. I want only to experience human emotions for all their splendor and reckless abandon. I cannot do that here on Polgara. I know it displeases you that I seek to leave Polgara, but High Controller Imorga, if this was not so paramount to my vitality and experience, I would not waste what could be my life's only chance to speak in your presence."

Gliding her fingers back and forth over the table in front of her, Imorga met the eyes of all her peers. Lita watched, hopeful, near desperate. She'd never desired something so badly in her life.

Imorga returned her stare to Lita. "I shall grant you one year in a human dimension. You must return promptly at the end of that time. If we are forced to retrieve you from that dimension, you shall forfeit all memory of your life away from Polgara. Do not forget, the existence of Polgara and the Pleasure gods and goddesses that serve here are a secret most of humanity is not privy to. If you in any way compromise our existence, if you bring undue attention to yourself, the same punishments will apply. I should hope your trip provides all that you seek. Lita, you have one year. You are hereby dismissed."

Chapter Two

೫

Lita knew she was going to die. Shivers wracked her frozen body, and her teeth clacked together uncontrollably. Ice-cold wind pierced her clothing, the flimsy material of her dress offering no protection from its harsh attack.

Something somewhere had gone horribly wrong. Whenever Lita had questioned Stephan about his dimension, he'd spoken of beautiful twilights over water and waves crashing onto sandy beaches. When she'd asked him where he would go if he could ignore his Shadow Walker duties, he'd talked about tropical islands where the sun shone all the time. So she'd chosen an island as her final destination in this dimension.

This place was not at all how Stephan had described an island.

Everything was miserably frigid and covered in an icy substance. If her travel bag hadn't included her toothbrush and other non-clothing essentials, she would have dropped it in a trashcan somewhere because none of the clothing she'd packed stood a chance against the chill.

Lights beckoned in the windows of the buildings towering over her. Although her feet were numb—her soft leather slippers completely soaked through—she forced herself to keep moving forward, hoping that she might find somebody who could help her, someone who could explain how Manhattan Island could be so cold.

A loud blaring noise caught her off guard and a bright yellow vehicle sped past, drenching her in dirty ice water. She looked down, not surprised to see small bits of ice clinging to her hair, and her nipples frozen peaks stabbing through the front of her dress. For just one moment she wanted to sit down and give up, or tread back into the trees where she'd arrived and beg the Controllers to let her return to Polgara.

But even though she'd never been so wretchedly cold, something about this world enigmatically called out to her, even through such misery. She turned down another street. If she didn't find some kind of shelter soon, she'd likely turn into an ice sculpture.

Another vehicle like the one from earlier stopped in front of her and a heavily bundled woman, arms full of bags and brightly colored boxes, emerged from its depths. One of her precariously placed parcels slid off the pile and into the ice on the ground. The woman didn't seem to notice as she headed toward a building.

Lita bent to retrieve the fallen item, her frozen fingers fumbling to grasp the small, cheerfully wrapped package. "Wait. You dropped something."

The woman pushed the door open with her foot and threw a glance back over her shoulder. "Whoa, thanks. You startled me. I didn't see anyone over my pile of goodies. Give me a sec to set these down and I'll grab it from you." The woman disappeared inside.

Lita stepped closer to the open door. Heat poured from inside and another involuntary shudder wracked her small frame. She closed her eyes and tried to soak in as much of the warmth as possible, reminding herself that if she ever got the opportunity to go to another dimension again, she would take the time to do some solid research.

Without any warning, strong arms surrounded her and she was lifted off her feet and pulled into the thawing heat of the building. She tried to grab hold of something to anchor her, instead dropping the package and her small bag of belongings. Lita opened her eyes to see a booted foot kicking the door shut, closing out the cold.

In the back of her mind an unfamiliar instinct kicked in that she should fight, run, hide, that she should be scared. But her empathic abilities kicked in as well and she knew without a doubt that this man was not someone she needed to fear.

Pressed against his body, Lita welcomed his warmth into her. She fought the urge to nuzzle deeper into the pleasurable heat. Looking down at the large arms surrounding her, she felt the strange compulsion to cover them with her hands, to see what they looked like together. As though he'd read her mind, he took her hands in his and began rubbing the life back into her fingers with a touch so gentle and caring, it nearly took her breath away.

She tilted her head back, wanting to see the face of the man whose touch echoed throughout every inch of her body. But all she could see were his eyes, such a dark blue they were almost black, staring down at her, calling her to him. Lita became lost. There were layers of life in his eyes. Something lost and something desperate to be reclaimed.

"Ben?!"

The voice echoed loudly in the empty hall, painfully jerking Lita out of the man's compelling stare. He cautiously separated himself from her, then disappeared down a hallway, a door closing quietly behind him. The expression on the woman's face was one of pure astonishment. "Well, I'll be goddamned. My brother, Ben...he hasn't shown interest in anything or anyone since... I don't know what got into him. I'm sorry if he frightened you. Ummm...are you all right?"

Lita's mind and body spun dizzily from the aftereffects of his touch and the look in his eyes. She'd felt as though she were being pulled within his mind, and if she were to let go and fall into him, he wouldn't hesitate to catch her, drawing her so deep within him she wouldn't ever want to resurface. Her words came out as a whisper. "Yes. I'm okay." Lita looked down the hallway where Ben had disappeared. "He didn't scare me at all." She returned her attention to the woman and gave her a small smile. "He just wanted to take care of me."

"Yeah, he's like that…or…used to be like that. He…" The woman let out a soft sigh and slowly shook her head, then her gaze returned to Lita and her eyes lit up with concern. "Wait. Is that all you were wearing? It's below freezing outside." She hesitated then reached for Lita's hand. "What's your name, hon? I'm Gail Stanton."

Lita let Gail take her hand. Her touch was sweet and caring, like her brother's. "I'm Lita."

Gail gently squeezed Lita's hand. "Such a pretty name. You know, it's Christmas Eve and well… Would you join Ben and me for dinner tonight?" Her face lightened in a sweet smile. "I understand if you have other plans. It's just that you brought some life back to my brother…please, let me give you something in return. I know Ben would be delighted to have a guest. Christmas was always his favorite holiday."

"I'd like that very much. Thank you." Comforting warmth swept through Lita as Gail took her by the hand and led her into the apartment.

* * * * *

Lita had never expected she would begin to experience stronger emotions after such a short time among humans. There was such freedom in knowing she was on her own, that she didn't have to answer to anyone but herself.

Even though she'd only met two humans so far, their hearts were good, and far from cruel like the Controllers had warned her about. Gail was a beautiful and kind soul, offering Lita food, clothing and even opening her home.

Ben was still a mystery. When Lita thought of him, it was as though she was stepping into the unknown. There was confusion and astounding beauty swirling together in a paroxysm of chaos.

Lita leaned forward and stared into the mirror, which was still foggy from her recent shower. She almost expected to see some type of visible change in her appearance. Other than the thick white sweater and leggings Gail had given her, she still looked like the same Lita. But inside, she *felt* so much. Confusion, joy, laughter, sorrow, anticipation, fear…even desire. Did all humans feel so much all the time? It was overwhelming, but she felt more alive than she'd ever felt before.

With a new bounce to her step, Lita opened the door and walked out of the bathroom. The mingled scents of dinner practically engulfed her, prompting her stomach to growl appreciatively. If her time in this dimension was starting with a meal that smelled this good, she knew it was going to be a great year.

Walking into the dining room, Lita stopped in her tracks, soaking in the awe-inspiring sight before her. It looked as though Gail had cooked a meal to feed hundreds of people. Or was this just another difference between here and Polgara? Did humans really consume *that* much food? There were plates and platters and bowls full to overflowing. A couple bottles of wine graced the table as well. Until that moment, she hadn't even realized just how thirsty she was.

Then her eyes met Ben's. Just like earlier, she felt drawn to him, and as though pulled by an unseen hand, she walked around the table and sat down next to him. "Is it okay if I sit…" Her sentence remained unfinished. Somehow she knew he wanted her close to him.

"Merry Christmas, Lita." Gail laughed as she came into the dining room with a plate of sliced ham and set it in the middle of the table. "Did you enjoy your shower?"

"It was wonderful, actually." Lita smiled up at Gail. "This all looks so delicious. There's so much food."

"Family tradition. We always have good leftovers during the holidays. But truthfully, this was easy to throw together.

You should see our place during Thanksgiving. I cook for days." Gail grinned and sat down across from them both.

Lita's attention shifted to Ben as he poured wine into a glass and held it out to her. Gail's gasp echoed in the sudden silence of the room.

Lita took the glass from him, letting the tips of her fingers graze over his. With just that little touch, the deep pull between them began in earnest and she lifted her gaze to his. Fear, pain, need, desire. Rampant emotions hurled toward her and she placed her free hand above his wrist, her anchor in the storm. He needed help. He was trapped inside. What had happened to him?

Lita forced her gaze away before she became lost. She took a deep breath to regain control, then managed a small smile. "Thank you, Ben. You read my mind."

She tried to remove her hand from his arm, but he covered her hand with his, stroking her fingers like he'd done earlier, soothing and calming. An apology.

Gail let out a ragged sob, pulling Lita further out of the trance Ben held over her. She looked at Ben's sister, who watched them both, her eyes wide in wonder, one hand fisted over her mouth, holding back her sobs. Gail lowered her hand to the table and nervously ironed out imaginary wrinkles in the tablecloth. Her voice was a soft whisper as she spoke. "You must be a miracle worker or something. My brother's been little more than a shell for over a year now." Tears streamed down her face. "Who are you?"

Lita froze. How could she answer that? "Just someone who understands what it's like to be trapped. How long has Ben been like this? What happened to him?"

Gail swiped a hand across her face, wiping away her tears. "I don't really know for sure. He was coming home from work, just like usual…he's a senior graphic designer. That night he was supposed to meet some co-workers for a drink but he never made it. I was beside myself with worry for the next three days because he was nowhere to be found. I looked everywhere I could think of. On the fourth morning I opened my door and he was just sitting there on the steps like he didn't know what else to do. I almost wasn't sure it was him because he was just gazing off...like he was completely lost in thought. I got him to come inside, but he's never spoken. And the doctors can't find anything wrong with him. He eats, takes care of himself, showers, gets dressed every morning...but he doesn't interact with anyone. It's like he's in his own world. Until now."

Lita's mind raced. She'd heard stories of demons that fed off the creative minds and souls of others. Usually, the victims ended up dead, or the small part of them remaining was so weak they could never find their way out again. But there were some that were strong enough, and their souls repaired themselves. Could that have been what happened to Ben? She knew he was trapped inside himself, that who he was still existed. She *felt* it. Maybe he just couldn't find his way out?

Gail took a deep breath and looked across the table at her brother. "The doctors think that one day he'll just snap out of it, that it's all in his mind. And maybe it is, but I can't imagine what could've happened to him to make him lose his way like this." Gail reached out her hand and placed it over Lita's free hand. "Lita, my brother was...is a good man. Everyone loved him. He had a good life. And he's all I have left. Whatever you have with him..." Gail lowered her head. "I know I sound crazy, but it's just that for some reason my brother is responding to you when he hasn't responded to anyone else. You give me hope. And for that, I thank you."

Lita smiled at the beautiful woman across from her and squeezed her hand, before pulling away from her grasp. Lita held up her wine glass in toast. "Merry Christmas, Gail. May all your hopes come true." The two women clinked their glasses as Lita silently prayed that she could help Ben find his way home.

Chapter Three

80

"Are you sure you don't mind sleeping on the couch?" Gail asked as she carried a stack of blankets into the living room. "I can sleep here if you want to crash on my bed."

"I'm sure. You've already given me so much. I'm not going to kick you out of your bed, too. Besides, I like it here. I've never slept next to a tree covered in lights before. It's beautiful. And so many gaily wrapped packages. I think I like this Christmas thing." Lita moved to the couch to help Gail lay out the blankets.

"I still can't believe you've never experienced Christmas before. Where did you say you were from?"

"A place far from here in spirit and location." Lita paused as Gail gave her a funny grin. "But I'm really happy to be here now."

"Full of mystery, aren't you? Okay, if you have nowhere else to go, can I convince you to join us in our celebration tomorrow? Eggnog and carols, and —"

Lita laughed. "I'd love to spend more time with you and Ben. Thank you for everything. You've both been so kind."

Gail finished making up the couch and turned and embraced Lita. "You're welcome. There's something special about you. I just know it." Gail stepped away, a light blush covering her cheeks. "If you need anything, just holler. I'll see you in the morning." She turned off the overhead light on her way out of the room.

Lita settled on the edge of the couch, not ready to snuggle comfortably under the blankets. Ben filled her every thought. The man he used to be was locked deep within himself, fighting to come out. But was there anything she could do to help him?

She wasn't a healer by conventional definition. Her touch couldn't fuse a broken arm or close a wound. But as a Pleasure goddess, her hands healed in other ways. She gave pleasure to soothe, and to help the mind, body and soul relax.

Would it be enough to bring Ben out of his locked-in state? He wanted his life back. She knew this by his touch and the look in his eyes. But to give him that chance, she'd have to walk a fine line to avoid calling attention to herself. The Controllers would pull her back to Polgara, erase her memories of this dimension and maybe even punish her further if they felt she'd compromised Polgara in any way.

For some reason, none of that mattered. She'd help Ben however she could and suffer whatever consequences came of it. Her mind made up, Lita rose to her feet, ready to head down the hall to the room she'd seen Ben retreat to earlier.

He was watching her, standing in the shadows at the edge of the living room. Somehow, she wasn't surprised. Ben knew her movements before she made them.

Silently, he walked toward her, still dressed in the dark green dress shirt and black slacks he'd worn to dinner. She stepped around the couch to meet him halfway. When they were close, Ben reached out and took her hand in his.

Emotion stirred within her, the lonely chaos she'd briefly sampled earlier. But a beacon of hope shone through as well. She couldn't let him down.

Together they walked down the hall and into his room, unsure of who was leading whom. They stopped at the edge of his queen-sized bed, a pool of moonlight washing over them with a subtle glow. Ben took both of her hands in his, and cautiously, Lita lifted her gaze and lost herself in his eyes. Her heart pounded painfully, making it difficult for her to breathe. For the first time, she was afraid of what she was going to do.

What if she couldn't bring him out of his locked-in state? What if she made things worse?

Ever so carefully, Ben's hands slid up her arms than neck, until he was cradling her face. With the softest of touches, he lowered his face to hers, until they were resting forehead to forehead.

Desire flooded through Lita. A desire to help him, but also so much more. A desire to be with him, love him, and take away his chaos. A desire to make everything in his world okay.

Lita raised her hands to his temples and began massaging his scalp. Every touch was meant to stimulate the senses and relax the body. She combed her fingers through the soft brown locks curling at the base of his neck. His slow exhale burned hot against her throat and she arched into him.

Oh Goddess, she needed this man, needed him to be healed, to be with her completely. Moving her hands to his face, she ran her fingers along the line of his jaw. The rough sandpaper feel burned against her fingertips. She wanted to feel that roughness as he kissed her neck, the scraping sting as he possessed her body with his mouth. She wanted to hear his voice growling out her name, feel him thrusting hot and hard inside her.

Lita stopped in mid-caress. This was a healing…not a seduction.

Then his arms circled her body, further pulling her against him. She trembled at the full body contact. Even through her clothing his touch excited her. And her touch obviously stimulated him. His rock hard cock pulsed against her stomach. She had to regain control, to remember exactly what she was trying to do.

"Ben…I need you to look at me."

He lifted his head, still keeping their bodies close. His eyes sought hers and she shivered under the onslaught. With raging intensity, his thoughts pummeled her. Chaos still reigned inside of him, his yearning to be free battling for survival. But the strongest emotion was his need for her.

Lita had felt craving and desire from her clients in the past. But she had never felt this depth of attachment, the feeling that his thoughts, even in the chaos, completed her. "You feel it too, don't you?" she whispered.

He answered by lowering his head and kissing her.

Any idea that she could remain in control disappeared as his kiss lit her senses. She stood in a whirlwind of tangled emotions, his and hers, joining together, filling her. It was impossible to tell where his thoughts ended and hers began. Resolutely, she let herself lose control, realizing that to bring him back, she had to merge with him without restraint.

The taste of him burned hot on her tongue, a mixture of peppermint and the sweet wine from dinner. Yet at the same time, she knew the way she tasted to him. It was an exchange of thoughts and hungers. All in one kiss.

In the back of her mind, behind the lust and pulsing desire burning her core, she saw a cord strung tight between them. A solid connection merging them together. Lita's heart rate sped up. It had to be a mistake.

Ben was her heart link...her soulmate. She'd seen it before in others, had known when a connection burned true between people. But Polgarans didn't have heart links—it went against their nature to be linked to only one other. Yet there was no denying it, and nothing could make it go away. They were bound forever, no matter the consequences.

And if Ben discovered that link within himself, he could use it to find his way out.

She didn't know where she found the strength to stop kissing him. When he tried to pull her back, she shook her head. "No, Ben. Undress me. And let me undress you."

As though he'd only been awaiting her invitation, his hands swept under her borrowed sweater and carefully pulled it over her head. She wore nothing underneath. His eyes glowed appreciatively and he knelt down in front of her and kissed each pebbled nipple.

Lita's knees grew weak at the simple touches he bestowed upon her. Years and years of sex with hundreds of people, and she'd never felt like this or craved so deeply. Why this man? Why now?

Love. It was that simple. His touches were more than just physically pleasurable. They reached to her soul, filling the emptiness inside of her she'd never before realized existed. How would she be able to return to her duties as a Pleasurer? Sex with anyone but Ben would be cold…meaningless.

But she couldn't think about that now. Now she wanted to feel loved and love in return.

Ben lowered his thumbs beneath the waistband of the leggings and tugged them off her body. He stayed on his knees, his hands holding her hips. Gently he placed a kiss at the top of her slit. Lita let out a soft whimper and sank down, letting his hands guide her to the floor.

Her hands shook as she unbuttoned his shirt. Inside her mind, she felt him pulling closer, using their heart link as a handhold, working his way fully out of the madness he'd been locked in for over a year. It was as though he'd wrested the control from her, and she was getting lost in his chaos. But this new experience didn't frighten her. Her body wanted him, yes. But so did her heart and soul.

When the shirt was removed, she discovered the strong muscles of his chest, shoulders and tight stomach. He was lean but toned and everything about him beckoned to her. She wanted hours to explore his body, days to learn every place he loved to be touched. Unable to stop herself, she moved closer, straddling his legs and ran her face over his chest, loving the feel and smell of him. She tongued his flat nipple, delighting in his masculine taste. He groaned and fisted his hands in her hair, holding her against him.

Lita could feel his cock throbbing through his pants, against her open pussy. Slowly she ground down against his cock, soaking the fabric of his pants with her juices. They both let out quiet moans.

In one swift movement, Ben stood up, taking her with him. He lowered her onto the bed, and then hurriedly removed his pants and briefs, freeing his cock from its confines. Newfound exuberance rippled through her body. Then he surged over her, the flesh of their bodies touching from head to toe. But he didn't enter her, not yet.

Lita knew there was more she was supposed to be doing. This wasn't about sex.

And then he kissed her and everything made sense. It wasn't only about sex between them. What they were going to share went far beyond anything that simple. Their minds and bodies were merging as they fought together to bring his soul out of where it was hiding.

This was about bringing him home.

Lita spread her thighs beneath him, wrapping one leg around his waist, inviting him to come inside. This was the first time she'd ever wanted a man so badly she thought she'd die without him inside her. One of his hands skimmed down her body and slid between her legs. He dipped a finger inside of her, slowly thrusting, pressing. Lita arched into his thrusts, wresting her lips from his so she could speak. "Ben…please. I need you. I need this. Come inside me. I'm yours, now. Free your mind and find me."

Ben's fingers grazed her skin, lighting a fire everywhere he touched. Finally he brought his hands back to her face, caressing her jaw, cheeks, even brushing his fingers lightly over her eyes. It was as though with his touch, he was memorizing her.

His hands came to a halt in her hair, holding her still beneath him. Then he looked down into her eyes. Lita gasped as the cord inside her pulled taut and a tidal wave of unleashed emotion rushed through her. The black chaos that filled him crumbled into nothingness as he sank into her, mind, body and soul. He'd broken free.

Heady outbursts of emotion rocketed through her. Hers, his, theirs. There was no separating them. Their thoughts mingled as their bodies mated. His cock filled her pussy, pressing against her womb with every downward stroke. She tightened her sheath around him, stopping him from pulling out, not wanting their joining to end. She could feel how badly he wanted to fill her with his sperm and knew he could feel her tension building inside. Back and forth, emotions, thoughts, desires flew and within moments they were both panting on the edge of fulfillment.

His hands cradled her face, holding their gazes steady as his thrusts increased in speed. The slick glide of his cock in and out of her became a branding on her soul. No lover had ever taken her so high. Lita stifled her cry as the first orgasm hit her, bursting inside her with explosive intensity. She kept her gaze locked with his and she knew he felt her pleasure.

He spoke then, the first words she'd heard from his lips. It came out in almost a growl, his voice hoarse from disuse. "Angel. Mine." Then he sealed his mouth over hers as his come flooded her cunt. Lita wrapped her arms around him. Holding him to her, feeling his pleasure, coming again with him, knowing she'd never be the same.

Knowing she had to disappear from his life by morning and could never see him again.

Chapter Four
December 21
One year later

ᔆᔆ

"And you're sure there's nothing we can do to convince you to stay on with us?" Dresden Mathers' deep voice filled the limousine. "I have some friends in the INS... You don't have to return to Poland."

Lita smiled up at the man who'd become like a father to her over the last eleven months. She looked around the car at Aimee and Mrs. Mathers—Colleen—and saw the family she'd always wanted and been blessed to have during her time in this dimension. How she wished she could tell them the truth about who she was and where she was from, make them understand that if it were her choice, she'd never leave. "I would stay if I could. You know that. But I have a duty to my people—"

Mrs. Mathers placed a hand on Lita's arm. "You're always welcome back, Lita. Always. Aimee loves you. We love you. You've been the best nanny we could ever have hoped for."

Tears filled Lita's eyes. "Thank you. I love all of you, too."

Aimee wrapped her tiny arms around Lita and leaned against her. "I'll miss you."

Lita stroked Aimee's auburn curls, a familiar, comforting gesture Lita had made hundreds of times. This time it brought an ache to her heart. Her time in this dimension was almost up. No more pillow fights with Aimee. No more excursions through Central Park. In three days she would step back through the portal and be a Pleasure goddess again.

But she was far from the same person who'd left New York one year ago.

She had come to this dimension to experience a life without boundaries, to understand the depth and range of emotions, to learn more about the human race in all its chaos and beauty.

New York had shown her what humanity was all about. Lita had grown to love the honking taxicabs, the buildings so tall they met the sky, and the bustle of people during rush hour. New York City teemed with life, a constant flow of contrasts—the best and worst of society living together in discordant harmony. Life was rougher, stranger and unpredictable in this dimension, but that's what made it beautiful.

Polgara, in all its perfection, could never match the vibrancy of humanity. It was a land of comfort and pleasure. But how could one appreciate comforts and pleasures without knowing pains and sorrows?

Lita sighed as she let her mind wander back to her first night here.

Ben.

The hollow emptiness inside echoed his name. He'd left a hole in her heart, showing her that the pain of loss never went away. She wondered what he was doing, if he'd gotten his life back, and if he ever thought of her.

Occasionally she felt a gentle tug on the heart link that bound them so closely together. Although she'd been tempted to open herself up to him again, to see if she could still feel him, hear his thoughts, be one with him, she'd firmly pushed the temptation away. Nothing could come of it. She couldn't change who she was, or the life that lay ahead of her.

Thank the Goddess for the memories, though. Lita had experienced love that night with Ben, a love that would haunt her for the rest of her existence. That was something she would never regret.

The car came to a stop in front of the hospital, and Lance, the chauffeur, got out and opened the door for the Mathers family. One last event as a nanny, then tonight she'd check herself into a hotel and spend her last three days just as a human. Walking the streets of New York, saying goodbye to the city she called home.

Lita gathered Aimee close and walked with the family into the hospital. She surrendered her cream wool coat and purse to the smiling coat check girl, then helped Aimee out of her jacket. A new children's wing was being dedicated tonight, and Dresden Mathers, head of the foundation that had donated the majority of the funding, was one of the guests of honor.

An extra sparkle of emotion and energy filled the air, buzzing across her skin like a lover's caress. At the same time, something else flickered to life inside of her, like a memory, or something nudging at the edge of awareness. Tinges of sorrow mixed with anticipation. It seemed to creep inside, filling her up until she could barely hold still. She looked around, trying to figure out what was affecting her so.

A string quartet played holiday music, and servers swept through the crowd with gleaming silver trays of drinks and hors d'oeuvres. The hospital was decorated for Christmas, tinsel, lights, mistletoe and holly filling every available space. Only one area remained clear, the wall at the entrance to the new wing, covered by a large black tarp. Scattered reporters and a news crew had parked themselves in the front, near where the dedication would take place.

Nothing in particular jumped out at her. And then it hit her. She was in a hospital. It had to be the residual emotions of the patients affecting her so strongly.

She let out a relieved laugh as the dedication ceremony began.

Just a few minutes into the ceremony, Lita felt a gentle tug on her hand. Aimee grinned up at her. "Lita. I need to go potty."

Lita smiled. "Okay, sweet cheeks, let's see if we can find a bathroom."

It was easier said than done. The hospital was a maze of rooms and hallways and it took them several minutes to find a public bathroom. Once Aimee was taken care of, they headed back toward the ceremony.

Lita made her way through the crowd, trying to get back to Dresden and Colleen. Suddenly she paused, goose bumps covering her flesh, the hair rising on the back of her neck. Something was wrong. People were pointing at her, their eyes wide in wonder, whispering words she couldn't hear over the noise of the crowd. Unsure, Lita picked Aimee up, holding her close. As a whole, the crowd's attention shifted to her, and they cleared a path for her to make her way to the front.

What was going on? Was she interrupting something?

Lita's gaze flitted over the guests dressed in their formal best, trying to find an answer to her questions. She froze as she saw what had everyone whispering in wonder.

The big black tarp covering the main wall at the entrance to the wing had been removed. A mural filled the wall, a larger than life image of a woman standing in snow, a filmy rose fabric delicately wrapped around her. Long, dark hair surrounded her upturned face, cheeks rosy from the cold.

But it was the almond-shaped violet eyes that made the mural come alive. The artist had captured a whirlwind of emotions in their depths. There were questions in the eyes, as well as need, love and a desire to understand life.

Aimee clapped happily, shocking Lita out of her trance. "Lita, it's you!"

Lita struggled to draw breath into her suddenly tight chest. How? What? Who?

There was only one answer that made sense. She searched the area for the man she knew was there. Her gaze was drawn directly through the crowd of tuxedo-clad men, to the only one that mattered. Ben stood just to the left of the mural, his eyes locked on her.

Their heart link flared brilliantly to life, pulling taut. Emotions crossed the distance. Disbelief, desire, need, love.

Then the second wave of emotions hit her with brute force.

Anger and betrayal.

Ben's mouth lifted in a grim smile. "Angel."

Chapter Five

ജ

Goddamn…his angel was real. A divine, heart-wrenching temptation, stepping through the crowd of people as beautifully as she'd come into his life nearly a year ago. All this time, he'd thought she was an ethereal angel from some other world, come to bring him back to the life he'd loved so dearly.

But so much for dreaming.

A knot had formed in his stomach the instant he had arrived at the hospital, and he'd thought it was just nerves. He'd given his speech, once again telling the story of his angel. It wasn't until this very moment that the last piece of the puzzle fell into place.

Bitter betrayal hit him like a punch in the gut, taking his breath away. She was someone's wife. The child on her hip made that abundantly clear. Then Dresden Mathers stepped to her side, leaning in close—familiarly. Lita nodded and brushed a kiss over the sweet cherub's head and transferred her into her father's waiting arms and out of the chaos of questioning reporters.

Ben's angel was the wife of *The* Dresden Mathers. No doubt living in an unimaginably luxurious mansion. He'd even liked Mr. Mathers when they'd met briefly, thought he was a good man. Ben snarled. They obviously had the same taste in women.

The night she'd stumbled upon his doorstep without so much as a coat had been some quick adventurous little escapade. Poor little rich girl. Slumming it up for a few hours of fun just to spice up her perfect little life with her perfect little family in her perfect big house. Why else would she have disappeared without a trace before morning?

Sure, Ben owed his recovery to her, but that didn't stop his heart from breaking. Lita had become the inspiration for his entire life, not just his paintings. He cursed himself. He'd pinned an otherworldly angel on a woman who was just that. A woman.

But something deep within him screamed that he was wrong. His chest tightened painfully, and his breath came in quick, short gasps. Like he just knew she was frozen in fear, terrified as the reporters closed in on her. Like she was shouting at the top of her lungs in sheer horror.

Without a second thought, he blasted through the sea of reporters, put an arm around her and ushered her toward the exit. The instant he made contact with her, his world shattered once more as her thoughts and emotions flooded his senses.

She wasn't married with children. She wasn't a liar. She was definitely a temptress, but that was just because of her beauty. Beauty only his loving angel could possess. He was shocked that any ill thoughts had crossed his mind in regard to this woman. How could he have made such horrible assumptions about her?

But how could he not? He'd spent the past year questioning both her disappearance and whether she was even real to begin with. Although part of him had known she had to exist. Even though he couldn't explain it, he'd never stopped feeling her. He didn't try to rationalize it. His life hadn't followed rules of logic since a dark and unfathomable evil had tried to rip his soul away.

Pushing through the crowd, Ben held Lita tightly against his chest, keeping out the throng of relentless story-seekers. He could hardly keep his voice from shaking as he spoke to the horde. "I'm sorry, but we have no comment. Please leave us be. I owe this woman my life."

The vultures kept shouting out their questions, following close behind them. Stroking her hair, Ben led her away, protecting her the only way he could. "Angel, are you okay?"

She nodded her head, but he felt a tornado of extreme emotions twisting through her. He tried to ignore the cameras flashing, recording their reunion for the ever-hungry press. After retrieving their jackets from the coat check, he helped her into a long creamy white overcoat. He couldn't help but wonder why she hadn't had it with her on the night they met. There were still so many mysteries about that night—about her—but his main concern was getting her somewhere they could finally talk in private.

Outside, he hailed a cab and instructed the driver to his place. They settled in as the cabbie sped away, their bodies only inches apart, their emotions even closer. Yet the distance seemed unbearable. Her whole body radiated an alarm he couldn't quite understand, but it was clear that the reporters had brought out a deep-seated fear. All he wanted to do was pull her into his arms and take away the chaos she was feeling.

Hesitantly, he reached over, taking her hands in his, warming them up just like he'd done when they first met, hoping she wasn't terrified of him as well. Lita's head shot up, her eyes wide. "I hadn't even realized they were cold."

"I guess I just knew before you did."

Those violet eyes he'd never forgotten filled with tears and she crumbled into his arms. He wrapped himself around her, holding her to him, this time planning on never letting her go. There were so many questions he wanted to ask, so many things he needed to tell her, but where could he start when the woman of his dreams showed up in the flesh?

Over the past year, he had used the link he'd shared with her to draw out his ideas and images so that he could paint her true to her beauty. Once the press had found out that his beautiful subject was the angel who'd healed him, his popularity had risen. His art was considered among the greatest for his ability to relay emotion. He didn't know how to tell everyone that he just painted what he saw in his heart for his beautiful angel.

When they arrived at his place, he threw a handful of money at the driver and helped Lita out of the car. He was afraid to move from her side, thinking that if he turned away she would disappear again. Once inside his place, he paused. He knew where he wanted to take her. Straight to bed to make her his, possess her until she never left his side. Primal instinct demanded that satisfaction.

Instead he helped her remove her coat, relishing the vision she made in shades of white. It was as though she'd stepped right out of his memories. His blood heated in response to the mixture of memories and her presence. Quickly, he shed his overcoat and tuxedo jacket, removing his cufflinks and rolling up his sleeves. They watched each other, the space between them simmering with longing and tension.

She spoke first, her voice so quiet he stepped closer to hear her words. "Is this your place? Gail…"

"Just me. I moved here after…" *you healed me…after you left me…* But he couldn't say that. "Years ago, Gail worked for the Red Cross. When I got better, she returned to the job she loved. She's in Africa right now, helping children."

"I'm glad she's doing what she loves."

"Me, too. She sends postcards or calls whenever she can. She's supposed to be back in late January."

Lita nodded then they both grew quiet again. He wanted to keep the conversation going, but his brain had apparently stepped out for coffee. *That's it! A drink! Maybe that'll help.* "Is there anything I can get for you? Something to drink maybe?" Placing his hand on her lower back, he slowly guided her into the living room where he hadn't quite finished decorating the tree before he'd left for the hospital dedication.

She smiled at him and his whole world brightened. "No, but thank you. I'm just a little overwhelmed." Her gaze fixed on the Christmas tree and her eyes seemed to glaze over. She rubbed her hands up and down her arms, seemingly lost in thought.

If only he could read her mind. The connection still flickered between them, but all he was receiving was a brash mix of confusion, fear and deep loneliness. Even though he sought some answers, she didn't seem to be in the right place to provide them. Would she leave again if he asked the wrong question? He didn't want to scare her away. If she needed to go slow, he could certainly do that as long as she stayed. At this point, keeping her with him was more important than anything. But curiosity still nagged at his heart.

He brushed by her, unable to stop himself from running his hand over her hair before he moved behind the Christmas tree. Damn he wanted to touch her bare skin, fist his hands in her hair and hold her still beneath him as he fucked her all night long. Clenching his jaw, he leaned down and plugged in the tree lights. His jaw loosened into a smile as her eyes lit up along with the lights. So damn beautiful… His cock twitched beneath his tuxedo pants.

Before his erect friend could make himself too obvious, Ben knelt down and opened the chest where he kept the Christmas tree ornaments. The stilted silence between them was painful and suddenly he couldn't take it anymore. "What have you done this past year? Where did you go after you helped me out?"

His questions hung in the silence. If she didn't reply, he'd know she didn't want anything to do with him. It wouldn't surprise him. She'd left him without a word once. Maybe he was just reading more into what they'd had. He'd never met anyone he truly felt understood him and who he might have a chance at understanding as well. Or maybe she had been sent to him by a higher power, but only to help him that one time. And the rest of his life, he'd be on his own.

But that wouldn't explain why she'd stumbled back into his life again.

Silently, she knelt down next to him, her knee pressing against his leg. With a small smile she reached into the box and removed a gift box shaped ornament. "I've been a nanny. But today was my last day."

While that wasn't exactly the answer he'd been looking for, he thanked his lucky stars that she'd even answered in the first place. He stood and offered his hand to help her up. She placed her hand in his and a jolt of awareness shot through him. Their eyes met and held as she rose to her feet. His heart rate increased as she laced her fingers with his. She'd given him the invitation he needed. Hopefully baring part of his soul wouldn't scare her away.

Finding himself short of words, he just spoke straight from his heart. "I can't tell you how glad I am to see you again. You've been my inspiration this past year. I-I've done so many murals and paintings of you... I've been thinking that maybe you were only a dream, that—"

He stopped as she placed her free hand on his chest and moved even closer to him. Her gaze lowered to where her hand rested on him and she brushed her fingertips back and forth over the polyester of his tuxedo shirt. Did she have any idea what her touch did to him?

Nervously, she took a deep breath and began to speak. "I left you last year because I was scared, because I didn't understand what had happened between us. But I've never stopped thinking of you. Every morning I wake up missing you. I've never felt like this before. I've loved you for the last year." Lita paused and lifted her gaze to his. Her eyes were strong though still tinged with fear. "I love you, Ben."

Everything else he'd planned on saying evaporated from his mind. She loved him. And he knew it to be true. Could feel her love for him wrapping around his heart. The heart that loved her back just as completely. He could think of nothing else but kissing her, being one with her. Dropping the ornament he still held in his hands, he pulled her to him, his lips crushing down on hers. She reacted with equal fervor, inviting his tongue through her parted lips, drawing him within her as though feeding a deep, longing hunger.

The kiss pulsed through his veins, heating his blood, bringing his cock from half-hard to full erection. Lita was everything in his life that was missing. He'd had a few one-night stands in the past year, unsuccessfully seeking an end to his hunger, but Lita was the only woman who could satisfy his every need.

Lita broke the kiss, her lips trailing along his jaw, her fingers fumbling with the buttons of his tuxedo shirt. She spoke through the kisses. "Ben, oh Ben. I need you so much."

Ben pulled away from her enough so he could look down into her desire-glazed eyes. "Tell me you won't leave me tonight, that you're not going to disappear before morning."

Pain rippled through their connection, and he clenched his hands into fists. No. She would not leave him again. He'd be damned before he let that happen.

Her eyes saddened and she traced a hand down the side of his face. "I won't leave you tonight. I promise you that. Let me be with you."

It would have to be enough for now. Later he'd make her stay, but now he needed to sate his hunger, to remember what it felt like to be whole again.

Growling, his primal side raging to the surface, he lowered his hands to her ass, grasping her fullness beneath his fingertips and lifting her off the floor. Her reaction inflamed him further as she wrapped her legs around his waist and crushed her breasts against his chest. She was his. Nothing and no one could tell him differently.

The bedroom was too far away. Somehow he managed the few steps to the couch without ripping the clothing off her body. She removed his bowtie and loosened his collar and her lips and tongue teased the flesh of his throat before moving back to his mouth. Desperate longing tensed his muscles. His head and cock pounded his mind with "Now, now, now," but his heart demanded he take the time to show her how she filled his world.

With a calm patience he'd been unaware he possessed, he eased her onto the couch. He remained on the floor kneeling over her, unable to pull his lips from the sweet sensuality of hers. She placed her hands on either side of his face, then slid them down his neck to his shoulders and tugged on his shirt. She'd managed to unbutton it completely and together they removed the garment. Her sweater, white linen pants, stockings and panties disappeared the same way. Ben marveled at the ethereal beauty before him. The glow of the Christmas tree lights seemed to dance across her skin. But before he could look his fill of his angel clothed only in the silk and lace of her bra, her hands locked behind his neck and she tugged. She wanted him closer. But as much as he wanted to give in, he wouldn't.

Instead, he worked his hands around underneath her grasp, then let his fingers sway to the curve of her breasts. He teased the tight velvet peaks of her nipples, letting the lacy roughness of her bra stimulate her further. He felt her emotions both relaxing and exciting as he moved one hand over her hip, letting his thumb just graze the top of her slit. She moaned and tilted her hips in response, her hands pulling at his shoulders once again.

He spoke against her lips. "Oh, no, Angel. I'm not done with you yet." He wove his hand back from her hip to cup her ass. "Last year, it was all about me. This time it's all about you." Kissing her one more time to stifle her protest, he slid his hand back over her hip, holding her still beneath him. Slowly, he trailed his tongue down, kissing her neck, fully tasting each inch of skin, doing what he'd spent a year imagining he would do if given another chance.

Minutes or hours later—time had ceased to matter—he made his way to her breasts, suckling each nipple through the lace before unclasping the flimsy material and removing it from her body. Her areoles looked like tight little rosebuds against the white of her skin and with hands and mouth, he continued making love to her breasts.

Lita's hands no longer coaxed him closer. They wound their way through his hair and massaged his scalp just like their first night together. Except this time, he felt like he was somehow trying to heal her. As though there was so much more behind her violet eyes that she had yet to share with him.

His hands and mouth moved lower, tasting her stomach, teasing her bellybutton, then as she arched her hips in silent plea, he willed himself not to let his primal instinct take over completely. The whimpering sounds of her desire further hardened his cock until he was sure his tuxedo pants would tear under the strain. His hand slid to her inner thigh and she opened her legs, as though she were a flower blooming for only him. Wetness coated her dark tendrils.

"My angel," he whispered, blowing lightly against her pussy. She gasped in response and lifted her sex to him, offering herself completely. "Mine," he said again as he inhaled her special sweet fragrance. "Mine," he repeated before he tasted her juices. Never would he have enough of this woman. He held her down as he loved her completely, gently nibbling and licking her labia, sliding his tongue through her folds, then suckling her clitoris until she came, moaning his name.

More moisture poured forth, coating his mouth as her body wracked with pleasure. He could feel everything through their emotional connection. The female orgasm had always astounded him, but sharing it with her, tasting her cream, nearly sent him over the edge. Love made the climax more powerful, the pleasure so intense he grit his teeth to keep from coming in his pants.

Hurriedly, he shucked his pants and underwear, practically chafing his cock in the process. He traced up her body kiss after kiss, his hands caressing, stroking as he climbed on top of her. She wrapped her legs around his hips. They needed to be joined as one. He entered her, burying his cock to the hilt within her spasming sheath. They found a matching rhythm, grinding, swaying, thrusting, finding pleasure in every movement, every touch, every emotion shared. Their mouths locked on each other as possessively as their sexes.

This time they came together, their minds and bodies so tightly interwoven the pleasure continued flowing between them until their bodies, unable to withstand any more, relaxed, and they fell asleep, still united in every way as one.

Chapter Six

ဆာ

Lita woke up with a smile on her face and Ben's cock thickening inside of her. Until last night, a year had gone by since she'd had sex, the longest she'd gone since becoming an active Polgaran goddess. Her pussy felt swollen and tender, but the moment he began to move inside of her, warm wetness seeped from her vagina, easing his passage. She let out a rousing moan as he began a slow, sweet worshipping, each stroke a quiet claim on her soul. Closing her eyes, she let herself simply feel every sweep of his hands down her body, every thrust of his cock, every kiss he placed on her neck, throat and face. More memories to hold on to.

"I love you, Lita."

She opened her eyes to see him watching her, his look both intense and tender. Even though their bodies were skin to skin and their heart link shimmered with their connection, she felt a frenzied need for more. With a fever born of desperation, she caressed her hands over his entire body, memorizing the feel of his skin beneath her fingertips, the play of his muscles as he flexed and moved above her. Lifting her legs, she invited him deeper. "More, Ben. Please. More."

His midnight blue eyes darkened to near black as he pressed even deeper within her core. Lowering his head, he suckled her breast. His tongue brought her flesh to life, sweeping in warm circles around her nipple. Then he lightly bit her erect nub. The resulting zing shot straight to her cunt.

"Ben!" she screamed, but he just chuckled around her breast and kept feasting. It was a game for him, biting then soothing, heating her flesh, then blowing cool air over it. She squirmed and begged beneath him, needing an end to the sensual torment.

As though he felt her breaking point, Ben slid a hand between their bodies and began circling around her clit, not quite touching the swollen bundle of nerves that would take her over the edge. Lita's breath came in rapid pants as the circles narrowed. Almost there…almost…and then he finally touched it. Starbursts shattered inside of her, wicked blasts of light and pleasure filling her from head to toe.

Holding her tightly, he stroked her hair away from her face and kissed her forehead.

"Ever made love under a Christmas tree?" he whispered between kisses.

"No. You?"

"No, and I think we should remedy that. This couch limits what I can do to you." Ben carefully slid off her body and reached along one edge of the couch, producing a fleece blanket and a knitted afghan. He spread the fleece blanket beneath the tree. The afghan remained folded but within arms' reach.

Lita placed one foot on the floor to stand up.

"Stop."

She looked up at Ben's command. "Just let me look at you for a moment. I've waited a year for this."

His gaze caressed her body with an almost physical sensation. Her body reacted, nipples hardening, a rush of liquid heat filling her pussy. Ready again for whatever he offered.

Just like one year earlier, she felt pulled into him when she looked into his eyes. For a moment it was as though she'd climbed into his mind, could hear his thoughts, see through his eyes. *The most beautiful woman who ever existed. Mine. All the love I'll ever need. My inspiration, my redemption, my soulmate. In one smile, she breathes life into me. My body quenches its thirst and warms all that is cold when I am inside of her. Show her my love, my passion, my hunger, such that she will breathe into me and make me whole.*

His thoughts filled her, warmed her, made her complete. Her emotions bubbled up inside. She wanted to cry and laugh, to sing and shout. Instead she just spoke the words of her heart. "I love you, too. Forever."

He held his hand out to her. "Come here, Angel."

She didn't need to read his mind to know what he wanted. With fluid movements, she shifted off the couch and walked toward him. His cock pulsed an angry red against the flat planes of his stomach. He'd given amazing pleasure to her and hadn't climaxed, so she'd return the favor.

She lowered to her knees in front of him and took the thick head of his cock into her mouth. He let out a quick hiss of breath through his teeth as she swirled her tongue around the head, mimicking the lovemaking he'd done to her breasts earlier. One of his hands twisted in her hair, coaxing her to take him deeper. Slowly she let him fill her mouth until his head nudged the back of her throat. Then she began rocking back and forth, suctioning him in and out, moving faster until his body trembled.

"God, Angel. You're killing me." Ornaments fell from the tree as he grabbed on to it. A strip of silver garland fell to the floor next to where she knelt, giving her an idea.

"Angel, what are you..." He let out a strangled moan as she wrapped the soft length of garland around the base of his cock, using the ends to tease his sac. His grip in her hair tightened and he began fucking her mouth in swift, sure strokes. He came with a roar, his salty fluid spurting down her throat. Pine needles rained from the tree he still held tightly in his grasp. She drank from him until he was empty, then reluctantly eased his shaft from her mouth.

She carefully unwrapped the garland from his relaxed cock. He sank to his knees in front of her, resting his head on hers, taking deep, gulping breaths.

"I'll never look at garland the same way again," he chuckled.

Taking the strand of garland from her hand, he wrapped it around her wrist, then circled his own. As he finished binding them together, he lifted his free hand to her face. They just stared into each other's eyes, not needing to say a word.

Together they lay down on the fleece blanket, covering up with the afghan. Several minutes passed as they held each other, kissing, touching, loving. Ben relaxed and soon his breath became deep and even as he drifted into dreamland.

Lita smiled lightly. She was warm, comfortable and for the first time in her life completely content. The man she loved slept next to her, their hands tied together, his head nestled into her hair, his body heat better than any blanket. Only one thing hampered her joy.

She had less than seventy-two hours left with him.

Returning to Polgara was an unfortunate given. But there was no way to explain that to Ben without causing a vicious fight. How could she tell him that she was a Pleasure goddess and that she gave freely of her body? He wouldn't—couldn't—understand. And even if she did tell him, what good would come of it? Under the best of circumstances he'd be given access to Polgara, and they could see each other on occasion. But what kind of life would that be for him?

As she pondered their quandary, she looked up at the Christmas tree. A crystal angel hung from a branch just within reach. Something about it called out to her and she reached up, taking it into her unfettered hand.

Air left her body in a swift rush as a vision filled her mind. Ben, decorating a tree, surrounded by three children. Laughter rang out as the kids took turns asking their daddy to lift them high to put their favorite decorations on the tree.

Then the littlest one, a young girl with her daddy's smile, handed Ben the angel ornament Lita held now, and said, "Daddy, tell us the story of the angel. How she saved you so you could be my daddy…"

Tears filled her eyes and the vision faded. She wanted to curse the Goddesses, to scream at the unfairness of it all. Her visions, while infrequent, were never wrong. Ben would have a family, he would find a woman who could love him, give him children, be with him forever. The fact that their hearts were linked must have been a mistake. Although she'd known she couldn't stay, and she wanted Ben to be happy, to be so clearly shown that the man she loved would find love with someone else…it was more than she could bear.

In his sleep, Ben murmured, "I love you, Lita." He kissed her cheek and squeezed her tightly.

A small glimmer of possibility flickered in her heart. Maybe she didn't have a choice about returning to Polgara, but at the very least, she and Ben deserved these next three days. She would have to give and take what she could, love a life's worth in that time.

Lita ran her free hand over Ben's back, memorizing the smooth feel of his flesh beneath her fingertips. He stirred, but did not awaken. She loved this man and nothing would ever change that. If all she had was three days, then she'd give him her everything in that time. No regrets.

Chapter Seven

ଛଠ

"Shopping? But I thought men didn't like to go shopping," Lita asked on Christmas Eve morning.

Ben grinned at her, looking just like a little kid. It was a sad reminder of the children he would have after she was gone. She brushed those thoughts away. Today was her last day with him and there was no room for painful thoughts when every second had to count.

Ben had told her he wanted to give her a Christmas to remember. Two days with him had already sped by much too quickly. It seemed the more Lita tried to hold onto her time with him, the faster the seconds slipped through her fingers.

They'd spent a day lazily learning each other's bodies all over again. Touching, tasting, loving. In between the lovemaking, they talked about their year apart, the changes in their lives. But Lita couldn't bring herself to tell Ben that she'd be leaving him on Christmas. Guilt gnawed at her gut, but she didn't know how to start.

They'd visited the Mathers' that first night and picked up her belongings, then Ben had taken her to his favorite café. The angels hanging in the window told them they were in the right place.

The next day they'd gone to one of Ben's favorite escapes from the city, making snow angels, tobogganing and having a snowball fight that escalated into a quickie in the snow. It was one of the best days of her life.

And today they were going shopping. Grinning from ear to ear, Ben wrapped his arm around her, leading her toward the door. "It's a family tradition. Gail and I wait until the last minute to get our Christmas shopping done, then we run around frantically trying to find the perfect gift. Let's go. This'll be fun."

Christmas music played over the speakers as employees in Santa hats rang up the season's final purchases. Hand in hand, Ben and Lita walked through the crowded stores, laughing at the last minute gift ideas each store was offering. They picked out a gorgeous hand-knit sweater for Gail and the newest books by all of her favorite authors. Ben bought a singing Christmas cactus and an ugly reindeer sweater for himself — another tradition he promised her, to buy things he could laugh about the rest of the year.

"So we'll meet back here in an hour, okay?"

Lita glanced up from the bin of Christmas ornaments she was digging through. "What? Where are you going?"

A sparkle in his eyes, Ben cupped his hands around her ass and yanked her against his body. "I can't shop for you if you're with me." He winked, dropped a kiss on her forehead and stepped away. "One hour."

"One hour. Okay. I'll be here." Lita watched Ben walk away. One hour seemed like forever when all they had was half a day left together.

She wandered up and down the aisles, trying to find something she could get for Ben while cursing herself for not telling him she was leaving. Just when was she going to break it to him? Five minutes to midnight when she grabbed her belongings, kissed him goodbye, told him it had been fun and walked out the door and back to Polgara?

Suddenly, a strong hand clamped over her mouth and an arm swept around her waist, sweeping her off her feet and dragging her into an empty storage room. Fear rocketed through her body. She fought against her assailant, biting down on his hand, screaming silently in rage.

A smooth golden voice purred into her ear. "Dammit, Lita. Shhh. It's me, Ty." He lowered her to the ground and she spun around to meet his eyes.

"Tynan? What are you doing here?" The question was barely out of her mouth when realization struck her. He was a Shadow Tracker. There was only one reason he'd seek her out. She scrambled backward away from him until she hit a wall. "No. I won't let you take me back. Not now. I still have twelve hours!"

Tynan stalked toward her and Lita crossed her arms, staring belligerently into his penetrating gray-green gaze. "I said no."

His long silver-streaked black hair fell wildly around his shoulders as he shook his head and gave her a wolfish grin. "Take it easy. I'm not here to take you back, Lita-love. Tresca asked me to warn you."

"Tresca? But how? And why? Warn me about what?"

Tilting his head to the side, he looked at her curiously, a frown creasing his brow. "I spent a session with Tresca yesterday. There's big gossip going on that you broke some pretty serious rules. Hundreds of newspapers around this dimension are running a story about a healing angel and the man who loves her. Reporters are researching your past. And you know what that means—too many questions are coming up without any shred of an answer."

Cold fear shot down Lita's spine as she slumped to the floor. She swallowed hard, trying to speak past the lump in her throat. "The Controllers are going to erase my memories, aren't they?"

Ty knelt down next to her, caressing her face, sorrow reflecting from his eyes. "Yes."

* * * * *

The diamond ring was perfect. Ben had looked in all three cases, but as soon as he'd seen this one, he'd known it was the one for Lita. A glistening solitaire with a baguette on either side. Simple but beautiful.

He completed the transaction and put the velvet box in his pocket. Tonight he would propose to her under the Christmas tree then convince her to marry him immediately. Next week. Tomorrow. The sooner the better.

But then sudden fear gripped his entire being. Lita was in trouble. Letting instinct guide him, he bolted to the back of the store.

Crashing through a door, he saw Lita in the arms of a long-haired man. *Bastard!* She wasn't fighting and didn't seem afraid any longer, but she was clearly shaken. The man glanced back at him before giving Lita a pointed look and taking off through the depths of the storage room.

Ben rushed to her and she looked up at him, her eyes weary…defeated. Whatever that bastard did to her, he swore, he'd… His thought was left unfinished as she wrapped her arms around him, resting her head on his shoulder. "What was that all about? What's going on? Angel? Are you okay?"

"Ben. I don't know how to tell you, but I know I have to." She spoke so softly he could barely hear her words. "Let's just go home…and talk. I don't ever want to be away from you. I love you too much for that to happen."

His heart did flip-flops in his chest. Was she going to leave him again? His worst fear realized twice in his life? "I love you, too, Lita."

The cab ride home was spent in silence but his thoughts whizzed loudly around in his head. From thinking everything was somehow going to be okay all the way to how stupid could a man possibly be to allow himself to be strung along like this. Lita just buried herself as close to him as possible. His heart went out to her, but he feared what she had to tell him would only hurt more than her silence.

When they finally set foot in his living room, it was everything he could do to keep himself from holding her. He needed the distance for clarity, otherwise he'd lose himself in her again.

They sat on the couch and she stared at her hands, as though afraid to speak. He asked her with his eyes and through their link to just talk to him, promising that no matter what she said, he would hear her out. But that wasn't an easy promise to make, especially with so much on uncertain ground. With each moment, he'd been simmering and the anger was getting harder to hold at bay.

Then she spoke. "I've got nothing else to lose."

"What?" He tried to keep the anger from his voice, but he couldn't completely remove the harsh edge. He softened and took a deep breath. "Angel, I just need to know. What the hell is going on?"

Lita took a shaky breath, then looked up into his eyes. "I'm not an angel, but I'm not a human either. I'm from a different dimension. A place called Polgara. The night we met was my first night in this dimension. I was given one year here, and tonight my year's up."

Stunned speechless, he backed away from her, his jaw agape. What the hell was she saying? Different dimensions? Although that would explain her curiosities about everything, her simple joy in things he took for granted. But no, that was absurd. Maybe she was just as lost as he had been when she'd found him.

But an inkling of belief wove its way through him. He *knew* she was telling the truth. Hell, he'd known from the moment he first saw her that she was different. And what they shared was different. He'd accepted it because he wanted it, but the connection they shared, that wasn't normal either. But it was *right*. Or at least it had been...

"I wasn't supposed to fall in love. Ben, where I'm from, the emotion of love doesn't exist to the depth it exists here. I'm a Pleasure goddess. I give of my body, but not of my heart or soul." She paused as though flailing through what she was telling him.

Did I fall in love with some kind of weird inter-dimensional prostitute? Each word falling from her lips was another blow to his heart.

Lita locked her gaze with his. It was obvious she was trying to remain strong, but her lower lip had begun to tremble. "The moment I saw you everything changed. You're my heart link. That connection that brought us together...Polgarans don't get that type of connection. But we have it! I know you feel it. Please tell me you feel it." A few tears streamed down her face, her eyes begging him to admit aloud that he indeed understood.

But he just couldn't bear to hold her gaze. He looked down and turned away. "I don't know what to make of any of this. You've made claims that should be impossible and to top it off, you were going to leave me without saying anything. Just like before." Hurtful words were brewing in his thoughts, but he couldn't find it within himself to start flinging them at her. She'd know how he felt. She would feel it through their...heart link...as she called that gnawing magnetic unexplainable connection which was the source of his greatest joys and harshest sorrows.

As she spoke, he looked back into her violet eyes. "No, Ben! I just didn't know how to tell you. I didn't want to fight. I ran away from you that first night because I was afraid, but it wasn't fear of what I felt for you. I couldn't explain how I healed you. And I'm not supposed to tell anyone about who I am or where I'm from. But I screwed up. The reporters the other night, they spread our picture, our story over newspapers everywhere. The High Controllers on Polgara saw it. They're going to punish me for my indiscretion. Ben, they're going to wipe my memory of my entire time here." At that, her tears finally broke. "They're going to make me forget you."

He pushed back across the couch and pulled her onto his lap, wrapping her in his arms. Her anguish through their link as strong as the betrayal he was feeling. "Lita, I…" *just don't know what to say. I'm so confused. So hurt. So in love with you. But I can never have more than a few short days and nights with you. How cruel can my life get?*

"I'm so sorry, Ben. I didn't know this would happen if I came here. I just wanted to see what human life was like. I didn't want to get involved or attached or… I never wanted to hurt you." She buried her head against his chest.

"When must you leave, Angel?" He soothed her with gentle caresses.

"I am supposed to return to Polgara just after midnight, but I'm not going to. I can't. I need to be with you."

"Then don't go to them. Stay here with me." He'd been afraid to speak those words before, afraid she'd leave him if he forced it, but now, there were no holds barred. "Lita, stay with me forever if you can. Don't go to them."

"They'll find me. The man who came to me today, he's a tracker. He came to warn me of what is to happen. If I don't return, they'll send more trackers after me. There's no escape."

"But you said they'll just wipe away your memories of me, right? We can start over, Lita. If we really are linked, no one can separate us. No one. I don't care how strong. No one. I won't allow anyone to take you away from me again. Angel, you are mine."

She lifted her face to his and kissed him, needing him as close to her as possible. "Ben, I am yours."

For hours, they sat in silence, kissing, touching, watching the clock tick the minutes by. Night came, and they sat in the dark, not moving, just holding each other.

Near midnight, Lita shifted in his arms, and he felt something in his pocket press against his hip. The ring. He'd been so caught up in the maelstrom, the gift had slipped his mind.

He removed the box from his pants and slipped the ring into his hand before dropping the box to the floor. "Angel, love. I need to ask you something."

Lifting her head from his chest, she gifted him with a small smile. "Anything."

"Marry me?" Before she could respond, he placed the ring on her finger then brought his mouth to hers. Her answer was in her kiss and the urgency between them. In a mad rush, they removed their clothing and Lita lowered herself onto his cock. The loving was simple. No words were necessary. They were together, nothing else mattered.

Midnight struck and they didn't move, completely meshed with each other.

Then his angel was swept away from him. He tried to hold on to her, but everything in his world faded to empty blackness.

Chapter Eight

ß

The tall, majestically engraved doors opened, affording Lita entrance into the High Chamber. She walked down the long stretch of open space, toward the tables where the Controllers presided, her back straight, head held high. Her hands were clenched into fists at her side, the engagement ring Ben had given her turned inward so she could feel the diamond pressing into her hand. *Never forget...never forget...never forget...*

Lita stepped onto the interrogation platform, automatically shifting into her stance of obeisance as the Herald announced her presence. She didn't even listen to his words. She knew why she was there.

Two weeks had trudged by since the night Polgaran security had ripped her from Ben's arms. She'd spent that time in the solitary loneliness of her room, suffering a range of human emotions—grief, pain, disbelief, love.

Now she was angry and scared. She couldn't fathom not having any memories of Ben. It was bad enough that she'd lost him, but to lose her memories, too...

Imorga's voice rang out in the chamber. "By my lead, Lita, you may naturalize." Lita lifted her head at the command to see Imorga regarding her...curiously? No, that couldn't be right. The look disappeared as Imorga continued. "You may speak to these offenses."

Lita squeezed her fist, feeling the sharp sting of the diamond digging into her palm. *Never forget...never forget...never forget...* "I am aware of the consequences of my actions. Not only did I bring undue attention upon myself, compromising Polgara and its entire people, I also did not willingly return at the end of my designated time. I did all of this with complete knowledge of the punishment due me upon my return. But with your permission, before you remove my memories, may I tell you a story?"

Imorga nodded her head thoughtfully. "It would please me to hear tell of your experiences."

Trembling both inside and out, Lita met Imorga's eyes and began to speak. "I spent a year among humans, embracing their emotions. I witnessed the give and take of humanity, saw the best and worst that their world had to offer. That world became a home to me, accepting me, teaching me.

"And I fell in love. Deeply, passionately, beyond anything I'd ever imagined love. Ben is my heart link. I can feel him, a part of me even now, no matter how far away he may be. I know he loves me, that he misses me, that he needs me, just as much as I do him. Not even erasing my memories will change that. When you're done, I may not remember his name, or his voice…" Lita choked on a sob but forced herself to continue. "But the connection between us will always be there. I will always love him, even if I don't know who *he* is."

The Controllers were silent in their regard. Lita wiped the tears from her cheeks and returned their stares. *Never forget…never forget…never forget…*

Imorga got to her feet and walked down the few stairs from the dais toward an open doorway. "Come, Lita. It is time."

Lita wanted to protest, but knew it would be to no avail. She'd said her piece. There was nothing left for her to do but follow Imorga out of the chamber and accept the punishment she had earned for falling in love. Anguish slowed the blood running through her veins until she felt as though she were moving in slow motion. They entered a hallway, lush carpets blanketing the floors, engravings and murals covering the walls. They walked in silence, moving through a maze of hallways.

After several minutes, Imorga opened a door and stepped inside. Lita squeezed her hand around her engagement ring again and took a deep breath. *Never forget…never forget…never forget…*

She entered the room, then froze, her eyes widening, her whole world going topsy-turvy all over again. Lita turned in a circle, soaking it all in. Paintings covered the walls of the room, in brilliant, vibrant color. Her life with Ben. Their first night together in the bed at Gail's place, their bodies awash in moonlight. Under the Christmas tree. Bathing together. Playing in the snow. Each scene meshing with the next, a timeline of love.

"God, Angel, I missed you."

Was that really his voice? Lita turned to the sound, afraid to believe it could be possible, until Ben stepped into the room behind her.

Then she was in his arms, not ready to question how or why, just so thankful he was there. Needing to remember his smell, his touch and the way only he could make her feel just by being near him.

His warm mouth lowered over hers. The kiss began soft and tender, a gentle caress of lips, a whisper of breath shared between them. But an urgency to make up for the last two weeks filled her and she nibbled on his lips then pressed her tongue deep into the sweet recesses of his mouth. He groaned and pulled her closer, the kiss becoming a duel of desire.

Their heart link shimmered in stunning glory, unwilling to be denied, almost blinding in its brilliance. Lita felt the warm glow of Ben's love heating her to her core, filling her up inside. She returned the love tenfold, and knew he felt it, too.

A gentle cough was the only reminder that they were not alone in the room. They separated their mouths but not their bodies, turning ever so slightly toward Imorga.

"Ben is an admirable artist, Lita. His use of light and color to bring his subject's emotions to life is stunning. Yet even more admirable is his devotion to you. That was made very clear over the last two weeks. I instructed him to tell me his side of the story. He looked around the High Chamber and requested permission to paint the story instead. An unusual request. But one which followed your initial unusual request. My permission was therefore granted and much deservedly, I might add."

Ben nodded to Imorga, then meeting Lita's gaze, winked and dropped a kiss on her forehead. Smiling, she turned back to Imorga, the questions beginning to flow from her lips. "What is to happen? What—"

"Very few things are more powerful than Polgaran law, Lita. You see, not even High Controllers can deny a bond between two heart links. For Polgarans that connection is a rare jewel, an anomaly not to be ignored. But your..." Imorga pursed her lips as though she tasted something sour, "indiscretions on the human level caused us great concern. You, I have little fear, will commit no further such indiscretions. However we in turn, questioned whether Ben could be trusted with our secret. As I gaze upon this room once more, I am quite pleased to inform both of you that our concerns have been allayed—his allegiances lie within the best of intentions. I trust he will do nothing to harm you or the Polgaran people. Lita, although Polgaran by birth, you are free to live life with your heart link. You must continue to keep Polgara a deep secret within your soul and live as a human, again and forever."

Tendrils of joy crept from her heart, filling her body, until only one tiny little bit of fear remained. "I have only one question, High Controller Imorga. I had a vision, of Ben with children of his own. My visions have never proven wrong, but Polgaran's can't..." Her question trailed off as a grin grew wide across Imorga's face. It was the first time Lita had seen her smile, and it made her beautiful and radiant and not someone to be feared.

"Lita, the moment you met Ben, the rules changed. A Polgaran goddess cannot be impregnated by anyone *but* her heart link. I do believe the family you envisioned has already begun." Imorga's eyes sparkled, as she lowered her head knowingly toward Lita's stomach. Then her expression became serious once again. "Lita, of the Damescine sect, high Platine quadrant, you are hereby relieved of your duties as Pleasurer and are free to live the life which fate has gifted you for it is a rare experience indeed."

Imorga turned and left the room, leaving Ben and Lita alone.

Lita turned to Ben as he lifted her hand. He twisted the ring so that the diamond was no longer clenched within her fist. Then he kissed her palm as though trying to remove the indentations etched from the diamond. His eyes locked hot on hers. "I love you, Angel. Marry me?"

Laughter bubbled up inside, the joy filling her completely. "Yes, Ben. Yes. I want to be Mrs. Lita Stanton."

Sweet and tenderly, his hands lowered to her belly. His eyes glowed with wonder. "A baby? Is that what she meant, Angel? Are we really going to have a baby?"

The heart link between them pulsed even stronger, and Lita focused on it, soaking in all the love between them. Then she looked closer at their heart link and smiled at the tangential lines forming there. New souls finding life from their love. She laced her fingers with his and looked up into his smiling eyes. "Yes, Ben. I do believe someday, we're going to have five."

Also by Ashleigh Raine

ဢ

Acting on Impulse

Ellora's Cavemen: Legendary Tails IV (*anthology*)

Things That Go Bump In the Night 2004

About the Author

෨

Sometimes two people meet, become good friends, and share a lot in common. When you're really lucky, you meet someone who understands you, who thinks like you, can finish your sentences and together, the both of you can create whole new worlds.

Ashleigh Raine is the pen name for two best friends, Jennifer and Lisa, who share a passion for strong alpha males that succumb to the women they fall in love with.

Both Lisa and Jennifer are married to their soul mates, who are the best support and inspiration. As Ashleigh Raine, this duo has many stories to tell, as their collective mind never stops creating fantasies that must be written down. They write larger than life stories, with adventures, hot sex, peril, hot sex, mystery, and more hot sex...but most assuredly they have a happy ending, usually with hot sex. Watch for many titles coming soon from this duo who are glad to have found their niche in writing erotic romances.

Ashleigh welcomes comments from readers. You can find her website and email address on her author bio page at www.ellorascave.com.

Tell Us What You Think

We appreciate hearing reader opinions about our books. You can email us at Comments@EllorasCave.com.

AUGUST HEAT
Lora Leigh

ജ

Author's Note

I've received many emails both for the sharing to continue and for a final healing with the August Brothers. This is the healing. So why did I wait? Because at the time of the completion of Heather's Gift, the August Brothers, I felt, weren't ready to let go of that final security line that had helped them survive a brutal, destructive past. They had survived. Perhaps not as you or I would have, but they survived. They had to realize themselves, for their own peace of mind, that the past was over and that dreams really do come true. They had to repair that final bond themselves, and learn how to be brothers again. Something that cannot be done overnight.

I hope you have all enjoyed the series. I hope you saw what I felt as I wrote these books. The strength of these men who had survived, who were strong, enduring. Men who had faced their worst nightmare and eventually overcame the obstacles that their very survival had put in their path. I hope you saw the love, the innate gentleness, and the underlying craving for the love of the women they had set their hearts on.

Love comes in so many forms. So many different faces and so many elusive ways, that who's to say what it can ultimately conquer?

God Bless you all this Christmas Season. And I hope you have enjoyed this Christmas addition to the August Family. May you all stay safe, happy, and most of all, loved.

Lora Leigh

Prologue
May

The contractions began late that night, and they began hard. Marly awoke from a restless sleep, a pained gasp on her lips as her rounded stomach tightened painfully. Imperatively.

She reached for Cade, to awaken him, to warn him, but he was already there, his blue eyes filling with panic as he flipped on the bedside lamp and stared back at her.

"Oh shit." She had never heard that particular tone of voice from him before.

Marly blinked at him in surprise, torn between laughter and concern as his wide eyes went to the rippling motions of the contraction that seized her heavily pregnant abdomen.

"Now, Cade," she tried to soothe him as she scooted to the end of the bed, "don't panic."

"Fuck. Sam! Brock!" Marly was certain his demented scream rocked the upper level of the house.

Damn. They were all going to panic on her now. She did not need this.

"Dammit, Marly, where are you going?" Before she could throw her legs over the side of the mattress Cade was moving to her, his hands trembling as he gripped her arm to keep her in the bed.

"Cade August, I refuse to have this child at home," she snapped, staring at him like the lunatic he was. "I need to get dressed. For that matter, so do you. I need the hospital."

Marly hadn't thought he could have gotten paler. But he did. In an instant his swarthy complexion went snow white as he swallowed tightly.

"Oh shit," he seemed to wheeze.

The door burst open and Sam, Brock, and their wives rushed into the room. Sam had a gun and a hard-on. Brock was just sporting the hard-on. Thankfully, Sarah and Heather had thought to drag on robes.

Marly closed her eyes helplessly. They still hadn't completely managed to still the terror that had gripped them during the months she, Sarah and Heather had been stalked. Annie still haunted them all.

"Heather was so right last year," she sighed. "Only you guys would still have a hard-on, no matter the situation," she moaned as she shook her head in resignation.

Another contraction seized her body, tightening her abdomen and rippling the flesh convulsively.

"Oh hell. She's in labor," Sam seemed to choke then as both he and Brock paled alarmingly.

"I don't want to have this baby here," she moaned, more than worried at the suddenly horrified faces of the men staring at her, as though she were some sort of aberration. "Sarah. Heather. Do something, please."

Thankfully, they did. Marly wasn't certain how they managed to get everyone dressed, including herself, and into the vehicles heading for the hospital. She was just thankful they had. The contractions were coming faster than Doc had told her they would be starting off, and though she fought to hide her fear from Cade, she couldn't hide it from herself.

She sat in the back seat of the Mercedes, Cade's arms wrapped around her, doing the Lamaze breathing and feeling like a panting dog as she tried to relax through the rapidly building pain. God, she was so thankful she had opted for drugs for the delivery. This was not comfortable. Not comfortable at all.

"Babe, you doing okay?" Sam glanced back as he sped through the night, his worried face reflected in the dim interior lights.

"Watch the damned road, Sam," Cade snapped as he held Marly close to his chest, his gentle hands stroking her distended abdomen as it contracted harshly.

"I'm watching the road." He turned back quickly as Heather's softly whispered reminder of the upcoming curves of the road added to Cade's order.

"I love you, Marly," Cade whispered at her ear as another contraction gripped her stomach.

"Fifteen minutes apart, Marly." Heather timed her. "Sam, honey, you'd better pick up some speed."

He picked up speed. Marly closed her eyes instead of watching the night pass by at a rate that came close to terrifying.

* * * * *

The contractions were less than five minutes apart by the time they reached the hospital. Thanks to Heather's call, nurses, orderlies, and Marly's no-nonsense obstetrician were waiting at the ambulance entrance when they pulled in.

For Marly, life had turned into a minute-by-minute count between contractions as she tried to relax against the overwhelming pain of the labor. It had also turned into a kaleidoscope of memories.

As though her life were flashing before her eyes, Marly saw the impacting moments of her years with Cade, from the day she had arrived on his doorstep until now.

How he had taken her, a gawky, awkward child, and dressed her in the finest clothes, given her everything a child could have wished for. He had showered her with all the love, security and praise that he himself had lacked in his life. Brock and Sam had followed suit. Throughout her teenage years they had raised and protected her, sheltered her, and by turns had overseen each adventure in her life. Had overseen them, and had eventually become the adventure. And now here they were yet again. The three of them, faces pale, voices hoarse, as the nurses worked around her.

Between contractions, preparation and the smooth transition from pain to woozy comfort, she watched the three men. They stood silently across the room, their gazes shadowed and worried, flickering with fear. But Cade looked tortured.

"I'm okay," she whispered, smiling for him as the pain receded. "We're both going to be fine."

He moved to her, careful to stay out of the way of the nurses until he could stand beside the hospital bed. Then he laid his head beside hers, his hands tangling in her long hair as he held her to him, his body convulsing with a hard shudder.

"I know," he whispered bleakly, his voice so haunted with pain it broke her heart. "Everything's fine. I know that."

But she could hear his fears. Fears that had only grown as the pregnancy progressed.

"He'll be as gorgeous as his daddy. And just as strong," she whispered, well aware of the fact that the child could be no one's but Cade's. She had made certain of it.

She had given each of them the illusion that they would be as much a part of the baby as Cade was, to keep that bond alive for them. But privately, she had ensured no other fathered the baby but Cade. He was her soul. Everything that mattered in this world to her.

As his hands tightened in her hair, his body trembling with emotion, Marly feared the changes that would soon come crashing into his life. She wanted her husband happy. Whole. The nightmares were gone, but she knew his fears still lingered. The fear of losing her. Of being alone, deep inside, once again. And she swore to herself in that moment, for Cade and for their baby, she had to make him face the final demon that haunted him. Him, Brock, and Sam.

* * * * *

Brock sat nervously on the uncomfortable couch in the waiting room. He held his wife close to him and watched the clock on the wall across from them. It amazed him. She amazed him. In little more than a year, Sarah had managed to fill his life so completely that he knew he could never ask for more. Yet he had so much more.

Beside him, Sam held Heather as they talked softly. As they both worried about the woman and child Cade was with now. Alone. His brothers weren't with him. But that was how it should be, Brock thought.

Until this moment, they had shared damned near every minute of that pregnancy with Cade. Had worried with him. Listened to his fears, saw his concerns. And as much as Brock was nervous now himself, he knew this final step was being taken as it should.

His fingers twined in Sarah's hair, his eyes narrowing at the emotion that had been forming inside him for almost a year now. He could feel the change in the air. From the moment they rushed into Cade's bedroom after his scream had disturbed Brock's careful sensual torture of Sarah's body, Brock had felt it. It moved like a wraith, weaving careful streamers of knowledge through his soul. He sighed deeply. No regret. No sense of nightmare. No overwhelming need to be certain he was still a part of the family, the bond that had saved his life for so many years. He had Sarah. With her, he could survive damned near anything.

"You okay?" She looked up at him, those whisky-colored eyes of hers soothing him as few other things could.

As always, Sarah sensed his feelings, his desires and needs, even before he knew himself.

"Do you know I love you?" he asked her softly.

A smile spread across her lips, through her gaze. "As I love you."

His arms tightened around her. Change could come, as he knew it would anyway. But as long as Sarah held him, he knew he would survive.

* * * * *

Why didn't he feel isolated? Sam sat beside Heather, his arm around her shoulders as her head rested against his chest, and frowned at that thought. Why wasn't he going crazy, the need to be in there with Marly and Cade overwhelming him? He was concerned. Anxious. Sam thought of all the things that could go wrong, but he wasn't frothing at the mouth to be certain. To share in it, to be assured Cade wasn't alone. That he himself wasn't alone.

He smoothed his hands down Heather's arms, distantly aware of the softness of her skin, the warmth of her body. She was talking about her sister, Tara. He knew what she was doing. Trying to ease his mind. To give him something else to focus on. He frowned. She did that often. When the memories haunted him, it was as though she knew. She knew and she went out of her way to still his demons, to fill his heart.

Strange. He hadn't seen that before. He had been married to her for well over a year, and was only now just realizing that.

"I told Tara this new assignment was a bad idea." Heather sighed against his chest. "But she thinks she knows it all. Ryder's not as easy to handle as she thinks he is. And Rick is just acting damned funny."

There was a thread of suspicion in her voice. Sam could feel it, but couldn't put his finger on what it was.

"Rick will keep her safe." He wondered if that was really what she was worried about.

"Yeah. He will." He heard the amusement in her voice. "Just like Cade will keep Marly safe."

Sam frowned. "Of course he will. Cade wouldn't let anything hurt her."

"Then stop worrying so much," she chided him gently. "I know you want to be in the delivery room yourself to be certain, but everything will be okay."

Sam frowned. "No. No, I don't." He hated the streak of selfishness that often filled him. "If it were you, I'd want it to be just us, Heather. Together."

He hadn't been jealous when Brock or Cade touched her, loved her. It filled him with a sense of security to know she would always be loved, always cared for if something happened to him. But sometimes…sometimes he wished he didn't have that need.

"It will be just us, Sam." She rose from his chest, turning to him, her green eyes dark with love, with dreams and life. "I promise you that. Just us."

His heart clenched. Something in his soul seemed to shift, though he wasn't certain what it was.

"I love you," he whispered.

She smiled that smile. The one that never failed to heat his blood, to mend his heart.

"As I love you, cowboy," she said gently, leaning forward, her lips touching his. "Always, Sam. As I love you."

Chapter One
October

෯

"Look. If you put the damned thing there it's going to throw the whole room off." Marly's voice was irritated, aggravated.

"It will make the room appear unique," Heather argued. "It looks perfect there."

"It's not even centered," Sarah piped in. "Really, Marly, that picture isn't going to work."

The picture in question was an aerial view of the house grounds. Unfortunately, Marly didn't want to move the large, older map-styled picture of the ranch from over the fireplace. It had been hanging there for as long as the ranch house had stood on that spot. She wanted both pictures.

"You could hang this one in the dining room," Heather argued. "It would look good there."

"I want it in here."

"It's not going to work."

"Only if you center it."

And the argument was off again.

Cade escaped through the doorway with a growing sense of male horror and split a direct path to the kitchen and the coffee he prayed was waiting there for him. He found the coffee. The coffee and Sam and Brock, heads lowered, resignation marking their faces.

"What the hell is going on in there?" Cade questioned the other two men. "They act like they're ready to tear each other's hair out."

"No, that was this morning. When the picture first arrived," Brock sighed. "They've been crazy ever since Marly had Drace. You gotta do something about this, Cade."

Cade crossed his arms over his chest and stared at Brock in no small amount of surprise. "And you expect me to do what?"

Drace was nearly six months old and growing daily. Cade had never known such a sense of love, of responsibility, as he did when he stared at his infant son. Nor such a sense of terror. How to protect him? No matter his age. To instill in him the strength of a man, the acceptance and the honor it would take to survive in the world.

"Hell if I know," Brock mumbled. "Those three women have gone crazy. I swear they have."

"Yeah. And they're wearing panties again, too," Sam bitched. "What's with that shit? I touch Heather and she pats me on the head like I'm Drace's age and goes about her business."

They were horny. They were all horny. Not that they had been cut off...exactly. Just seriously restricted. Cade hadn't anticipated this. Drace was his pride and joy, but there were days he exhausted Marly. And during those days, being with Sarah or Heather wasn't the answer, either. The shift in the family dynamics had come about slowly, but it had settled like a comfortable shirt across their shoulders.

"I feel like I'm a fucking kid again," Sam sighed. "Trying to seduce my favorite girl. Heather's worse than a virgin some days."

They were bitching about it, but Cade could hear a thread of amusement, feel the slowly building tension and anticipation growing in them all. He shook his head and headed for the coffee pot. He'd be damned if he knew what the three of them were up to, but he knew it was something.

"And they keep mentioning presents," Brock pointed out. "What do you buy them? Hell, I can't think of anything they don't have that we can afford."

"I offered Heather a trip." Sam sounded more than bemused now. "Anywhere she wanted to go, for however long. Thought she was going to cry. And not because she was happy, either."

Uh oh. Cade turned back to them slowly.

"Yeah. Same with Sarah." Brock shook his head. "I took her to look at new cars, and she acted like I broke her heart."

Cade had tried several different suggestions with Marly. She smiled. Acted enthusiastic over each but there was no missing the sadness in her eyes. Christmas was only weeks away now. There wasn't much time left and he had no idea what the hell she wanted.

"Has Sarah even given you any hints?" Sam asked Brock desperately. "Hasn't Heather mentioned anything to her?"

"Not a damned thing," Brock griped. "I even asked her what the others wanted. She told me to stop being a man and to figure it out." Insulted male ego echoed in his voice. "How does one stop being a man?" he grunted irritably.

"By being a woman," Sam snickered. "Want us to buy you a thong for Christmas, bro?"

Brock hurled a biscuit at his cackling brother, hitting him in the forehead even as Sam tried to duck. Crumbs rained down as it broke apart, littering Sam's broad chest with the baked flour.

"Cut it out. Both of you." Cade grabbed for one of the few remaining biscuits. Heather had made them, obviously. They were light and flaky, damned near melting in his mouth when he bit into one.

"How about a housekeeper?" He frowned as he thought of all the extra work involved in the house now. "Someone to just come in through the day."

They all stilled. At any given time during the workday, they could sneak in for a few minutes of heated, lusty sex wherever they found one of the women. Cade sobered at that thought. Or at least it used to be. He frowned. He hadn't touched Sarah or Heather since Drace's birth. He was spending too much time trying to get into his own wife's pants. Like the other two, she was as hard to seduce these days as a nervous virgin.

"Yeah, maybe that would be a good idea." Sam straightened in his chair. "Hell, Heather gets out of bed too damned early to fix breakfast anyway. I never get to touch her in the morning anymore. That could work."

"At least we don't have to worry about a housekeeper walking in on anything anymore," Cade said wearily. "Damned if I want any more talk circulating around town about our lives. I'd like to see it settle down a bit before Drace is old enough to go to school."

The other two sighed. They had talked about this before. They had never given much thought to what those in town gossiped about. They were careful of their wives' reputations, and were feared enough that nothing was said or done to hurt the women. But they knew how cruel and thoughtless other children could be. It wasn't something they wanted Drace to suffer.

"Might be a good idea," Sam said slowly. "Thanksgiving is coming around. We could have a big dinner. Maybe let the girls invite some of the friends they've made. The best way to ensure Drace's future is to make certain he has the loyalty needed to overcome anything that gets thrown at him."

Everyone had hated old Joe so badly that torturing his boys had been a favorite game. Cade would be damned if he would see his son tortured that way.

"Okay." Cade breathed in slowly. "I'll call Marie and see if she can find us someone."

Marie had been their housekeeper while they were growing up. She was retired now, living comfortably on the fund Cade had set up for her years before. She would be more than willing to help. They were still her favorite boys, she claimed each time they drove over to make certain she had groceries, medicine, whatever she needed.

"Good plan. But that's not going to fix Christmas for us," Sam warned him. "A housekeeper is not a good enough present."

Cade shook his head. "Damned if I know yet. I'll see if Marly is any more forthcoming tonight than she has been in the past weeks. We might get lucky."

Chapter Two

ဢ

She wasn't. Cade stared at Marly in the privacy of their bedroom after putting Drace to bed, a frown on his face.

"You don't want a housekeeper?" he asked her, confused as frustration flashed in her expression after he made the offer.

"A housekeeper is fine, Cade." Oh, he hated that tone of voice. Where the hell had his sweet, passionate little wife gone?

"Then what was with the look?" He faced her, hands on hips, his eyes going over her overly dressed body. "And what's with the clothes? What happened to your dresses, anyway?"

She frowned darkly. "It's getting cold, Cade. I like my jeans."

"Not that damned cold, it's not." He felt like a sulky child and he was certain he looked like one. "Dammit, Marly, you look good in the dresses."

But she looked damned fine in the jeans, too. They molded her body like a second skin, smoothing over her slender legs, emphasizing her small waist and flat stomach.

"I like the jeans for now." She shrugged. "We'll discuss dresses when it gets warmer. Unless you want me to freeze to death, that is." She arched a brow in question.

Cade's eyes narrowed.

"Fine. This room is plenty warm anyway. Wear the jeans outside it, but at least take them off while you're in here."

Her eyes rounded as though she were scandalized. "What if Drace cries? I'm not trotting into my son's room naked."

79

Cade wanted to roll his eyes. "He's a baby, Marly. You breastfed him, for God's sake."

"That doesn't mean I intend to run around naked in front of him." She crossed her arms under her breasts.

Cade's mouth watered at the sight of those soft mounds beneath her light sweater. His cock throbbed. He was walking around in a nearly constant state of arousal.

"Then put a robe on." He forced the words past his gritted teeth. "Marly, baby, you're pushing a desperate man here."

What was that glimmer that flashed in her gaze? As though she were stilling a flare of anticipation. How long had it been since he had paddled her ass for playing games with him? He hid his smile. Let her keep playing. He couldn't wait to watch those tender curves redden; hear her screaming for release.

The baby's nursery was on the other side of the bathroom. Pretty much protected from the sounds of her arousal and completion. He checked the monitor at the side of the bed. It was on. No danger. His hands itched to touch her. Hell, it had been before the baby was born since he had sunk his cock up her tight ass. He could take her, show her the dangers of pushing him so far. Hell, that was most likely why she was pushing him. She loved it as much, if not more, than he did.

"A desperate man," she snorted softly, her eyes filled with warmth and amusement. "Really, Cade. You act like you haven't been touched in months."

His eyes narrowed at the deliberately provocative sound of her voice. Her nipples were hard. He could see them beneath her sweater.

"Days," he growled.

She gave him a moue of false pity. "Poor baby. But I'm sure things will settle down soon."

Cade knew she was more than aware that he wasn't about to go to Sarah or Heather, so he wasn't exactly certain what the hell she was up to. And from his conversation with his brothers earlier, the other two women were no more forthcoming than his own wife was.

"Is this about Christmas?" he finally asked her point blank, wondering what the hell was up with the subtle little game he sensed was being played. "Am I supposed to be catching hints that I'm missing about presents?"

He saw it then. A flash of fire in her eyes. Almost a sense of frustration or anger. Okay. So this was about hints.

"Marly, tell me what you want," he chided her gently. "I'm not good at the hint, baby. You know that."

"I don't know what you're talking about." She shrugged, but he could feel a sense of hurt involved.

She knew damned good and well what he was talking about and she had no intention of enlightening him. Something tightened in Cade. A sense of fear. Could he be wrong? Maybe this wasn't about Christmas after all. Was he losing her? He had heard horror stories of the changes in women after the birth of a child. Marly was young. Had she really been too young to know what she wanted? To understand the commitment it had taken to love him? Had he destroyed it all?

He tried to still the rush of agony that resonated through him at the thought. The need to take her, hard and deep, to make certain he still held at least that part of her. He tightened his body instead. Steeled himself against the nightmares that rose inside his soul.

She had lost everything he had tried to give her from the moment she had been brought to him. Her innocence. Her fairy tale dreams of love and marriage. Her fantasy of her mother and a mother's love. It would be enough to destroy anyone. Especially someone as gentle, as filled with love, as his Marly.

"Look at you," she sighed. "You're closing up on me. Freezing me out, just like you always do. I hate it when you do that, Cade."

He watched her quietly. He saw love in her eyes. They were soft, shimmering. But there was something more, and that unknown quality had the potential to be his worst nightmare.

"What do you want, Marly?" He kept his voice cool, kept a tight rein on the emotions clashing inside him.

Her gaze flashed with anger. "I want you to stop expecting the worst," she snapped. "Any time you don't understand something going on inside me you lock up. Like you expect me to start spouting hatred and judgmental accusations. It's like even now, you can't accept just how much I do love you."

The pain in her voice robbed him of breath.

"Marly, no." He strode to her instantly, his heart breaking at the tears suddenly shimmering in her eyes. "Baby, you can't cry," he whispered desperately. "Whatever you want, I swear, you can have it. But you have to tell me."

She surprised him by shaking her head, moving away from him.

"Not this time." She breathed in roughly. "This time, Cade, you have to figure it out."

He blinked in surprise. "Figure what out, Marly? Dammit, I'm not a mind reader."

"Too bad." She shrugged.

"Too bad?" he asked her softly, his lust rising sharply at the deliberate challenge he could feel pulsing in the air now.

"Figure it out, Cade." She wasn't angry, but she wasn't far from it.

He watched as she paced over to the window, staring out at the wintry night, tucking her hands into the pockets of her jeans, refusing to say anything more. Refusing to acknowledge him.

Cade realized then that she had been doing this a lot lately. All three of the women had been. Distancing themselves in very subtle ways, making him, Brock and Sam crazy as they fought to figure out the problem. He'd had enough. Since Drace's birth he had tried to be gentle, tried to be the lover a young, innocent woman should have. Tried to make up for the way he had taken her, pushed her, in the beginning of their relationship. She might not tell him what the hell she wanted, but he was damned sick and tired of trying to guess, trying to make up for something he wasn't totally certain anymore that she regretted.

"The hell I will," he muttered, jerking his shirt off, determined that if he wasn't going to get answers, he was at least going to get that tight little ass she was driving him crazy with. First she would submit, then he would get answers.

She turned back, her eyes wide as he stripped. Shirt, boots, pants. His cock was like a length of hot steel, driving him mad with the lust sweeping through his body. And there she stood, her gaze surprised. As though she didn't know what he was pushing her toward.

"Cade." Her voice was hesitant. "The baby…"

"Is asleep," he growled, the fingers of one hand going to his cock as he watched her. Damn, he was going to explode just watching her. "Strip."

"Excuse me?" He would have laughed at the offended shock in her tone if he didn't know damned well that was lust glittering in her eyes rather than fear.

"Now!" He kept his voice hard, visions of her naked, on her knees, his cock tunneling between her lips suddenly driving him insane.

"I don't have time for this, Cade. I'm tired."

"Damned good thing I'm not." He walked to her, grabbing her close, his lips grinding down on hers as he ripped the sweater in half.

She groaned beneath the kiss, but her lips opened, her tongue tangling immediately with his as the pent up violence of his need swept through them both. God, how long had it been since he had taken her like this? Since he had driven them both crazy with the hunger building inside him?

He divested her of her jeans just as quickly, certain the zipper had been stripped with the heavy hand he used to part the material. Fuck it, he thought, one less pair of the bastards for her to tempt him with.

"Cade." Her voice was sharp with the denial that her body contradicted.

His hand caught in her hair, dragging her head back as he stared into her eyes.

"Take the panties off." He bared his teeth, fighting the need to throw her to the bed and pound inside her with a force that would send them both screaming into release.

"No." Her eyes narrowed, her breasts heaving, the hard points of her nipples raking his chest with lashes of fire.

"No?" He released her hair, hooked his fingers in the elastic band of the scraps of lace she called panties and jerked them down her legs as he pushed her back on the bed.

In less than a second he had her gloriously naked, her legs spread. His body tightened at the sight of glistening female cream on the bare mound between her thighs. The small lips pouted, parted, revealing her swollen clit, the tiny entrance to her tight pussy. His cock jerked as she tried to close her legs.

He let her fight. He remembered clearly the excitement that whipped through her when he pretended to let her struggle. She kicked free, turned and attempted to jump across the bed.

Cade pushed her flat to her stomach, moving between her thighs, spreading them, one hand holding her back to the bed, the other moving between her thighs.

Their groans shattered the stillness of the room as his fingers raked along the little slit of her cunt, circled her clit and moved down, parting the silken folds until they could delve into the hot recess of her body.

Silken muscles tightened on two plunging fingers as her vagina convulsed. Cade was mad with lust now. There was no time for foreplay, no time to prolong the exquisite agony. His fingers gathered the satiny juices lying thick and wet on her pussy and spread them back, opening the little bud of her anus, preparing it for the invasion of his finger.

He positioned his cock at the entrance of her vagina. Teased the opening to her hot ass. In the next second he invaded both with forceful thrusts that had her screaming out beneath him.

God. It was so good. Hot. The muscles of her cunt clenched with biting force around the thick shaft of his erection. Her anus convulsed around his finger. Both channels milked at his flesh as his scrotum drew tight and hard against the base of his cock. He was only seconds from release. Thankfully, so was Marly.

With one hand he held onto her slender hips, watching the penetration of his finger into the ultra snug anal opening and began to fuck her with hard, deliberately powerful strokes.

Perspiration poured from his tense body as he fought the need to come fast and hard. He wanted to pour himself into her. Mark her forever. Make her scream her satisfaction. Just as she was screaming his name, begging him for more.

Her vagina rippled around his cock. It convulsed as he thrust into her hard and heavy, relishing the tight grip, the building heat. She tightened on him like a fist, her grip desperate, causing each entrance to forcibly part the spasming muscles, making her scream from the biting pleasure/pain as he groaned from the building pressure in his cock.

"Take me. All of it." He clenched his teeth against the pressure tightening in his scrotum. The exquisite agony of holding back, feeling her tighten around him, plunging inside her until her cries rose, whipped around him, filling his soul until she exploded beneath him.

"God! Marly!" He buried his finger deep inside her ass as he plunged every inch of his tormented cock inside the erupting volcano of her pussy and released his control.

His back bowed as heat arced from between his thighs, up his spine, burying in his mind and exploding with lightning-fast sensation through his body.

He could feel his semen rushing from the tip of his cock, vibrating inside her spasming pussy, and couldn't hold back his own cry. It poured from his soul. Desperate. Filled with his dreams, his needs, his fears.

Spurt after spurt tore though him until he collapsed weakly against her. She was trembling, just like he was, fighting for breath as the storm slowly passed.

"Now, tell me what the fuck is going on," he growled at her ear. "Any more games, Marly, and I swear, I'll tie you up and torture the truth out of you."

Actually, he thought that might not be a bad idea. As soon as he managed to catch his breath, that is.

Chapter Three
November

ઈઝ

"This isn't going to work like this," Sarah muttered as she, Marly and Heather sat in the hot tub in an enclosed grotto and relaxed after a night of exhausting sex.

The house had echoed with all their screams the night before and they hadn't even been in the same room. It seemed the men were growing tired of trying to guess. And the women were growing tired of their thick heads refusing to take a hint.

"God, I'm so tired." Sarah had her head thrown back on the padded edge of the tub, eyes closed. "Brock is going to kill me at this rate."

Strangely enough, they had yet to attempt to gang up on them. If they did, Sarah had a bad feeling this little plan of Marly's was going to go from sugar to shit real fast.

"Have faith," Marly murmured as she sipped at the cool wine she had poured for them all earlier. "Enjoy the moment's respite. You have no idea in hell how hard it was to steal it."

For two weeks Cade, Brock and Sam had waged a steady, ever growing sexual war against their wives. The wives gave the clues; the knotheads ignored them and demanded answers. Sarah sighed. Brock was going to keep ignoring the clues long enough to piss her off and she would end up giving the game over to the men. She wasn't much for games anyway. It was her idea to just lay the law down to them and have it over with. Marly and Heather were certain that wouldn't work. Sarah needed some sleep. The idea was looking better to her every day.

"How bad do we want this?" Marly asked them.

Sarah lifted her head and sighed heavily. "Pretty damned bad," she muttered.

"The idea's a great one," Heather answered wearily. "The execution of it is just getting tiring as hell, though."

"Then we finish it." Marly's will was a hell of a lot stronger than Heather had given her credit for.

When she first met Marly McCall, she had never suspected that beneath that sweet smile, the wicked glint in her eyes and her gentle demeanor existed a backbone of steel. She was proving differently, though. She had outlined the plan while still in the hospital after giving birth to Drace. Her voice had echoed with determination then. It was steel-hard with it now.

"How do we finish it?" Heather asked curiously. "They aren't taking the hints, Marly. As you can see."

"They will." Marly seemed to have more confidence in the men than Heather did.

"At least you have a baby as an excuse to rest," Sarah grumbled as she sipped from her wine. "Brock is killing me, Marly."

Marly snorted. "Oh, is that pain I keep hearing in your screams then?"

Heather laughed. Sarah wasn't above begging loud and hard once Brock got started. She always did say Brock was the most patient of the three men. And it wasn't that it wasn't enjoyable, Sarah thought wearily. It was just getting harder and harder not to give him what he wanted.

"Bite me," Sarah said tiredly as she leaned her head back again.

"Uh-oh. Brock," Sarah heard Marly mutter as the sliding door whispered open and a step sounded behind them.

Sarah's head raised in alarm as she turned around slowly. And there was Brock. Gloriously naked, his erection straining, throbbing heavily, as he caught her gaze and moved slowly toward her. Oh hell. She licked her lips in anticipation, feeling the moisture flooding from between her thighs.

"Brock, you were supposed to help Cade." Marly sounded more than nervous now.

"Drace is sleeping fine, Little Bit." There was no smile. He didn't break his gaze from Sarah's. "You can go check for yourself or stay and wait until Sarah takes care of this little problem she caused earlier."

Sarah had a feeling she was going to pay for teasing him only seconds before leaving him with the other two men to watch the baby. Drace usually stayed up for hours in the evening.

He stepped into the hot tub, his cock, thick and delicious, at level with Sarah's face now.

"Your choice," he growled.

Sarah shivered deliciously. She opened her mouth.

Instantly she was filled with the thick male flesh pulsing so demandingly. Her lips closed over it, her tongue flickering against the head teasingly as her hands rose to grip his thighs. She was aware of Marly and Heather moving from the hot tub, fleeing from the sexual tension beginning to build in the grotto.

Brock's hands gripped her head as he began to thrust in and out of her mouth. This was his retaliation. He always gave her the choice to begin with. She could ease the demands of his body, which she usually teased to a fever pitch, with her mouth or between her thighs. She always tried to stay in control. But she knew damned well what would happen next if she wasn't extremely careful.

"Such a hot little mouth." His words washed over her, spurring her own lust. "So tight and wet. That's it, baby. Lick my cock. Just like that."

She normally loved how very vocal he could get in his hunger for her. He never failed to tell her how much he enjoyed her touch. How hot her mouth was. How very good her tongue felt.

"There you go, baby. Suck me. Suck me harder, Sarah." Her lips were wrapped around the turgid heat, suckling deeply, drawing him as far into her mouth as comfortable. She was quite adept at nearly taking him to her throat and then swallowing almost convulsively.

She did this now. Allowing the head to sink to the entrance of her throat, working desperately to swallow his flesh as he groaned in delirium. Oh, he loved that. His thighs trembled, pre-come leaking from the tip of his cock, salty and sweet at the same time. Then she drew back, savoring the taste that exploded on her tongue as pearly liquid dripped from his cock. He was close. So close, she could feel it.

His balls were tight against the base of his shaft, his breathing loud in the grotto, almost strangled with pleasure as he drove as deep as he dared into her mouth once again. Her fingers cupped his scrotum, caressed it as her other hand stroked the remaining length of his shaft not buried in her mouth.

"Fuck. Yes, baby," he groaned. "Swallow my cock, Sarah. God, it's good. Too fucking good."

He was muttering his pleasure constantly now. A litany of scattered explicit phrases that had her flushing with heat, her vagina pulsing with need. She was already pleasantly tender from his lusty play hours before. She had a feeling she would be exquisitely sore before it was over with.

"Sarah. I'm going to come." He always warned her first. Gave her the chance to pull back, to let him finish in the depths of her pussy rather than spilling his seed in her mouth and making him harder, hungrier, for the flesh between her thighs.

As always by now, she was craving the taste of him, nearly demented in her need to feel the hard wash of semen blasting down her throat. Like a favorite dessert, she couldn't deny herself. Her lips tightened on him, her stroking hands intensifying the pleasure as his hand buried in her hair, fingers clenching, his hips thrusting harder, faster into her mouth.

The burst of his release had her groaning in pleasure. The tart taste of his semen washed over her tongue. His cock stroked over it, spilling the rich essence as she tried to swallow the flesh coming so close to her throat.

Hard, liquid pulses of pleasure accompanied by his throttled shouts of release washed through her. Sarah wanted to cry out at the depth of her own satisfaction. Even without her orgasm, knowing she brought her husband to the point of such pleasure never failed to heat her entire body. Never failed to keep him hard, make him hungrier than ever before.

He pulled from her mouth with a lusty growl, his hands gripping her waist, pulling her up until she sat on the padded edge of the hot tub. There were no preliminaries. He spread her thighs, bending her back, then watched as he sank every hard, hot inch of his cock deep inside the slick portal awaiting him there.

"Brock," she cried out, as helpless as always to still her own vocal enjoyment of the act.

"That hot little mouth is like an aphrodisiac," he growled as his head lowered, his tongue licking at the hard point of one nipple. "I can't fuck you enough, Sarah. I can't get enough of the pleasure, baby. I can't come hard enough to ever sate the need I have for you."

She almost climaxed at the power of emotion echoing in his voice. He always hungered for her. She knew that. Reveled in it. Loved it. Her cunt tightened convulsively around the thrusting shaft, her clitoris throbbing with each stroke of his pelvis against it. He was destroying her. Stroke by stroke, by each whispered entreaty, each earthy vow.

"Harder," she cried out at the carefully paced strokes. She needed him now. Needed him to take her hard and fast before she poured out every secret he demanded that lay in her soul. "Please, Brock. Fuck me harder. Now."

He chuckled against the curve of her breast. "You know better than that, baby."

She groaned. "Please, Brock. Please."

"Give me what I want, Sarah." He burrowed deep and hard, parting the muscles of her vagina with a shatteringly slow thrust, stroking each nerve, each tissue, with destructive pleasure. "Come on, baby. I promise I won't tattle."

She knew better. Knew if she dared voice the need he would never be able to keep it to himself.

"Now, Sarah." He stroked inside her harder, deeper. Then pulled back with such exquisite hesitation her back bowed as she fought to end the sensual torture.

"No. Please, Brock, please take me harder." She shook her head, tightening on him, her flesh spasming with the need for release. Hot, liquid desire spilled through her vagina, gushing around the pulsing shaft as she begged for more.

"Anything you want, baby," he crooned an instant before he slammed inside her, hard and fast. "Tell me, Sarah."

She could hear his control weakening. His cock pulsed, throbbed inside her.

"Oh God, Brock. You're so thick. So hard." She shook her head, so immersed in the pleasure, the need to climax, that she was reaching her own breaking point.

"Sarah," he groaned, fighting for his own control. God help her if he ever found out how weak he made her. How much she wanted to give him what he asked for.

"Tell me." He retreated until only the head of his cock remained inside her. "God, Sarah, don't you know I'd give you the universe itself if I could? Just tell me what you want."

Desperation and pain filled his voice. Sarah's eyes opened, and she stared into the dark depths of her husband's tortured gaze.

"I love you, Sarah. More than my own life." His hands clenched on her hips. Sweat glistened on his face as his expression drew into lines of painful need. "Please, baby. Please don't hurt anymore."

And he knew. Tears filled her eyes. It wasn't just a game. He knew how desperately she needed, he just didn't know what she needed, and she could see the pain that caused. A pain she wanted to ease, yet she knew that the revelation in words could cause more harm than good.

Her fingers lifted to his cheek, trembling as tears spilled down her own cheeks. She loved him. She needed him. But she needed him whole.

"My heart," she sobbed, unwilling to hold it back any longer. Her hand fell to his chest, flattened over his heart. "Mine, Brock. My soul and my life. That's all I want. All of you." It was as much as she could give. But was it enough?

Brock stilled. His eyes widened. She felt his hands tighten with bruising strength on her hips as something glittered in his eyes.

"Always yours," he whispered. A second later he was plunging so hard and deep inside her, so fast and desperate, she felt her soul soaring from her body as she erupted around him a second before his climax exploded inside her.

Deep, hard, pulsing spurts of his seed vibrated deep inside her, throwing her higher as her womb erupted in an orgasm that had her screaming, her head falling back, her pleasure filling the air as her thighs tightened on his, holding him deep, taking every drop of ecstasy he spilled.

They collapsed on the heated wood surrounding the hot tub, their breathing rough, ragged.

"You have a lot to learn about me, Sarah," he whispered breathlessly. "And there's a hell of a lot you're not seeing. Now, baby, ask for what you want. If you dare."

She watched as he raised his head, staring down at her, his expression, for once, closed, cool.

"Brock?"

He moved away from her, watching her, his expression dark, controlled.

"If you can't trust me that far, Sarah, trust me enough to give me your every dream, then you can't trust me to love you, either. Can you?"

She shook her head, her chest tightening in pain. "I know you love me. I love you, Brock."

"Do you?" He rose to his feet, his eyes never leaving hers. "If you did, then that trust would be there. You would open your eyes as you expect me to open mine, and see what's right in front of your face. When you can do that, let me know. We can talk then."

Chapter Four

ଚ୬

"This isn't going to work." Sarah tried to still her panic as she faced the other two women the next day. Brock had been too silent the night before. He had watched her too intently, too knowingly. He knew, and the very fact that he hadn't said anything was scaring her to death.

"Settle down, Sarah." Marly moved to the living room door, checking the dining room and entry hall before closing the door quickly. "We don't need the housekeeper to hear us."

"Not to mention the men." Heather paced the room. "This is getting too damned difficult. We're only weeks away from Christmas, Marly."

"What happened, Sarah?" Marly asked as Sarah sat down heavily on the couch.

"God, this is such a mess," she groaned. "I did my best, Marly. I swear I did. I was nice and vague, just like we agreed, but I think he guessed. He guessed and now he's madder than hell that I didn't just tell him. I knew this was a bad idea."

She glanced up as Heather and Marly shared a worried look.

"What?" she asked warily.

"Cade isn't speaking to me, either." Marly was wringing her hands, her blue eyes wide, upset. "He came to bed last night and just gave me this really strange look before he kissed my forehead and rolled over and went to sleep. He didn't say anything. He always talks to me before we go to sleep."

"Sam was acting strange, too." Heather pushed her fingers through her already rumpled hair. "God, this is such a mess. And it shouldn't be this damned hard. We shouldn't have to play games like this, Marly."

"Do you have another suggestion?" Marly was growing increasingly frustrated now. "Dammit, both of you know how we tried to talk to them before. It didn't work then. Why would it work now?"

They were all silent. Sarah frowned as something Brock had said the night before continued to haunt her. That the answer to what she wanted was right before her eyes. Her heart had slammed in her chest then, and it did again now.

"Marly?" She raised her eyes to the other woman. "They've stopped."

Marly shook her head as she stared at her in confusion. "What?"

Sarah frowned as she considered the past nine months. "Think about it. Admittedly, we haven't given any of them much of a chance to try, but they don't try, either. They've stopped."

Heather and Marly stilled. "We realize that, Sarah." Heather sighed. "But it has to continue this way."

Sarah shook her head demandingly. "No. Listen to me. Think about it. It's completely stopped. No little butt pats. No hot little looks. The whole nine yards. It's stopped."

Marly and Heather both watched her in bemusement. Had they somehow gotten what they were fighting for, without fighting for it? Had the men not paid any attention to their careful avoidance of being alone with any of them, other than their chosen husbands, out of choice?

Marly sat down slowly. "She's right," she whispered, looking at Heather in surprise. "I know Cade. All the avoidance in the world wouldn't work if he got horny enough to go after it. They've stopped on their own."

They had been so concerned with their subtle maneuvers to be certain there was no opportunity for the three men to catch one of them alone, or to try to seduce them into their erotic, heated play. They hadn't realized that the men weren't trying to do so.

"Now what?" Heather asked softly. "How can we be certain they won't want to try to reestablish those relationships later?"

Sarah breathed in roughly. "I'm certain, Heather. Brock is madder than hell right now." The very thought of that terrified her. "He pointed out to me, rather coolly, that maybe what I wanted was right in front of my eyes and I had refused to see it. I think he's right. We've been so concerned with protecting them, with trying to feel our way through this for the past year, that we haven't noticed the change in them." And that broke her heart. "We didn't see that it wasn't our machinations, but their decision to stop themselves."

She watched the other two women pale. "God. We're in some deep trouble here." Marly swallowed tightly. "A pissed August male is not a good thing."

Heather snorted. "What are they gonna do? Divorce us?" she asked them both in irritation. "Okay, so we fucked up. They were a little less clueless than we imagined. But they still haven't figured out exactly what we want. I say we tell them straight out and see what happens."

Marly and Sarah both shot her a look of incredulity.

"Get real!" Marly snapped. "That might work with Sam, and you can go for it if you think it will. But not Cade. You forget his sense of responsibility. His determination to keep this family together. This will break his heart if we do it your way, Heather. I won't risk that."

"It's not like we want to move to another state, Marly," Heather argued. "For God's sake, he would be able to see the house outside his bedroom window. Dammit, as much as I love you and Sarah, and the other brothers, I want my own home. I want my own family, too."

There was a wealth of pain, of growing despondency, in the other woman's words. There was the dream they all held. Their own homes. Their own families. The freedom to bring children into a full, productive family unit rather than the unconventional lifestyle they lived.

It had been different when they married. New to the sexual excesses the men provided, they had been flying on sensuality and the freedom to give in to the more extreme fantasies they all had at one time or another. But now, with Marly's pregnancy and Drace's birth, they had found a core of need inside them that terrified them all. Possessiveness. They wanted their husbands to themselves. They wanted their own homes. Their own families.

"So what do we do?" Sarah asked them both softly. "We can't destroy them. We can't hurt them for our needs. Where does that leave us?"

"Damned if I know," Marly finally sighed bleakly. "But we have to do something now. Because sure as hell they're all three onto us, and they won't wait long before they hit us with it. We have to be prepared."

Damn. Sarah had a feeling the next few days were going to be less than pleasant.

* * * * *

"They're plotting again." Cade looked up from the baby he held securely in his arms to Sam as he walked into the nursery.

Brock was already there. He stood at the window, silent, morose. He was letting this affect him too deeply. Feeling too guilty over something that could be fixed. And Cade was certain it could be fixed.

Drace cooed in delight as Cade continued to rock him, his drowsy blue eyes staring up with an innocence that could only be found in a child's eyes. Eyes so much like Marly's. Drace's features were more like his father's. It made Cade wonder what their daughter would look like. And he was damned determined he wanted one. A fiery little bit of temper and beauty like his Marly, driving them all crazy with her less than logical ways. And his Marly could definitely be less than logical.

He smoothed a finger over Drace's cheek, smiling as the baby giggled and latched onto his fingers. He was already crawling. Put the little imp on the floor and he would be off and struggling to find some kind of adventure that was less than safe. He looked like his daddy. Acted more like his mommy.

"Did you hear me, Cade?" Sam stood by the closed door, and Cade knew his brother's eyes would be glittering with anticipation and amusement.

"What now?" He winced as Drace bit into his finger, the small, barely visible teeth stinging the hard pad of flesh.

"Well, at least they know we're onto them." There was laughter in Sam's voice. Only God knew how that lightened Cade's heart.

Drace yawned, his little eyelids drifting down as he gnawed contentedly on Cade's finger.

Cade snorted. "I was onto them days ago. Sarah just affirmed it." Brock had been furious with himself when he came to Cade and Sam and revealed the nature of the women's wishes.

"We should have seen it sooner," Brock murmured.

"We did, Brock," Cade reminded him of their conversation months after Marly's pregnancy had been confirmed. "It was our decision to stop. We just didn't know how far they wanted to take it."

A year ago, it would have killed something in him to see his brothers and their wives leave his home. They had been a part of each other for so long, he didn't know if he could have survived it then. Drace had changed that, though. The thought of the other children Marly had talked about wanting had cemented the decision. He didn't give a damn what the townspeople gossiped about, but he couldn't face the pain it could bring his children. Couldn't face the thought of raising them in any way that wasn't conventional.

He wanted to take them to Sunday school. He wanted to join the fucking PTA, for God's sake. He could never do that comfortably as long as their lifestyle continued as it was. Besides, he wanted his wife to himself. As much as he loved his brothers, as exciting, intense, and filled with eroticism as their sex lives had been, he no longer needed the affirming bond that had saved them over the years. He needed Marly. He needed their children.

"She could have said something." Cade could hear the regret in Brock's voice. "I should have let her know she had the freedom to do so."

Cade looked up as Sam snorted. "Come on, Brock, they love driving us crazy. You know it and I know it. And we love it. I've called the contractors and they'll be out here next week. Let's let them have their fun while they can. Then they can make it up to us for not trusting us as they should have. As soon as I show my sweet little honey what a bad girl she's been, I'm sure she'll do just that."

Cade hid his smile as he looked up from his sleeping son to his brother's smug expression.

"I think we should push them just a hair bit further." He leaned back in the rocking chair, lifting Drace to his chest, his heart clenching at the gentle weight of his son resting against him. His hand smoothed over the baby's back.

"Yeah?" Sam would be all for the game.

"How?" Brock was always more suspicious.

"We make them ask." Cade kept his voice low. He had no desire to disturb the baby's slumber.

Brock moved from the window until he could face his brother.

"And we do this how?"

Cade watched the other two men. The changes in them all in the past two years were amazing. They laughed. They hugged sometimes. They had even found a way to discuss the events that had nearly destroyed them so long ago. They had healed. And it was the tender acceptance and fiery love of their plotting wives that had sealed the open wounds in their souls and allowed them to live again.

"Easy." Cade smiled. He had been planning this one all day. "We force it out of them." He looked over at Brock. "You know what makes Sarah the wildest. Stop having mercy on her and playing with her. Let her know the game is being played in earnest now. If she wants something, she has to trust you enough to ask for it." His voice hardened, as did his own resolve.

He loved Marly more than he loved his own life, but like Brock and Sam, it bothered him that she hadn't realized how he had drawn back from touching the other women, how he no longer needed any touch but hers. He didn't like the thought that she felt she had to lead him through a decision this important. He wouldn't allow her to play with their lives that way.

"When?" Sam was, of course, the most amused by the whole deal.

Cade shot him a chiding look. "You're enjoying this too much, brother."

"Of course I am," he chuckled. "I've not had this much fun out of Heather in months. It pisses me off she wouldn't come to me, but I figure once it's all said and done, she'll realize the error of her ways."

Cade winced. He had a feeling if Sam wasn't careful his little redheaded wife would be waving her gun under his chin. Damn, she could get mean when she wanted to.

"Tonight," he decided, rising to his feet to place Drace in his crib.

The baby was spread out in innocent abandon, chubby little legs sprawled, arms thrown back above his head. He refused to sleep on his stomach any longer. Cade drew a light blanket over the sleeper-covered body and swallowed past the knot of emotion building in his throat. His son. It never failed to amaze him that he was a part of anything so perfect.

"Now." He changed his mind as he smoothed his finger over Drace's cheek once again. He was as perfect as his mother was. But unlike his mother, a hell of a lot easier to manage. For now.

Chapter Five

ഌ

Heather knew trouble was brewing when the door to the living room opened and the three men walked in. Damn. Separately, they were too good looking for any woman's peace of mind. But together they were dangerous. Tall, dark-haired, bodies built like sin and gazes as wicked as hell itself.

Dressed in jeans, scuffed boots and T-shirts that showed their perfect muscles in stark release, it was enough to send her body humming. But when she looked at Sam, it kicked into overdrive. He was hard. They all were. But that hard-on was for her. She could see it in his eyes; in the way his gaze went over her body, lingered at her breasts, her thighs, then moved back to snare hers.

They stopped just inside the doorway, arms crossed over their chests, staring back at the women with cool, arrogant expressions. Confidence seemed to vibrate around them. Control. Resolution. Hell, she had a feeling the three of them were in a shitload of trouble now.

Cade shook his head as he tsked at them softly. "Ladies," he sighed patiently. "I can see we've evidently not been keeping you well occupied."

Heather's brow snapped into a frown. Oh, she really didn't like that tone of voice.

"And you figured this out all on your own?" She almost winced at Marly's confrontational tone.

Cade shot his wife a chiding look. "Beloved." His grin was wolfish. It made all of them nervous. "You are, I'll assume, the ring leader in this little farce."

Marly snorted. "You know what assume does, babe. Makes an ass out of you and me." The cliché was delivered with more than a little heat.

Cade's gaze flared with lust. Hell, Marly was going to be screaming louder than the rest of them would be.

"Bad move, girlfriend," Sarah muttered from Marly's side.

Brock's brow lifted sardonically. Usually not a good sign. His gray-blue eyes were glittering with lust, a hint of anger, and a possessive glitter that should be curling Sarah's toes.

"Nothing to say, sweetness?" Heather's attention was caught by Sam's sardonically voiced question.

Heather shrugged lightly, fighting the grin that curled her lips. Hell, it wasn't like he would divorce her. Right?

"Oh, I have plenty to say, hotshot," she murmured as she let her gaze heat and drift over his body. He was one damned fine looking man, she thought. It never failed to amaze her that she had managed to gain this man's love. "I've just been practicing patience."

Sam grunted. It seemed he wasn't buying that one.

"You ladies ready to state your demands yet?" Cade asked them, his voice hard, his gaze hot as he watched his wife. "The game is getting old."

"Says who?" Marly was definitely fired up now.

Sexual tension thickened in the room, making Heather shiver with the anticipation of what was to come. They had all settled rather well into married life. The sex was great, but the past year or so had been lacking in some of the kinkier aspects of sexual play between herself and Sam. She realized now that it wasn't just something she had missed; it was something that had begun to fill her with a fear she had refused to acknowledge. The fear that Sam was growing bored with her. That he no longer needed her as he had before.

That revelation caused her chest to tighten painfully. They did have, to an extent, exactly what they had been fighting for and they had been too frightened of the changes in their lives to see it.

"Says me, Marly." Cade moved into the room, advancing slowly on his wife as she became increasingly more nervous. "You should have known the game came with a price, baby."

Heather glanced at the other woman. Her eyes had widened in surprise. Punishment had normally been the exquisitely sensual torture of the three men driving her insane with pleasure. Heather frowned. Surely the men didn't think they were going to resume the sharing to placate their tender feelings? After more than a year of shying away from it, Heather wasn't about to allow it.

She stepped in front of Marly, surprising them all.

Cade stopped. His brows lowered ominously. He intimidated the hell out of her, but she wasn't about to let him know it.

"No sharing." She was tired of the game herself. Her gaze went to Sam, desperation welling up inside her as she met his hard gaze. "I mean it, Sam. No more."

"Are you saying you didn't enjoy it, Heather?" Cade asked softly, his voice suspiciously bland.

Fear, pain, and not a little regret rose inside her. "You know we all did," she snapped furiously. "But enough is enough, Cade August. It's finished."

"It was finished over a year ago. You ladies were just too damned stubborn and determined to have it your way to notice it." A spark of hurt, of anger, tinged his voice.

"You didn't say anything," Heather argued forcibly. Hell, how were they supposed to know? They were avoiding the men during that time as much as possible.

"Say anything?" Brock snapped. "Damn. Why would we? We weren't trying to fuck you, Heather. That should have been enough."

Exasperation laced his voice but filled all their expressions.

"Well, excuse me for not noticing you weren't getting hard-ons for all of us." Heather threw her hands up helplessly at that point. They were men. Dammit. She knew better than to argue with one of them. "It's not as though you informed us of this bright idea at the time."

"Sam." Cade's voice was carefully controlled now. "Would you come collect your wife so I can drag mine from behind her? Might be a good time to prove you don't need help handling her."

Sam's throttled laughter had anger surging hard inside her. She clenched her fists, braced her body. She would be damned if she would be treated like a child.

"Heather?" Cade caught her attention by simply cupping her jaw with his larger hand and turning her head to meet his gaze again. What she saw there had her stilling in surprise. Warmth. Kindness and caring, but the spark of lust that glowed there for his wife wasn't there when he gazed at her now. "You will always be my sister. Always loved by me. Always a part of me, just as Sam is. Nothing, and I mean nothing, means more to us than your, Sarah's and Marly's happiness. No matter what you want. No matter your needs. If it's ours to give, then it's yours."

The vow, made so simply in a voice hoarse with emotion, had tears filling her eyes.

"But Sam's still going to make you think twice about playing games with us again." His wolfish smile was followed by her gasp as Sam moved in from the side, gripped her arm and began to pull her away from Marly. Brock was behind him. Sarah was thrown over a broad shoulder as she gasped in surprise. When she protested, a large calloused palm slapped her vulnerable rear lightly.

Heather wasn't certain what happened to Marly. But the other woman was laughing. Not that she thought laughter was entirely appropriate under the circumstances.

The look on Sam's face was unnerving. His eyes damned near glowed with lust, with love and an intent determination. Heather had a feeling the holidays were definitely beginning to look up.

Chapter Six

⁊∙

Sam dragged Heather from the living room. She gave him just enough of a fight to appease her sense of pride. She wasn't going to just lie down and let him have whatever he wanted. That might spoil him. Or her. She wasn't certain which. One thing was for sure, he was a man unwilling to take no for an answer.

He pulled her through the entryway and up the curving staircase. Each step was deliberately paced, as though he were holding onto his control by a thread. His expression, the few times he glanced back at her, was a study in sensuality. He wasn't going to go easy on her. But quite frankly, she'd had enough *easy* in the past year to last for a while. She wanted her man back. Hard-driving. Demanding. Dominant. She loved the gentle Sam. But she craved the bad boy sex he had seduced her with in the beginning.

He pulled her into their bedroom, slammed the door behind them, then ripped her shirt from her back. She stared down at her bared breasts in surprise and shock. He had never ripped her clothes from her before.

"Do you have any idea how hard it's been to treat you gently? To show you how much I love you? How much you mean to me?" His low, hoarse voice had her eyes widening in surprise. Was he hurt? Had she hurt the one person she would rather die than wound?

"Sam?" She reached out for him, then gasped in surprise when he gripped her wrists, anchoring them behind her back before his lips lowered to hers.

His kiss was pure carnal delight. His other hand gripped her jaw, forcing her mouth open for the smooth penetration of his wicked tongue. Once inside, he became rapacious. Starving. Bending her backwards as he pressed his jeans-covered erection into the hot vee of her thighs, his lips, teeth and tongue forcibly seducing her with lustful intent.

Heather cried out, her fingers curling into her palms as she fought to rub the hard nipples of her breasts against the rough fabric of his cotton shirt. She moaned at the electric thrill that shot through them, arcing between her thighs, dampening her pussy further at the pleasure.

He held her securely as he backed her through the room. Each step was rife with anticipation, building in sexual tension as she waited for the feel of the bed behind her legs.

Heather had only a second to realize she was at the edge of the mattress before he pushed her down, his hands moving quickly to the snap and zipper of her jeans. Releasing them, he jerked the material down her legs then ripped her panties from her hips.

"Look at you," he growled as he stripped hurriedly, staring down at her, his face flushed, his lips heavy with sensuality. "So damned tiny my lust for you terrifies me at times. Each time I watch my cock burrow into you, I'm amazed you can take me."

There were times it amazed her.

"Sam." She was panting with excitement now.

"I hope you're ready for me, Heather," he said softly as he freed the heavy, thick flesh of his cock from his jeans.

She licked her lips nervously. He was raging hard. The plum-shaped head pulsed in demand, the skin over the steel-hard shaft stretched tight.

"Turn over." Her gaze flew to his as he muttered the order.

She knew what he wanted. In that second, she was well aware that the bad boy she had missed so desperately was back. And he was back with a vengeance.

"I haven't…" She shook her head quickly. She wasn't ready. She had stopped preparing herself for it when his lovemaking had become more tender, though no less hungry or demanding.

He smiled tightly. "That's when it's better, baby. So tight and hot I know my head will come off when I shoot my come inside that sweet ass. When I hear you scream, because you don't know if it's pleasure or pain."

His jeans were discarded, his shirt thrown to the floor as he turned and removed the tube of lubricating gel from the bedside table.

"Turn over, Heather. Don't make me tie you to the bed."

She shivered at the demand. At the thought of being tied down.

"Like that thought, do you?" Several silk ties were snagged from the drawer then. "Let's see how much."

She fought him. She wasn't about to give in without a fight. She struggled and cursed his easy strength as he dragged her up the bed, held her down and restrained her wrists to the slats of the headboard, spreading her thighs as he positioned himself between them. She was laid out for him, thighs spread, her cunt so hot and wet she could feel the juices lying thick along the tender lips.

"Damn, I could almost come just looking at you." He leaned forward instead, his lips covering a painfully hard nipple as Heather cried out, arching against him, helpless now, wary of the streaking excitement that flashed through her blood stream. She liked it. Liked being vulnerable, tied down for his pleasure.

"Sam." She bucked against him, so desperate for his touch now she knew she would go insane if he didn't hurry and fuck her soon.

"Uh-uh, baby." He raised his head, his lips wet from his ministrations at her breast, his eyes dark, ravenous. "It's time to see what you're tempting. Next time you play games with me, Heather, you'll think of this."

Oh yeah. That was really going to scare her, she thought. Then he pulled one of the toys that had gone unused from the table by the bed. Her eyes widened as he pulled it from its protective package.

The thick, supple dildo was nearly as large as his cock. He smiled wickedly as her eyes widened.

"I haven't shared you all these months, Heather, for a reason," he informed her silkily. "We made the decision. Me. Cade. Brock. No more sharing. Do you want to know why, baby?"

She shook her head, her breath catching as he pushed several pillows beneath her hips, elevating her, lifting her to give him better access to the small entrance she knew he was determined to take now. After arranging her as he wanted, he squeezed a thick row of the lubricating gel on his fingers.

"Yes, you do." His voice was soft now, dangerous in its completely sexual intent. "I'm going to tell you anyway. Because when I do this…" His fingers tucked into her anal entrance. "And hear this…" He pushed two into her slowly, surely, as a long, tremulous cry tore from her throat. "I want to know it's all for me."

Heather's back arched as he filled the small opening with his fingers, stretching her, sending a fiery pleasure streaking through her body so destructive she feared she would never survive it. Her cunt pulsed, gushed, sending its slick juices to mingle with the lubrication he was applying to the small channel, making his entrance that much easier. But it had been a while since he had taken her there. She was unprepared, the muscles tighter, exquisitely sensitive.

"Damn, Heather." He grimaced with anticipation as she watched him. Watched as he tracked each move his fingers made in and out of her gripping channel. "Baby. It's going to be so good." He glanced up at her then, smiling wickedly as she trembled from head to toe.

His fingers thrust inside her slow and easy, parting the muscles, stretching them, preparing her as she cried out at the heat and pleasure-pain assaulting her body.

"It's been so long," he growled, his voice tight with anticipation. "I've been dying to burrow back inside your sweet little ass, Heather. Starving for it. I won't wait any longer. And I'll never wait again."

His fingers plunged inside her again. Deep. Wide. Heather dug her heels into the mattress, lifting closer to him, bucking against each entrance to drive him deeper. She was drunk on the sexuality thickening around them, damp with perspiration, with the heat raging through her body.

"Ready now, baby?" he crooned, his voice dark, anything but soothing as he lifted her closer, raising her legs until they rested on his wide shoulders, and positioned his erection for entrance.

"Sam…" She stilled as she felt the broad head of his cock beginning to part the tender opening.

"I love you, Heather." The softly spoken words, so filled with emotion, with hunger and need, washed over her. "You are my life. You are the only bond I need. The only love I crave. Only you, Heather."

She screamed as his cock pushed slowly, relentlessly, into her anus. Not with pain. With streaking pleasure so intense it burned her alive, sent flames flickering through her pussy, her womb, making her insane with the combination of carnal delight and emotional excess.

As he pushed with hot deliberation into the ultra-tight channel, his fingers weren't still. His thumb raked her clit. His fingers played with the bare lips of her pussy, sliding in teasingly as he made a slow advance into the hot grip of her ass. She was dying with ecstasy. Heather bucked against him, trying to drive him deeper, gasping then crying out at the biting streaks of pleasure as her body accommodated the thickness of his cock, until he was fully seated in, every throbbing inch buried in her backside as the muscles convulsed around it.

"There, sweet baby." He was breathing hard, fighting for control.

Heather stared up at him, dazed, her anal channel on fire, filled, stretched, awash in such stinging pleasure she feared the coming orgasm.

"Now," she gasped, moving against him, trying to force him to begin the deep hard thrusts that would eventually send her spinning into her climax.

"Not yet, baby." He picked up the dildo then. "I won't share you anymore, but I'll be damned if I'll do without that certain little cry that pierces my soul when you get fucked like this."

"Sam. I can't stand it," she cried out as he rubbed the firm head of the fake cock against her vaginal entrance.

He stretched her anus so tightly, filled it so deeply, that she feared what would happen to her own state of mind if he pushed that dildo up her pussy. She was already poised on such a peak of sensation it was mind destroying.

She had done this with his brothers. Felt their cocks straining in her body, her mouth, and hadn't known this intensity of sensation.

"Too bad, baby," he whispered gently. "Because here it comes."

She could feel every thick inch, every manipulated ridge, every damned nuance of the fake cock as he began to work it slowly into her already tight pussy. She thrashed in his arms, screaming out as the pleasure tore through her body with bursts of heat so blinding it nearly took her breath.

When he had the device firmly, deeply embedded within her, he began to move. Oh God. It was too much. He pushed her legs back, coming over her, bracing his arms at her side as he stared into her eyes.

"Now." He pulled back, his cock nearly sliding free of her snug anus before he pushed back in a long, smooth stroke that had stars flashing in front of her eyes.

The dildo buried in her pussy moved with each thrust. Slow, shallow strokes that caressed nerves rarely exposed to such sensation, rarely stretched in just such a way. She tossed her head as her muscles tightened on him as he groaned in pleasure and lost the last bit of control. She loved it when he exploded in just that manner.

He began to fuck her in earnest then. Each hard thrust inside her anus, each rasping of the dildo up her pussy pushed her higher, turned her into a creature of sensation, hungering, craving each second of the countdown to ecstasy. And he was driving her to it. Hard, blistering thrusts up her ass that kept her poised on that edge of pleasure, of pain, left them both gasping, moaning, desperate.

Her pussy rippled and she knew he felt it in the desperately stretched tunnel he was powering into. Over and over. Fierce, desperate thrusts as she felt her body tighten, her womb clench, her pussy spasm.

"Now." She tried to scream as she strained against her bonds, feeling her orgasm building, surging…destroying.

Unconsciously, the muscles of her anus clamped harder on his thrusting cock, her pussy clenching on the dildo as every nerve ending in her body exploded. Seconds later, she cried out again as she heard Sam's ragged groan, felt his cock throb, expand, then felt the hard, heated jets of his semen blasting into her anus, triggering another, deeper orgasm and taking her breath along with it.

"Love you. Love you. Oh God, baby. How I love you." Sam collapsed against her, raining kisses over her face, her lips, as his body jerked, trembled, his own release rippling through each muscle and tendon.

Heather fought to catch her breath, but the aftershocks of the orgasm stole it each time. She shuddered beneath him, her own voice husky, ragged, as emotion rushed through her.

"I love you, Sam." Tears dampened her cheeks, wet her lips. "I love you so much. But I need our own home." The dam had broken inside her. "I need our own family, our own babies. Dammit, I want my own picture over my own fireplace."

She was sobbing now, barely aware of him pulling free of her, removing the dildo and gathering her gently in his arms as he released her bonds.

"I want it all," she cried into his chest. "I want all of you."

She would never regret the time she had spent with his brothers, the sexual escapades, or the wildly erotic knowledge that she could have one or all, whenever it pleased her. No recriminations. No guilt. But she no longer wanted that. Had never truly wanted it for longer than it had lasted. She had what she wanted, what she needed, right now in her arms.

"Shh, baby." His lips stroked over her cheek. "It was always yours, Heather. Always. All you had to do, baby, was tell me. All I needed was to know."

"But you needed your brothers." She shook her head, hating her own tears. "You needed that bond."

"Heather." He pulled her head back and she was amazed at the depth of emotion she saw in his gaze. "This, with you, is all I've ever really needed. Without this, no bond on earth could save me, baby. My soul would wither away and die. You saved me, Heather. I'm so sorry you didn't feel you could come to me. Didn't feel you could trust me with your dream. The wounds healed slowly, baby, but you healed them. I'm all yours. Always."

The truth of his words glistened in his eyes, in the single tear that tracked down his cheek.

"Our own home," he whispered then. "Our own picture over our own fireplace." He placed his hand on her abdomen. "Our own baby." His voice lowered, becoming reverent, awed. "I want our own baby, Heather."

In his voice, in his eyes, she saw the need, the dreams she had been afraid he would never have.

"Our own baby." Her hand covered his. "I love you, Sam."

"And I love you, Heather. Forever, baby. Forever."

Epilogue
Christmas, One Year Later

෨

There were three houses where once there had been one. Within sight of each other, front yards facing the center of the main ranch yard. Each different. Each distinctive to the couple who resided within.

Cade stood at the large window of the suite of rooms he and Marly had renovated to allow them a view of the other houses. The bedroom was larger, filled now with Marly's gentle, sometimes whimsical, tastes. But despite the feminine touches, it still retained the more dominant flavor that the old room had. Heavy dark furniture, large chairs, a wide bed. Not that he ever let her get far from him.

It had been a year since she and the others had plotted and planned the final downfall of the August men. Cade smiled. Being taken down had never been so good.

"Aren't the lights pretty?" Marly moved beside him, snuggling against him as he wrapped his arm around her waist.

The lights were indeed pretty. Each house had been strung with a multitude of festive colors. Lighted icicles dripped from eaves, while candy cane colors wrapped around porch posts, and multi-colored blinking confections surrounded windows. It was a winter wonderland of holiday delights. Drace had loved each and every minute he spent watching them. And soon, there would be a baby brother or sister to share the excitement.

He ran his hand over Marly's distended abdomen, amazed at the life he could feel pulsing beneath it. Twins. It terrified him. Heather was expecting as well. Sarah had just given birth to Brock's daughter. A golden-haired little heartbreaker they would all be hard-pressed to keep the beaus away from later. The ranch was filling with life. With laughter. With love. With dreams he never thought would be his own.

"Thank you." He pressed a kiss to his wife's riotous curls.

She looked up at him, her brilliant blue eyes misty with emotion.

"Thank you," she whispered. "For both our dreams, Cade. For daring to dream with me."

Their arms surrounded each other, both their gazes returning to the view, and the future stretching ahead of them.

About the Author

ഃ

Lora Leigh is a wife and mother living in Kentucky. She dreams in bright, vivid images of the characters intent on taking over her writing life, and fights a constant battle to put them on the hard drive of her computer before they can disappear as fast as they appeared. Lora's family, and her writing life co-exist, if not in harmony, in relative peace with each other. An understanding husband is the key to late nights with difficult scenes, and stubborn characters. His insights into human nature, and the workings of the male psyche provide her hours of laughter, and innumerable romantic ideas that she works tirelessly to put into effect.

Lora welcomes comments from readers. You can find her website and email address on her author bio page at www.ellorascave.com.

Tell Us What You Think

We appreciate hearing reader opinions about our books. You can email us at Comments@EllorasCave.com.

MAKE ME BELIEVE
Shiloh Walker

శం

Chapter One

ഇ

"Nikolai."

The gleaming black head didn't so much as lift in acknowledgment.

But the leader knew he was aware. In nearly nine hundred years of walking the earth, those large green eyes had rarely missed anything

"You did not come to our meeting." The boss's voice was grim, aggravated, and firm. Nikolai should have been intimidated.

Nik's soft sigh filled the room. He closed his heavily lashed eyes, a thick lock of black, silken hair falling into his eyes as his long-fingered, graceful hands stilled on the small sculpture he held. *The Council can go fuck themselves.* He didn't say it out loud, but he suspected his captain heard him all the same.

"How many times must I tell you? 'Tis bad enough in the eyes of the Council that I have chosen an unmated man as my successor—"

"One of three."

The low, deep timbre of his voice still held the rich hints of Russia, the echoes of his homeland from centuries past.

"It doesn't matter if you are one of a thousand. You are unmated, you shirk our traditions, you do not act as one of us, dress as one of us."

"Renounce me," Nikolai suggested pithily as he continued to carve an angel from a piece of crystal. Dreamy blue eyes narrowed in concentration, though he was fully aware of the concerns of his mentor—once his master, now his friend. But Nikolai had more important concerns on his mind than whether or not the North Council chose him.

Once, it had been the most important thing to him.

Once…

* * * * *

Chelly lowered herself gently down onto the couch, afraid her body was going to shatter. The papers in her hand sealed her fate.

The bastard was trying to take Bryan from her, saying she was unfit, losing her mind, dreaming of places, men, worlds that didn't exist. Certainly not fit to take care of a normal boy, much less a handicapped child, one with special needs.

"Our son isn't handicapped, you cold-ass son of a bitch," she hissed. Then her emerald green eyes narrowed. He couldn't hear. That didn't mean he was less of a person. *Damn him!* "My son. *My* son." Drawing her knees to her chest, she rested her cheek on them and sighed shakily. "*Nikolai*…this is all your fault."

Of course…what good does it do blaming it on you?

You aren't real.

I am going crazy.

She had first had dreams of him when she was small, just five. Right after the death of her parents, on Christmas Eve. They had been out doing some last minute shopping. A desperate druggie, looking for money, needing that next fix and her parents had been wealthy-looking targets. He hadn't cared he had robbed a child of her parents, her focus, and on Christmas Eve, the most magical day of the year.

It would have stopped being so magical that day.

But a gentle, smiling man with kind, caring eyes had come to her in her tear-filled dreams and whispered soothing things, promised her that her parents were well and together and she would see them again, she just must be good and patient…and she mustn't cry so…Christmas was coming. A man who made magical things happen as he spun snowflakes from his hands, and made rainbows come alive in midair while she watched.

A man who had eyes that glowed in the dimness of the room, and curving, pointed ears.

Damn Christmas!

He had laughed at her outburst and picked her up, cuddled her, stroked her downy, golden curls. *Da, da, you feel this way now, I know. But not for always. Sleep, little one. Sleep.*

That was the first time he had come to her, though not the last. Her imaginary friend wasn't the typical one. Hers was a tall, handsome man, with hair that billowed down to his waist, impossibly blue eyes, and curved pointing ears…*elf* ears. A handsome, fairy tale prince. And as she went from girl to teen, he became the focus of all her daydreams, her first teenage crush, a man who didn't exist.

This imaginary friend who never went away, who knew her better than she knew herself.

Nikolai, who had guided her through her teenaged crisis and turbulent college years with his infrequent visits in her dreams, with his wry smile and dry wit, his low, husky laughter and that exotic voice that sent shivers rushing down her spine even thinking of it. Anytime life had gotten too tough, Nikolai had crept out of her subconscious and guided her through the toughest times—was it any wonder she had fallen in love with her fantasy?

It wouldn't have been so bad if she had kept the knowledge completely to herself. If she hadn't taken to writing her daydreams down in journals, or letters to him. Which was how Nate had found out about Nikolai. He had found the journals inside the wooden chest in her home office, filled with years of lovingly written words—page upon page of thoughts, letters, and sketches of the man who wasn't real.

Chelly had laughed it off.

She didn't realize how very real Nikolai was to her. It was written all over her face, in the way her eyes softened, her mouth, the way her entire body seemed to relax and go into preparation for his touch. Nate had seen it—and hated the man whose image was vaguely similar to his own.

Idiot…why did you ever write to him? Slamming her head back against the wall, she stared outside, tears streaming down her face. Chelly could have explained away the sketches. But the letters…how could she explain away years and years of letters?

And she should have listened when Nikolai had warned her, hell, threatened her about marrying Nate when she found out she was carrying Bryan. She had fully intended to take care of the baby on her own, but Nate had talked her into it, lulled her into thinking he truly loved her, the pompous bastard.

Nikolai had warned her—

"Damn it," Chelly hissed, clapping her hand over her mouth in horror. "I'm doing it again."

Maybe Nate was right, maybe she was crazy.

Chapter Two

&

"I am real, you contrary little minx," he murmured into the mirror, narrowing his eyes, frowning as she buried her face against her knees. Why was she so sad now, his little angel? His time with her was bitterly short, and it had been nearly six months since he had seen her and the little one last, just a few days after she had broken her union with that bastard who was so unworthy of her.

Nik waited, waited for her to whisper to him, the words that would bring him to her. But they never came. A thick, bitter swell of disappointment rose in his chest and he clenched his fists as she rose from the window seat, *alone*, scrubbing her tears away, and squaring her shoulders.

There was a determined look on her face, a look he didn't like.

What was his little minx up to?

Nikolai shook his head and pulled himself away from the mirror, away from the woman who had called to him for years. So much to be done. Christmas was only a month away, and he had much to do, they all did.

He did not have the time to sit around and yearn for the sloe-eyed minx who had haunted him for years.

Rhys would love to see him now, yearning and sighing after a young mortal he could never have. Just another thing to make him even more melancholy, another mark against him in the eyes of the Council. Rhys was unmated as well, but at least he was not a somber, unsmiling bastard, as he so often pointed out to Nikolai.

With a grim sigh, Nikolai turned away from the mirror and focused on the task at hand. Work. There was work to be done.

He would worry about Chelly after Christmas.

Or when she called him.

When she needed him, she'd call.

But the call never came.

Even after a year of waiting, the call never came.

* * * * *

One Year Later

Gone…

Missing…

Every mother's worst nightmare, and Chelly was living it. Nate hadn't returned Bryan from his visitation. Had, in fact, absconded with him—along with his new fiancée—clearing out their house, and fleeing the state. Chelly paced the living room as cops and federal people surrounded her, talking around her and through her, but rarely to her.

Chelly jumped every time the phone rang, and slept only in stops and starts. Last week, with shaking hands, she had flushed her medicines down the toilet. Medicines she hadn't needed—she wasn't depressed and she wasn't suffering from hallucinations or delusions. Her headaches still plagued her and would take a while to go away, but she would no longer pretend that she was delusional and needed medicine just to keep her ex-husband happy. Hell, he had taken Bryan away from her anyway.

As she paced the room on the eighth day of Bryan's kidnapping, she grew aware of how quiet the room had fallen. Slowly, she turned and met Agent McKiernan's faded gray eyes, his tired face. He gazed at her from across the room as he started toward her and she realized he held his cell phone. Cell phone...

Tearing her gaze from it, Chelly started to back away.

No.

"Chelly...they've found your ex-husband and his fiancee. And your son..."

* * * * *

After nearly a year without it, he felt her. Nikolai jerked up in the middle of a vast lake of silken sheets, the midnight blue comforter falling to his waist, his chest heaving raggedly as he struggled to breathe beyond it.

Her pain was tearing at him.

Nikolai felt it in his heart like a great ripping beast.

It was her need that pulled him, her hunger, her wishes. More often than not, she merely pulled his consciousness into her dreams, and he would try to soothe whatever troubled her.

Oft times, her misery was great—she took on much and she did too little for herself, ignored her own heart, her desires, her needs. He made his way to the darkened bathroom and threw on the light, staring at his pulsing almost feverish eyes, before the mirrored reflection dissolved away and revealed Chantelle—for the first time in almost twelve months.

A hospital room, darkened, lights and machines pulsing and beeping, small plastic tubes going to and from the child.

Heaven above, what has happened? Nikolai's hands gripped the edge of the counter and his vision blurred for a brief moment. Swallowing convulsively, he reached out and pressed his hand to the mirror and flexed it, watching as Chantelle's body flinched as he slid inside her mind, probing and seeking...

Ahh, there would be no simple soothing this time, Nikolai knew. Staring through the mirror, he studied the child. Bryan was a happy, rather astounding child, he knew. And he lay fighting for his life. Mortal bodies were so frail. An old scar, very old, low on his belly, was proof of that. Nikolai had been mortal...once.

A wounded child, grievously wounded, in Russia nearly a thousand years ago, he had been hunting with his father at the age of nine. His father hadn't survived the thieves' attack on their camp. Nikolai wouldn't have. But Alisdair had come upon them that wintry, frozen night as he lay bleeding to death from the ragged knife wound low in his belly. He still clutched the knife he had used on one of the thieves as he tried to protect his father's fallen body.

Da... Mortal bodies were frail.

Chantelle lay with her head against the bed linens on the narrow hospital bed sobbing.

The boy was still young enough...he could be made elf-kin.

But the mother...that option simply wasn't there. But he would have her, nonetheless.

And she wasn't likely to forgive him easily either.

He waited until she had fallen asleep. She was weary—once sleep held her in its bond, there was no waking her, but he brushed his mind to hers and whispered of sleep just to be certain. Then Nikolai went to the boy and hunkered down beside him, cupping his face and easing inside his mind. *Ahhh...the pain...so young to feel such pain...*

He felt the boy's sudden jerk, his startlement as he recognized a phantom touch in his mind. Then his fear... "Do not be afraid, boy, I come to give you a good thing," he whispered. "To take this kind of pain away forever and ever."

"Nonononononono...Mama!"

In reality, all the boy did was whimper, but it was enough. Wrapping his arms tight around the child, Nikolai opened his eyes, a flash of moonlight falling across them as he stared at Chelly just as she woke. "No more pain, Bryan, I promise."

* * * * *

Chelly awoke to see a familiar, glowing pair of eyes — dreamy, soft, and blue — awash with light, the face in shadow, as a man lifted Bryan, still hooked up to various machines and monitors. And they were gone, before she could even draw in the breath to ask who in the hell he was.

But she didn't need to.

Chelly knew those eyes. They haunted her dreams, both sleeping and waking.

Nikolai…

The soft, husky voice rolled through her mind even as she opened her mouth to scream as nurses came running in. Shooting up out of her chair, she flipped on the lights and whirled around, staring at the room. He was gone. Well and truly gone. Not out the window, or the door, just *gone*. Her breath left her lungs in a shuddering gasp and her teeth were chattering as she stared at the nurses who started to ask where the boy had gone.

And she had to whisper, "I don't know…"

But she did. Chelly knew.

He was with Nikolai, a fey creature who shouldn't exist, a man who had eyes that glowed, and exotically curved ears, a smile that turned her insides to mush, her knees to jelly, and made her heart flip over in her chest.

And that fey, magical being had her son.

Gritting her teeth, Chelly felt the anger start to build in her gut.

Nik had her son.

Chapter Three

ಬ

"Where is my son?"

That low, furious female whisper rasped through Nikolai's rooms and he lifted his gaze away from the still child who lay on his bed. Ganessa looked up from Bryan and smiled sympathetically. "She will be so angry."

"Angry is better than heartbroken, *da*? He would not have survived such grievous injuries, Ganessa." Long, silken hair spilled like an ebony cape around his broad shoulders as he knelt beside the bed, stroking one hand over the boy's downy, golden locks. Nikolai lifted his gaze to study the healer who had come to assist him and he shrugged. "Her anger I can handle. Her broken heart I cannot. And the boy—I love this child. He has a hold on my heart, and has had since his birth. First because he came from her, but then because of who he is."

Ganessa smiled at Nikolai, shaking her head. "I wish you luck. A woman's wrath is a terrible thing. And mortal anger..."

Nikolai arched a brow at her. "I was mortal, Ganessa. Once." Lowering his eyes back to the boy, he asked, "How is he faring?"

"Well. He is younger than most that are brought into the kin-bond. Elf-kin isn't a pleasant journey to make, but he is taking it better than the older children. He will sleep through it all and wake with no memory of the accident that nearly killed him. But his mama needs to be here when he wakes. Hadn't you best bring her here now?" Ganessa asked as she ran mental hands through the boy's spirit and psychic self and her physical hands over his healing body. Lastly, she cupped her hands over his ears, lingering, wondering.

Nikolai grimaced. "*Da*. And what a pleasant task I go to."

* * * * *

Nikolai couldn't possibly have just come in here and taken my son...

But that means he is real.

But a man doesn't just appear and disappear.

He did! The cameras didn't record anybody entering or leaving this floor – Chelly was almost ready to put a pillow over her ears to drown out the voices in her head. But she was pretty damn certain it wouldn't work.

It had been Nik. Which meant he was real.

Slowly, Chelly turned her head and looked at the security guards and various administrative staff and nurses who had gathered in her room. Chelly smiled a brittle, false smile, her eyes wild and bright as she said in a high, nearly hysterical voice, "Excuse me. I need a minute alone."

Once in the bathroom, she leaned over and splashed water on her face, leaving it running as she straightened to stare into the mirror. Her soft green eyes were snapping and glinting, harsh and full of threat as she rasped quietly, "Nikolai...where is my son?"

There was no answer for a long moment.

Then the mirror started to fog...maybe it was the heat from her breath. Maybe she was nuts. Would that explain why the surface rippled like water?

When Nikolai's face appeared in the mirror, Chelly had to stifle a scream. She'd hoped he would answer. Had prayed. But so quickly? Long, glossy black hair spilled around broad proud shoulders, two thick braids at each temple keeping the hair from his face, displaying the fine, arrogant bones of his handsome face, the high arch of his brows, and a polite, quizzical smile.

Polite? Quizzical? Like he hadn't just kidnapped her son.

"Where is my son?"

Like a voice from a well, Nikolai's voice came echoing and rippling, caressing her ears. *"Here...with me...healing. Your mortal doctors cannot save him. We can."*

"Bring him back." Her voice was a furious, snapping hiss and Chelly's hands clenched in fury as rage coursed through her. He had just taken him, like Nate. Even to save him...*why didn't you take me, too?* A soft little voice whispered inside her head. And the more rational part of her added, Nikolai is nothing like Nate.

But she had been separated from her son for too long, and rationality had never been one of her finer points.

Nikolai smiled. *"There is no coming back. He is here – here he stays. Come and join him or stay there, but he will live, know that, Chantelle."*

No coming back?

"Um, excuse me, ma'am, are you all right in there?" a soft voice asked from outside.

"I'm *fine!*" Chelly bellowed, tossing the door a dirty look before glaring at Nik.

He smiled beatifically.

Chelly could have throttled him. From one kidnapper to another. "You can't just take a woman's child, Nikolai, without... well, period. You just don't do it!"

You would prefer I wait and ask and waste his time? He had precious little, Chantelle. His body was broken, and he was fading. Da, you know this is true. You felt it.

Chelly's heart stuttered and her mouth quivered before she firmed it. Yes, she had...frustration went shrieking through her and she reached out, intending to slam her fist against the mirror before demanding he take her to Bryan.

She'd find a way back, damn it, from wherever *here* was. But darkness swarmed up and caught her, and she fell screaming into it, feeling warm, strong arms come around her and hold her.

. And that familiar voice purring in her ear, *"At last...you are here. At last. And you will* not *be finding a way back."*

* * * * *

Chelly could smell Bryan, the familiar scent of baby lotion, flannel pajamas and fabric softener. And pine, musk, the rich, delicious scent of male — familiar. Nikolai.

Her eyes flew open.

Nikolai sat in a chair across from her, staring at her with dark, brooding eyes. *Hungry* eyes. A small smile curved his mouth as he studied her, watching her as she pushed up on one elbow, staring at him with wide eyes. His gaze moved from hers down to her mouth, the line of her neck, to linger on the curve of her breasts, following the covered lines of her body beneath the silk blankets. Chelly felt a hot, slow pulse in her loins and a sigh shuddered through her, her nipples stiffening as her sex started to heat.

A soft, muffled sighing sound came to her ears and Chelly tore her eyes away from Nikolai. With a cry, Chelly threw back the blankets and stared down at Bryan, who lay in the bed beside her, curled up on his side, knees drawn up to his chest, his face cuddled into the pillow as he sighed in his sleep. And he held his beloved bear, a ragged, much repaired little stuffed creature she had received from her mother when she was born. The bear she had left at home. "Bryan..." she whispered raggedly.

Though he couldn't hear her, it never stopped her from talking to him, even as he slept. Bryan had been born deaf, and he would die deaf, but he was a smart, precocious little boy and he was learning at the same rate as other kids his age, he just needed other tools to help him learn. Chelly started to reach for him and pull him to her, but her hands faltered and slowed and she settled for just stroking his brow after she remembered his injuries. "You can't keep him here. He needs—"

"Your boy is fine, healing quite well. Pick him up, hold him. You need it." Nikolai rose in a slow, fluid motion from his sprawl and lifted Bryan in strong, gentle arms, placing him in her lap even as Chelly stared at him, sputtering blankly.

"He is fine." He covered her lips with two fingers and whispered, "*Da*, he is fine. Look at him, as he is now, not what you last saw." As Chelly watched, Nikolai unbuttoned the small one's pajama top, revealing his plump little body, free of all bruises, scrapes and scars. Which was impossible.

Bryan had a punctured lung, broken ribs, a broken leg, a concussion, internal bleeding, so many cuts and lacerations, and bruises, so much trauma on such a small body…*how?*

They were all gone.

"*How?*" Chelly asked, running her hands over Bryan's smooth skin, reaching back to probe the back of his scalp where a four-inch gash had been sutured closed. No sutures. No gash. No *scar.* Nothing. Like it had never happened. "This isn't possible. What in the hell is going on?"

"We healed him. Well, Ganessa did. She is a Healer among us." Nikolai's gaze lingered on Bryan's face, a soft, loving look, and then it fell away and Chelly felt her belly sink to her knees. Something wasn't right.

But then, a soft, muffled little voice whispered against her neck, "Mama?"

"Oh, baby…"

"Mama, I can hear, they fixed me all better," and Bryan lifted his head away from her neck and smiled up at her with eyes that glowed, just barely.

Chapter Four

ℬ

Chantelle stood staring woodenly at Nikolai and Bryan as they played in the middle of the room. It was too opulent to call it a living room, a sea of golden gleaming wood, covered with jewel-colored rugs and white furniture that hugged and cuddled your body as you sat down. Her little boy could hear, for the first time in his life. She should have been ecstatic. She was, in a way. But he wasn't just Bryan anymore...was he? His eyes gleamed at her in the dark, and he had asked Nikolai if he'd learned how to make magic rainbows. Bryan knew about the magic rainbows. Nikolai had been paying visits to her son. It brought a bittersweet smile to her mouth before she recalled the man's answer.

"*Da*. Magic rainbows and more. You will be able to bring much joy to many, many people."

Chelly had little doubt of that. Bryan had a gift for bringing joy to all around him. But he wouldn't be going home with her. How could she take home a boy whose eyes glowed in the dark? A boy who would learn how to make magic rainbows and spin little snowstorms in his hands...a boy who would grow into a man that would never age. So she was staying here—with *Nik*. If he had asked her, or if she had asked to come here, or anything other than having her choice taken away...

Chelly hated not having the choice.

The traitor. A little voice whispered in her head, *He saved Bryan.*

I know that... She felt like a petulant child, but she also felt as though she was losing her son as she watched Nikolai patiently draw a lacy pattern of ice in the air, only to have it disintegrate the minute Bryan touched it. And then they started all over again.

Jeans clung lovingly to Nikolai's muscled thighs and cupped the bulge at his crotch, while the cotton of his shirt stretched over his flat belly and the taut wall of his chest as he laughed at Bryan's squeals of delight. The masculine laughter faded as Bryan launched himself through the misty wall of pseudo-ice and wrapped his arms around Nikolai's neck, laughing and chortling with glee. Nikolai's face softened and his lids lowered as he wrapped his arms around the boy's little body, cuddling him close.

And the picture hit Chelly right in the solar plexus, bringing tears to her eyes, and a knot to her throat. Bryan had never thrown himself like that at his father. Not once. And from the look of sheer awe on Nikolai's face, it was a rare pleasure for this man, and one he realized he liked too much.

He kidnapped us. He didn't give me a chance to say yes or no to any of this.

This bizarre change had been forced on Bryan, and Chelly would have welcomed it. All he would have had to have done was say it before he had done it. But he had done it, and left her in the dark.

Turning on her heel, she walked away.

"So Bryan is what now? Magic?"

"Elf-kin." Nikolai entered the room slowly, feeling the tension in the air, tempted to reach out and touch her mind, but refusing to trespass. He had already taken her away from her home, her life. Even though he knew she would have gladly come to save her son, he had not asked. He wouldn't take anything else.

He knew, *da*, he knew good and well why she was so angry with him. And truly, Nikolai couldn't blame her. But what was he to do?

"Elf-kin," she repeated drolly, rolling the words over her tongue, then pursing her lips and staring at him over the rim of her coffee cup. French vanilla cappuccino. He had recreated it just for her, like the recipe for French onion soup and guacamole. And he had learned to make grilled cheese sandwiches for Bryan. And chocolate chip cookies. Of course, those were rather tasty—no wonder Alisdair was so fond of them. "Exactly what is elf-kin?"

"A mortal with an open mind, a gifted channel, that we choose to make a blood bond with. Our blood mingles, mixes with his, reproduces with his, and in time, changes his. And since he is so young the changes will be quite…thorough. The younger a child is when he is made kin, the more complete the change.

"He would have had some gifts anyway, Chantelle. You already knew he is a special boy. How special, I cannot even begin to tell you. A deaf child who can already speak, and he is only three years old? But the gifted channels in his mind are wide open now and his potential is unknown, vast, limitless. He—"

"You look the same as you did twenty years ago," she spoke softly, interrupting him, staring pensively over his shoulder. "Elves…they really exist. And they don't age. At least not the way humans do, huh?"

"*Da,* not the way humans do." Nikolai moved closer, cupping her face in his hand, stroking his thumb over the curve of her bottom lip. Threading his hand through her golden brown curls, he stared down into her eyes, absorbing the feel of her skin, the scent of her. "So pretty, so soft. Been wanting you, I have, for several years. How long will you stay angry with me?" His lids drooped, lashes hanging low over his eyes, as he studied her mouth. His other hand, big and warm, came up to rest on the curve of her hip.

Chelly's eyes widened. Her mouth was dry. Other parts were…not. She could feel the hard swell of his cock against her belly, throbbing and pulsing. A deep, aching need opened inside her as her heart started racing a mile a minute, and her nerve endings began sizzling. Blankly, she said the one thing that came to mind. "Are there elves in Russia?"

"Hmmm. Elves, elf-kin and elf-mate as well." He cocked his head as he responded and a ribbon of hair fell over one muscled shoulder, thick, black and shining. His eyes moved from her mouth down the line of her neck to focus on the movement of her chest as she sucked a breath in and tried to remember how to breathe again.

Chelly followed the gleaming lock of hair as it curled over his chest, her mouth watering. The rippling muscles of his belly almost vibrated and as she stared at him, a hungry growl rumbled out of his chest.

Slowly, unable to keep from touching him as he moved closer, nudging her belly with his sex, she rested her hands on the rock hard, warm wall of his chest, flexing her fingers against the smooth skin there and smiling a cat's smile as a shudder vibrated through him. Hypnotized, her eyes slid further downward, staring at the bulging swell of his sex under the blue fabric of his jeans.

Jeans? "Elves wear jeans?"

"Would you prefer pointy shoes with bells?" he asked blandly, as his eyes started to glow brighter and hotter.

Her brow creased in confusion and she shook her head. "I always thought of elves wearing..." her hands roamed restlessly and settled on the swell of his biceps without her realizing it and she shrugged her shoulders as pictures of flowing gowns, tunics, and cloaks moved through her mind. "Ummm, bells? Why would you wear bells and pointy shoes?"

Just then, outside, a bell tolled. And Nikolai rolled his eyes. "*Eynou*, we know it. Five bleeding days, we have. We will get the work done, have we ever failed him yet?" he grumbled, stalking to the window and jerking the drapes closed.

Five days…

What happens in five days?

Chantelle's mental clock filled in that blank.

Christmas.

"*Da,* Christmas."

Her eyes widened and she swallowed the lump in her throat. She hadn't said anything out loud. She knew it. So how had he heard her anyway? Could he really read her thoughts the way it had always seemed?

Yes, he could. His lips curved up in a smile as he stared at her, his head cocked to the side, his black hair falling over his shoulder as he studied her face, following the trail of her thoughts. And as he followed them, the smile slowly fell away and his face grew pensive.

She turned her eyes back to the sparkling, crystalline vista outside one of the other windows, then back to the outrageously magical, beautiful man in front of her with his gently curved, pointed ears and eyes that glowed. The view reminded her of how, when she had been younger, he had carved little statues and sculptures from what looked and felt like ice. In a low hushed voice, she asked, "What is going on?"

"You are in my home, the Northern Reach. Mortals have called it the North Pole for many, many years."

"And the 'him' you haven't failed?" There was a hysterical giggle building in her throat. Oh, man. If Nate had any clue…

"You mortals know him as Santa Claus."

Chapter Five

&

It took the little minx a very long while to stop her giggling.

A very long while.

Nikolai finally left her to it while he went about his job. As Head of Interworld Communications, he had many responsibilities. It was his job that had first led him to Chantelle a few short decades ago. Such a sad little child she had been, having her family taken at such a young age. It wasn't an unusual thing, alas, but it still broke his heart. But she had broken it even more, as she defiantly sobbed out her frustrations against Christmas. Her spunk had endeared her to him, so much so that even after those first few years, he had kept going back to check on her.

But then she had grown up.

And he had fallen in love. The kindly, gentle guidance he had always felt compelled to give to her had turned into a burning, driving desire to own that green- eyed little wonder. Deep inside his soul he knew this woman was the only woman he would ever love. He ached and burned for her, like he had for none other, in all his many centuries.

Nearly nine centuries he had walked this earth, and so many ladies he had known—fleeting loves—some lasting a few years, others only nights.

And now he was in love with a mortal.

Who was even now smothering her laughter and trying to dry her tears while she struggled to accept the truths he had told her.

And her child — that wide-eyed little boy whose body was changing inside with every rapid beat of his heart — was playing with a toy that the mortal world would not see for another fifteen years.

Oh, what a wonderful life.

Nikolai smirked and settled down to work, his long-fingered hands playing over the grid in front of him, his psychic skills connecting him to the children of the world, and then he relayed the needs and wishes back to the workroom. Rhys was in control there, the lunatic. Who would want to be in control of all that chaos?

Five days.

Da, more than enough time. Time enough to fill the wishes of the children, but time enough to get his? Ah…that was the question, wasn't it?

As they stepped outside, Chantelle braced herself for what was certain to be biting, bracing cold. Though Nikolai assured her it was very mild, she didn't believe him. Or her mind didn't. Her heart did, otherwise, she wouldn't have let him carry her son out that door without a coat, blankets…

It felt like springtime.

"How?" she asked, turning around and staring into the distance at the snow- covered landscape outside Nikolai's house.

"Environance-dome. The technology for building it will be in your scientists' hands within a few more years. We keep the temperatures moderated to sixty-five degrees through the majority of the work season. Once December is over, we will allow nature to take its course, but for now, it is much easier for us to work if we do not have to bundle up like bears every time we cross the threshold." Nik pointed to the myriad reflective lights over each house and explained, "Those provide camouflage on the outside, making it seem as though we are not here, muffling our presence. It's quite advanced but it is—"

"No," she interrupted. "Please. Don't explain it to me."

He shrugged, smirking a little at the pained look on her face. She wasn't really interested in technology. Like some of the elves. Even Alisdair was not fond of technology, though his job required he have a decent understanding of it.

Nikolai smiled down at the little boy who cuddled against his chest. Bryan stared around them with huge, wide eyes and a big smile. Unlike his mama, who stared with suspicion and a narrowed gaze, occasionally rolling her eyes at the garb many of the people wore.

Nik preferred the more comfortable clothing favored by mortals, and over the past few decades, it had disgusted the Northern Council to see some of the younger elves wearing similar clothing—jeans, sweaters. *T-shirts.* He grinned widely as he recalled the sheer horror in one Councilman's voice.

"We will see if he is available, since you continue to giggle and disbelieve," Nikolai told her drolly. "Do not be too disappointed when you see that he doesn't have the flowing white beard and hair."

Chelly ignored him as she stared with wide eyes at one lady who wore skintight velvet breeches in deep garnet red, a flowing white shirt, and a vest to match the breeches. The woman was lovely, with her upswept hair revealing the lovely arch of her ears, a higher, more curved point than Nikolai's, and her slightly slanted eyes that twinkled merrily as she caught sight of Nikolai.

"Are you looking for the boss?" Her lilting voice carried the music of Ireland as she stopped beside them, reaching out absently to caress Bryan's hair as she spoke to Nikolai. She smiled with friendly curiosity at Chantelle before turning her gaze to the boy and Nikolai, waiting for an answer.

"We are, *da.* Brenna, this is Chantelle, and her son, Bryan. They are going to be staying with me for a time," he said, not glancing at Chantelle as he spoke. He felt her resistance and urge to argue, and the equally strong need to stay some place where her son was safe, loved, able to live a normal life. Her husband hadn't really wanted the boy—not really. He had just wanted to strike out and hurt her. She had given him a child who was less than perfect.

A growl of rage struggled to surface in Nik's chest and if the man wasn't already dead...Nikolai had to remind himself of what he was, and how wrong it was to wish ill on the dead. And it didn't work. Bryan was as perfect as any child could be. His hearing had mattered little. A gifted child, and his own father had shunned him, and then he had taken him away from his mother and endangered him—

"Bryan, aye, I know of you, little brother. Welcome. We will talk, you and I. I will tell you of the real elves, the sidhe, and fey and leprechauns and selkies as well. Don't be listening to this Russian brute too much," Brenna teased, ruffling Bryan's hair and chucking him under the chin.

"You talk pretty," Bryan said, looking up at her with a winsome smile.

Charmed, Brenna lapsed into Gaelic and lowered her head to kiss him on the nose as he giggled. "Welcome to the Northern Reach, little brother." Then she turned her eyes to Chelly.

"Welcome, Chantelle." Brenna gave her a broad smile. "Though I canna see how you will tolerate this bear's surly moods for more than a week. The boss is in his office. The Council is nagging him, telling him he should at least try to look more...rotund." She poked Nikolai's lean belly with one finger and said impishly, "Whatever will they do with you?"

Nikolai smiled and shrugged as she moved away.

"So we get to see him, huh? Santa Claus? I wonder if I'll find out why I never got that black cat I wanted when I was ten," Chantelle said. "You'll have to do something pretty impressive to make me believe."

Nikolai wisely didn't respond as they rounded the corner. He loved this walk. The hall was of golden oak, polished and gleaming, the windows of stained glass, each one made to resemble the last reigning Claus. Soon, a portrait of Alisdair McNeil of Scotland would join them as he retired back to his homeland. He had sat in the office at the end of this walk for three centuries, the tenure for each Claus, and he was ready— very ready, and very tired, very sad, since his wife had died suddenly less than a decade ago.

Elven folk tended to live well into their second millennia. And Brielle had only been eight-hundred-fifty-two years old. Alisdair had never quite recovered from the loss. He would retire, and quietly grieve.

And a new elf would take his place.

Nikolai knocked on the carved wood of the door and waited until the heavily accented Scots voice invited, "Enter, Nikolai. And ye'd better be in a better mood than you have been these past months. I'm in no mood to tolerate you after listening..."

Alisdair's voice trailed away as he caught sight of Bryan and Chantelle. His eyes, twinkling blue, gentle and soft, settled first on Bryan. The boy, usually so nervous and shy with strangers, looked at the bearded man and smiled. Broadly and easily. And he said simply, "Hi, Santa."

"Hello, Bryan. Did you like the trucks and trains you got last year?" Santa/Alisdair asked as Bryan squirmed out of Nik's arms, trotted over to the chair and climbed up onto the older man's lap.

Bryan nodded vigorously.

Alisdair laughed. "I thought you did. Especially since you played so hard one of them was broken by New Year's Day. But your mama fixed it all up, didn't she?"

Nik heard Chantelle's soft gasp and he moved behind her, resting a strong hand on her waist as her body started to sag.

146

"And what of this year? What do you want for this year, lad?"

"I already gotted it—my ears are all fixed. And we never thought they could," Bryan said, grinning hugely. His freckled nose wrinkled and he scratched it with a small hand. "The words sound funny, and sometimes people talk too fast. But I can hear, and Mama's voice is so pretty."

Chelly muffled a sob against her hand as Alisdair smiled gently at Bryan. "Your hearing isn't a gift we gave you for Christmas. That didna come from us—not exactly. It came from the Maker. The One who made Christmas possible. So it's not the present we needed to talk about. And we can talk nice and slow, and use some sign language as well."

Alisdair went on as he stroked Bryan's head, speaking slowly, staring into the boy's face, signing a few words from time to time as he said, "I remember your mama. Chelly, your grandparents called her when she was little. And she wanted a black cat when she was oh, ten, I think. But she's allergic to cats. She did not go finding that out until she was in high school, but we knew. Can't go getting her a present she wouldn't be able to keep."

Make me believe.

Nik heard the words circling around in her head and felt the impending dizziness just as she started to sway. He caught her against him and carried her out the door with a quick thought to Alisdair to occupy the boy. He was already doing it, with a pleased smile. Playing with children was something he never got enough of, and something he truly enjoyed.

Chelly awoke back in that wide, sumptuous bed, her heart racing, her mouth dry, and her head woozy.

She was in the North Pole.

She had seen Santa Claus.

He was real.

The presents last year…the ones she didn't think she had bought, and convinced herself she had. They had come from here, they had to have.

And Nik…Nikolai was one of his elves. Nikolai was truly an elf. Truly magic.

"Da."

She barely saw him move and then his mouth was against hers in the darkness of the room and his thoughts were filling her mind. *So many, many years I have ached to touch, to taste,* he told her as hard hot hands slid up her torso, around her ribcage and up her back, until he was cupping her neck and angling her lips up for his kiss, pushing his tongue deep inside her mouth, groaning greedily, hungrily.

Nikolai.

One of his hands fisted in her hair while the other went racing down her body, cupping and molding her breast, pinching her nipple until she was squirming against his body. Dropping to his knees and staring down at her, his electric blue eyes glowed hotly in the dim room as he watched her. Gripping the edges of her shirt he tore it open, and fastened his gaze on her breasts, hidden still by the lace of her bra.

"Lovely." His voice was deep and guttural as he ran the roughened tip of his finger over the edge of the bra and smiled as she shivered, arching up. Sliding his forearm under her and lifting her up, arching her higher and taking one pebbled nipple into his mouth, drawing deep and suckling hard, he had her moaning and keening against his mouth. Her legs straddled one of his thighs, and she rocked against him, riding the muscled length of his thigh and whimpering.

Nik felt the throbbing of his cock and groaned as she rubbed her belly against him, her small soft hands roaming restlessly on his shoulders. They dipped in his hair and fisted as she clasped him against her breast and the frantic movement of her hips increased. Nostrils flaring, he caught the desperate, hungry scent of her body. She was close, very close to coming, and through the barriers of their clothing he could feel how hot she was, how wet she was. Hungry little moans rose and died in her throat as she pushed her tongue inside his mouth, her nails biting into his shoulders.

He moved his lips down her pointed little cat's chin, and bit lightly before kissing a hot trail down her throat. Lifting her up and closing his mouth over the hot, erect point of one swollen nipple, he listened with sharp satisfaction to the little scream that filled the room. "*Scream again, Chantelle.*" His mental voice purred inside her mind, pushing beyond the surprisingly tough shields so he could murmur inside her head. "*Come for me, let me feel it.*" He tugged at the fastening of her jeans as he whispered to her, stroking the bud of her breast with his tongue and teeth, worrying it gently, then roughly as he worked her jeans down lower and lower. Palms on the firmly rounded cheeks of her ass, he caressed the crevice there before stripping away her jeans and silk panties and tumbling her onto her back, staring hungrily down at her, pushing her thighs wide.

Eynou, she had removed the hair from her mound, except for a narrow little path of hair right at her pubic bone, leaving the lips of her sex smooth and bare. "Hmmm, look at that," he purred roughly, sliding one finger through the cream gleaming in her folds. He slipped his finger into his mouth and groaned hungrily. "What a taste you have, sweet. Oh, what a taste." He sprawled between her thighs and opened her, plunging his tongue deep inside her as she arched up with a weak, wild cry, climaxing at once against his mouth.

He worked two fingers inside her, feeling her tighten around him and shudder as she twisted and whimpered under his hands and mouth. The sweet clasp of her cleft hugged his fingers and Nik swore as his cock pressed into his belly, burning him like a branding iron. He wanted, badly, so badly, to get inside her. The chaotic whirl of her thoughts filtered through his mind and he knew he could have her, but he didn't want her to regret it later.

She had to stay, had to want it.

As if she had been reading his mind as clearly as he had been reading hers, she whimpered, "Nik, please. Damn it, you don't know how long I've wanted this with you." She opened her eyes and stared up at him, her gaze gleaming with want, need, and tears of sheer frustration as she surged up and pressed her mouth hungrily to his. Eating at his mouth, sucking his lower lip into hers, she gasped when he caught her hands and pinned her to bed, crushing her body beneath his.

"Know this." His voice was a rough growl in her ear as he wedged her thighs apart with his and reached for the buttons at his fly. "I want badly to take you, mark you as mine. And if I do, you *are* mine. I will never let you or the boy leave me. Mine to keep. I cannot leave the Northern Reach. My destiny, my life is here. Are you certain?"

In reply, Chantelle reached down and pushed his hands aside, sliding the buttons of his fly free and shoving the denim of his pants aside, catching his hard, heavy length in her hands and sending a rumbling growl through him as she stroked him with soft, cool hands. Nikolai shuddered, lowering his brow to press against hers. "Mine to keep, *da*?" he asked, staring with near desperation into her eyes, as he pressed the tip of his cock against the wet portal of her sex.

A slow feline curl of her lips had his heart leaping in his chest.

He used one big hand to tilt her hips up as he surged slowly forward, hot, wet tissues closing over the engorged head of his cock as he stared down into her eyes. Her lids lowered to half-mast and her tongue slid out to wet her lips as a sigh shimmered out of her. "Nik…"

At the sound of his name on her lips—in that heavy, sultry voice—his control snapped, and he pushed deep, driving hard and fast into her, until he was lodged hilt-deep. The head of his cock rested at the very mouth of her womb as her eyes opened in shock and she screamed out his name, her nails biting into his skin.

He moved higher on her body, shifting so that he was riding her clit with each stroke, and she started to convulse around him, the clasp of her pussy tightening around him with each deep, driving thrust as he caught her thrashing head, fisting the gleaming golden-brown locks around one hand and pushing his tongue deep into her mouth, feeding on her taste.

Chelly sobbed into his mouth as he caught one thigh in his other hand, pushing it high, draping it over his arm, opening her wide so he could fuck her deep and hard. She wailed, her head falling back, away from his hungry, greedy kiss. His avid, seeking mouth found one hard, pebbled nipple and fastened onto it, sucking it deep, until it was pressing against the roof of his mouth and throbbing.

"Mine to keep…"

His mental voice filled her mind, a soft, seductive caress, a sharp contrast to the thick, burning fullness of his cock invading her cleft. She screamed out his name as she started to come again, opening her eyes and staring up at him as he pushed onto his knees and caught her clit between his thumb and forefinger, staring down and watching the play of his fingers on her body.

She stared hypnotized at his body, the gleaming muscles of his chest, covered by a light film of sweat, the rhythmic play of his washboard belly as he pushed his thick cock inside her. Something odd…a twisted, puckered scar, old, low on his belly, between his hipbone and his navel caught her eye, but then his cock twitched, and her mouth went dry as she stared at his sex, ruddy, and gleaming wet with her cream—the sheer erotic sight sent her screaming into another orgasm, and this time she felt his cock jerk, and the hot flood of his come as he climaxed inside her.

He crushed her body into the soft mattress, his mouth coming down on hers as he pounded his hips against her, growling deep in his throat, biting her lower lip, his tongue seeking out hers and tangling with it hungrily as they both went flying into orgasm. A series of hot, rhythmic contractions from her drew out his climax until he finally collapsed atop her in exhaustion.

"Where's Byran?" she asked numbly once she was able to breathe again. She still couldn't feel her toes. Or her fingers. She wasn't sure she could feel her hands or knees either. She was going to have to take stock in a few minutes. But first things first. Bryan.

"With Alisdair." He had rolled onto his back, taking her with him and now he cuddled her slim body to his chest, smoothing one hand down her naked, gleaming back, sighing in contentment. One of her hands ran over his pecs, flattening over the pounding of his heart. He felt her smile slightly.

"Your heart is racing as fast as mine." Then she lifted her head, her feathery brown bangs falling into her cloudy, sleepy green eyes. "Alisdair, you said? I don't want my son with somebody I don't know, somebody I've never met. Even if you know and trust him—"

"You have met him already. You were just in his office a while ago," he reminded her, reaching up and brushing her hair away from her eyes. "And Alisdair is more trustworthy than any man you will ever meet."

"I've only met Suh—hell. I can't even say it. It doesn't seem real."

"That is more a title, like Mr. President, or His Majesty. His given name is Alisdair, not Santa Claus. And Bryan is with him." Nik's lids drooped as she shifted and sat up atop him, staring down at him.

A dry laugh escaped her lips. "My son...my son is being babysat by Santa Claus. Oh, that's rich. That's a good one," she said, sighing and shaking her head.

"I'll be sure to let him know how amused you are."

Her nipples puckered and tightened in the cool air and she smiled as his eyes slid from her face down to her torso, darkening to cobalt, glowing in the dimness of the room, a palpable heat flowing from them to caress her. "So lovely. You like to tease me, *da*?"

The husky, low timbre of his voice flowed over her like a caress, tightening her flesh. "I like knowing you want me, knowing you are real. I've dreamed of you, for so long." His hands came up to rest on her waist then stroke upward, until he was cupping her breasts in his hands, pinching and tweaking her nipples until she was shifting and rocking against the thick, hot length of his cock.

She braced her hands against the broad, golden expanse of his chest, staring down into his bewitching eyes. His black hair was spilled beneath him, like a silken, black cape, and the carved, exotic bones of his face captured her eye and made her chest hurt, he was so beautiful. And he kept staring at her like she was the most beautiful thing he had ever seen.

"*Da*, you are," he murmured, reaching up, twining his hands in her hair and pulling her lips to meet his, shifting his hips and piercing her, sliding his cock inside her, where she was wet from him. "Most beautiful, most lovely. And mine to keep. And I will make you believe that, Chantelle. You will see."

He breathed the words against her mouth before plunging his tongue deep inside, stroking her tongue, her palate, everywhere he could reach, as he slid his hands down and cupped her ass, moving her in a slow, steady rhythm and rocking his hips up and down, pushing his cock deep and high, piercing the very mouth of her womb.

As a long, shuddering contraction gripped his cock, Nik pulled his mouth from hers and buried her face in his neck, gritting his teeth and holding onto his control. *Not yet…not yet.* He ran his fingers through the crevice of her bottom and felt her quiver. Shifting, he moved her body so that he could stoke her clit. The hot, silky cream of her sex coated him, and her cleft hugged him tightly, making him swear silently as she started to come around him.

With a rough groan, he threw control to the wind and drove his shaft inside and fucked her roughly, setting his teeth into her shoulder and listening to her scream out his name. Gripping her ass with one hand, he wet one finger with her cream and started to probe her rosette with the other. Feeling her shudder and sob and go into spasms around him, the hot, silken little hole gripped his finger tightly even as his cock jerked and he pumped her full of his seed.

"Hmmm, sweet, sweet little Chantelle," he purred into her hair, cuddling her against his chest, rubbing his chin against her hair as she gasped for air. "Mine…"

A wave of bitterness washed up out of nowhere and she sighed against his chest. "You made certain of that, didn't you? I'm stuck here, aren't I? Bryan can't go back into the real world now, can he? My place is with my son."

And to that, Nikolai had no answer.

Chapter Six

ை

Christmas Eve in the North Pole.

No, the Northern Reach. Chelly stood watching as people hurried around her. She wasn't the only mortal. As she stood in her borrowed jeans and sweater, cuddling Bryan against her chest, she saw more mortals rushing by than she could count.

It was easy to pick them out.

The humans, including herself, were less...vibrant.

Lacking something. The elves had larger eyes, Bambi's eyes, Bryan had called them, almond-shaped, large and gleaming, in brilliant jewel-tone hues. And shimmering, gleaming hair. Even their skin seemed to glow with vitality and health and...*life.*

The humans were...human. Pretty, handsome, some more so, others plain.

But then her eyes started to pick out a human she thought at first was an elf. Eyes that gleamed, not quite as brightly as an elf's. But more than a mortal's, a human's would. Hair that shifted and swirled and gleamed with a life of its own. A fire inside.

Not wholly human.

But not elf either.

"Elf-touched, elf-mated," Nikolai murmured behind her, sliding one brawny arm around her waist.

He brushed his lips across her head as she jumped, and Bryan laughed at the look on his mama's face. "Nik fwighten Mama? Mama jump." The boy clapped and tugged, jerked and squirmed until she set him down and he made a beeline for the window to the workshop, trying to rise up on his toes and peer inside. "Can't see nothing…magic windows."

"The Northern Reach is full of magic." Nikolai was murmuring to her as they watched the small child pace back and forth, casting awed glances at the workshop. Such a frantic pace inside. Nik had taken a short, quick break to come see her, but then he must go back. Too much to do, too little time to do it in. Would she understand? "I want to share that with you. Chantelle, please…"

Chelly stood stiffly in his arms, folding her arms over her belly, rubbing her hands up and down against some inner chill. "Elf-touched? What do you mean?"

"They've mated with one of my kind." He gently turned her in his arms, taking her hands and lifting them to his mouth. "Joined souls, minds, life essence. Their bodies are mortal no longer. They are not truly elf, but not truly human, either. My mate…this is what you are to me, have always been. I've just been waiting for you. I could have taken the time to explain before bringing Bryan here, but he did not have the time, so I did what I knew you would have wanted, *da*?"

Chelly felt her breath leave her lungs in a hot, shuddering rush as Nik's lashes lifted, revealing the smoky, smoldering depths of his cobalt blue eyes. "I wish to share that with you, all of my long life, all of my heart. I have loved you since you were eighteen, Chantelle, and I shall love you for all the years that I walk upon this earth. I do not wish to spend those years without you. And I hate feeling your anger and helplessness."

Helplessness…a choice taken from her.

Yes, he had saved Bryan, and brought her here against her will.

Lifting her eyes, she met his and just mutely shook her head. And then she turned away from him.

She only heard his rough sigh, but she knew when he was gone. Chelly could feel his absence in her heart.

"You made the right choice."

The voice was friendly enough.

There was no reason for her to dislike the owner of it so intensely before she even saw the emerald-green eyes appraising her so thoroughly. None at all. But she did. Meeting that intent stare, she patted Bryan on the back and told him to keep playing. He studied the visitor with distrusting eyes before going back to the brightly colored picture in front of him, one hand gripping a chunky crayon tightly.

Then she rose in a fluid motion and met the man's eyes. "I beg your pardon?" she asked, lifting a dark brow. Her eyes, a softer green than the elf's, were blank and polite.

"Nikolai is infatuated, but you cannot truly believe he would love a mortal, can you?" He smiled as he said it, as if to take the sting away. "You are a sweet thing, I've no doubt. But surely, you can see this is not a fated thing."

Chelly studied him with curious eyes. He was a handsome, almost angelic man, with long golden blond hair that fell just below his shoulders, and those big green eyes. "You expect me to believe that Nikolai doesn't know his own heart?" She smiled in return, just as politely, sliding her hands into her pockets and cocking her head.

His eyes glinted, flashed, with what looked like amusement but it was gone so fast, she couldn't be sure. "Elven men are quite captivated by mortal women—" He moved toward her in a smooth, stalking gait, muscles rippling and flexing under his clothes.

A mountain lion. Her head spun dizzily for a brief moment, then she shook it and threw off the odd, muffled feel inside it, the nagging sense of fear that resided inside her belly. It didn't feel right, didn't feel like her. And as soon as she thought that, the fear fell apart, and he was in front of her, glaring angrily at her. "Captivated by your stubbornness, your charm, the way you cling to your short, insignificant lives—"

Chelly narrowed her eyes and spat, "Insignificant? You pompous, self-righteous bastard. Insignificant? Because I won't live forever?"

He smirked at her. "No, because you could have. Because you could have had everything you had ever wanted…and you turned it down. Because you fear tomorrow. All mortals do. And that fear robs you of your joy of today."

He turned on his booted heel, an old-style boot. His old-style velvet breeches matched the same impossible green of his eyes. He smiled at Bryan, who stared at him with a rather ambivalent stare now, instead of outright distrust, and left in smirking silence.

That fear robs you of your joy of today…

Oh, hell.

Chelly knelt beside Bryan and ran her fingers through his downy soft blond hair. "What have I done?"

Chapter Seven

ಬಿ

Alisdair's voice filled the chamber just as Rhys was closing the door behind him with a self-satisfied smirk. She was thinking hard now. And about time too. Rhys didn't know how much longer he could tolerate Nik's brooding.

"What exactly did ya hope t' accomplish by that, Rhys?" said a low, silky voice.

The room was empty.

Rhys turned around lazily, a whimsical smirk on his lips as the tall red-haired giant went from nothingness to a mist, to a solid, massive mountain of a man. His blue eyes were no longer twinkling, but snapping with anger, his full sensual mouth drawn tight with rage as he stared at one of his successors.

"An empath should know better than t' use his gifts to induce such fear on a person, a mortal. Such a sweet girl, she is, an' ye go causin' her fear and doubt and distrust. What is going on inside that head o' yours?" Dair demanded, his voice booming, his mouth grim and angry.

"I've no idea what you're talking about," Rhys said smoothly.

That fear robs you of your joy of today... Rhys grimaced as his voice echoed through the corridor. Alisdair snarled angrily, "I guess I should be thankin' ye. Chantelle has loved Nikolai for years and years. But her pride and fear is what keeps her from telling him. You just pushed her into acknowledging how foolish that is—"

Rhys smirked. "I know." His golden hair fell in a curtain around his face and he shoved it back behind with one hand, as he met the boss's eyes. "Why else would I have gone there? After all, Nikolai is my best friend." Then he turned on his heel and ambled down the hall, whistling under his breath tunelessly as Alisdair stared at him in bemusement.

Over his shoulder, Rhys called out, "Both of us being made Successor to the Line didn't change that."

* * * * *

Alisdair was weary when he returned to the Northern Reach at noon the next day. The last few children in Berea and Nome, Alaska, were opening their presents as his shiny black boots settled down on the polished wooden floors of the Great Hall. There was a dim echo in the back of his mind where he could hear their jubilant cries, some disappointed groans— those always made him smile—some bittersweet. Like Chelly's had. She knew now that the black cat she had wanted would not have worked out.

But many children would never understand.

Ah, well.

One voice in particular drew him this morn...and it was close. It took only a thought and the rich red velvet he wore faded away and was replaced by a flannel shirt that hugged his massive shoulders and faded jeans that clung comfortably to long, muscled thighs. The Council had covered their eyes and all but whimpered when the boss had also started wearing the comfortable mortal clothing.

He ran a hand through his red hair and tucked it behind his pointed ears before knocking on the door to Nik's apartment. Nikolai wasn't there. Out sulking, Dair imagined. When Chelly opened the door, and he studied the soft, sweet-smelling mortal in front of him, he decided that was understandable.

But needless. She was as miserable as Nikolai, aching and yearning for him. It was there in the misery in her eyes, in the slump of her shoulders, all over her face, in every line of her body.

With a wide, brilliant smile, Dair held his arms out to the boy and then they were gone.

Chelly looked down at herself with a gasp.

Because so were her clothes.

Nikolai was in the process of chopping wood. A tedious, back-breaking job, guaranteed to leave him aching and sore, which was why he had chosen it. He had been at this task for more than four hours when suddenly the axe was gone and he was being flung through time and space as his clothes were stripped away.

"Damn it, Dair, what in the name of Hell are you doing?" he snarled as he battled against the superior elf's power.

He heard the distant echo of his friend's laughter as he landed bare-assed in his room. "You've a week, man. Don't be wastin' it," the Scot told him.

He lifted his eyes to see Chelly standing over him, her eyes wide and luminous with shock, need, and love.

He barely had time to stand before she flung herself at him.

Her mouth covered his, her tongue pushing its way into his mouth, hungrily, desperately as her hands raced over his body, squeezing each muscle, massaging and rubbing every body part she could reach as she urged him backwards. Nik growled and reached for her waist and rasped, "Now." The bed was too damn far away. Grabbing her slim hips, he lifted her and guided her legs around his waist, arching and using the muscles in his back and thighs to bury his cock in her cleft to the hilt.

"Nik…" His name fell from her lips on a ragged moan, her eyes wide, the pupils dilated and dark as she arched up against him.

"Do not turn away from me," he whispered, fisting one hand in her hair and pulling her mouth to meet his, staring into her eyes as he kissed her hungrily. He sucked her tongue into his mouth, and bit down, then he pulled away and nibbled hungrily on her lips before rasping out again, "Please. Do not."

"No. I won't." Her arms came up, winding around his neck. "I won't. I couldn't." His cock jerked inside her and she cried out, twisting against him, the slick swollen tissues of her pussy caressing him as she moved herself up and down.

Sweat gleamed on his powerful, nude body as he worked her up and down on his impaling sex. "Scream for me, *dushechka*…Come, let me feel it," he purred, one hand gliding down and pressing against the pink rosette. "I've a need to take you here, and soon. You're so tight…so hot. Push down for me."

Chelly shuddered and screamed as he pushed one finger past the tight ring of muscle, working it in and out slowly, gathering cream from her sex to ease his passage until he had seated his finger in fully. She arched up against the new invasion, feeling tightly stretched, invaded, and *hot*. Her womb contracted and she started to come, as Nikolai rumbled against her ear, "Ah, yes…that's it. Let me feel…"

Rhythmic, waving contractions caressed him and Nikolai's cock jerked, then he started to pulse and jet his seed deep inside her, seeking out her mouth and moaning as he kissed her, pushing his tongue inside her mouth, taking in more of her sweet, addictive taste. The silken walls of her pussy hugged and stroked him, tightening, relaxing, tightening, until he thought he'd go mad with it.

On legs that shook, he carried her to the bed, keeping his sex still buried inside her as her head slumped against his shoulder. Soft, weak little moans fell from her throat as he bent his head and kissed the exposed arch of her neck. "I love you, Chantelle."

"I love you, too, Nik. I'm sorry. I've got this pride thing…and I couldn't let it go, just being snatched away from everything I know and brought here." Chelly opened her eyes, blinked sleepily as he laid her on her back and started to surge over her, moving deeply. A low, rough keening sound came from her as he pushed her legs wide and pulled away, sprawling between her thighs and burying his face there, catching her clit between his teeth.

She fisted her hands in the black silk of his hair and screamed when he stabbed at the sensitive little bud with his tongue while he worked moisture from her cleft lower, easing his finger in and out of her ass, until she was lifting eagerly for that caress. Then he started to use two fingers on her and she shrieked out his name and came, waves of hot pleasure washing over her with each little biting thrust.

He mounted her and drove in with one deep thrust, feeling her silken wet pussy close greedily over his cock, the scent of her body rising up and filling his head, taunting him to near madness. Leaning down to her, Nik covered her mouth and caught her wrists, pinning them overhead. "Mine for always…you swear?" he rasped against her mouth.

"Yours always, I swear."

With a triumphant, savage grin, he rode her fast and rough, until they both went tumbling into bliss, Chelly screaming out his name, raking his arms and back with her nails, as he suckled one nipple deep and growled out her name, slamming his hips against her as he flooded her with a hot wash of come before they slid into sleep, gasping for breath, and holding tight to each other.

"Have you chosen your Successor?"

Dair smiled as he stroked the head of the boy who cuddled against his shoulder. The Council had not looked pleased when he strolled in carrying a mortal's child. Granted, this child was now elf-kin, with the glowing eyes and the bloom of magic already growing under his skin.

But the Council was stodgy and had always been so.

None but Council and Successor had ever breached these chambers.

Dair smirked inwardly.

But outwardly, he pasted on a polite smile and said, "Nikolai. As you know, he has always been the one I say is the ideal Chosen one."

A soft-spoken, sweet-tempered elf spoke up, shaking her head as she said, "The man is unmated. He is a grim, melancholy creature—"

Dair dropped one lid in a wink as he made sure the boy was still deep in slumber. A bit o' magic made sure he would stay that way as he pictured the looks on a few more faces... *"Hold onto your hats, my friends—"*

"Damn it, Dair, what are you doing?"

Chelly was on her hands and knees, a look of rapture on her heart-shaped face. Dair had fast eyes, but he caught no more than a glimpse of berry-colored nipples and a slim body, firm ass and thighs before Nik had his mate covered with bed linens as he rolled out of the bed, his cock wet and shining from her body as he glared angrily at both Dair and the Council.

Chelly was a bit slower to react, her eyes blinking sleepily as the last bit of climax rolled through her and her body shuddered with it.

"As you can see, Nikolai has a mate, and a very satisfied one at that," Dair said with a smirk he didn't bother to hide this time.

Chelly heard voices and squealed as Nik settled down on the bed, bringing her against his side and murmuring to her as the Council studied the grim, hard-as-iron man going as soft as a newborn snow rabbit's fur as he cuddled his mate up against him and stroked her gently, murmuring into her hair.

She flushed red and he smiled, a smile as wide as Dair's, and the Council fell silent.

Dair felt, under his magic, the boy trying to wake. He sent a silent thought to Nik and Nik blinked, used a bit of his magic to don some jeans before he looked up at the Council. "I had planned on a bit more formal meeting, but this lady has agreed to become my wife, my mate. My life," Nik announced just as Dair allowed the boy to waken.

Bryan saw Nik and squirmed his way out of Dair's arms, taking off toward him with a laugh.

Nik caught him with a smile, and added, "And this…this is my son."

Not one Council member argued as Dair turned over the reigns of Leadership to Nikolai later that day.

They did, of course, wait until they were more formally dressed.

Also by Shiloh Walker

ಬಿ

About the Author

୫

They always say to tell a little about yourself! I was born in Kentucky and have been reading avidly since I was six. At twelve, I discovered how much fun it was to write when I took a book that didn't end the way it should have ended, and I rewrote it. I've been writing since then.

About me now... hmm... I've been married since I was 19 to my high school sweetheart and we live in the midwest. Recently I made the plunge and turned to writing full-time and am looking for a part-time job so I can devote more time to my family—two adorable children who are growing way too fast, and my husband who doesn't see enough of me...

Shiloh welcomes comments from readers. You can find her website and email address on her author bio page at www.ellorascave.com.

Tell Us What You Think
We appreciate hearing reader opinions about our books. You can email us at Comments@EllorasCave.com.

JUST A LITTLE MAGIC
Kate Douglas

&

Chapter One

છ

The lights on the Christmas tree twinkled and glittered, reflecting off the few gaily-wrapped packages beneath its fragrant boughs. The dying fire cast a soft glow about the formal dining room of the small cottage, throwing the holiday decorations into muted shadow. The scent of a well-seasoned roast blended with the piney smells from the fresh greens trimming the mantel.

Beth Adams watched the expensive beeswax candles on her perfectly arranged dinner table sputter and die as, one by one, they burned out.

Sort of like her plans for the evening.

Face it…just like my plans for the rest of my life.

A soft clink disturbed the silence, the bottle of champagne settling among the melting ice cubes. She reached for the bottle. No point in wasting good, chilled champagne.

Steve was a jerk. He would never have appreciated her grandmother's bone china with its gilded design, or her great-aunt Audrey's beautiful silver service—one reserved for only the most special occasions.

He wouldn't notice the expensive brand of champagne, or recognize the fact Beth had prepared for a very memorable evening.

Steve couldn't help it if he was culturally, emotionally and intellectually challenged. She'd honestly thought he was cute enough to compensate for the occasional lapse in…well, just about everything.

"How could I be so stupid?" She rested her aching head in her hands and fought tears. He wasn't worth tears. He certainly wasn't worth the effort she'd gone to tonight.

She'd never before pulled out the china, the crystal goblets, the gorgeous silverware. Never opened her heart and her home with so much expectation.

Only for special occasions…

A wedding proposal on Christmas Eve definitely came under the special occasions heading. Steve had been hinting at something big, something special, something just for Beth, all week long. Not just little hints, either.

Of course, she'd been so sure he was planning to propose. She didn't expect him to pick the perfect setting, so she'd created it herself. They'd dated for months. Tall and slim she wasn't, but her ample curves were in all the right places and her auburn hair waved and curled in shining splendor almost to her waist. The sex had been good. Not spectacular, but okay. At thirty-two, Beth figured she was willing to settle for okay.

She was not, however, willing to settle for a boyfriend who thought a satellite dish for her TV was the perfect Christmas gift.

Especially not when she'd been expecting a diamond ring.

She went hot and cold all over, remembering how stupid she'd felt, standing out there in the snow, dressed in her dark burgundy velvet gown designed specifically for seduction, asking Steve what he was doing on her roof.

"Isn't it great, honey? Merry Christmas! I got you a satellite dish for the TV. You can get the Sports Channel, Playboy TV—why, you can get almost two hundred channels with this thing!"

She'd opened her mouth, but nothing had come out. She'd opened it again, swallowed, blinked. "That's my big Christmas surprise? A satellite dish?"

"Yeah. Cool, huh?"

"No, Steve. It is definitely not cool. Take it away. I don't even watch TV. Why would I want a satellite dish?"

"Uh, to make watching TV more fun? I really miss seeing the games when I'm over here. And think of all the fun we could have with the Playboy Channel."

Suddenly, Beth realized her entire relationship was there, encapsulated within those few words. Steve didn't have a clue who she was, didn't care what she wanted. Did she really want to marry this schmuck? Create more little schmucks?

Clear as the driven snow, as fresh as an ice crystal and not nearly as painful as Beth would have imagined, it all coalesced into a single amazing thought.

This was not the man she wanted to marry. Thank goodness he hadn't actually asked her, because she would have said yes.

Not a smart move. Not smart at all. Waking up to Mr. Sports Channel every morning?

"Go home, Steve. Go home and take your satellite dish with you. Have a merry Christmas. Watch the Playboy Channel on your own TV because you certainly won't be watching mine." With her dignity intact and her head held high, Beth had quietly gone back inside the house and closed the door.

* * * * *

She poured another glass of champagne from the half empty bottle. A bit splashed on the linen table cloth, but she leaned over and licked it up with her tongue. The same tongue that could have been licking Steve. *The idiot.* She focused on the small pile of opened gifts resting in front of her, gifts from her girlfriends at the office.

Irene's package was really interesting, nothing more than a little egg with a remote control. Of course, once Beth figured out where the egg went, she realized someone else really needed to work the remote to get the full effect. She giggled, thinking of the possibilities. Margaret's present was more obvious—a lifelike purple penis, complete with extra batteries.

She stared long and hard at the phallus, comparing it with Steve's. His was nothing like this monster! She flipped the switch and it pulsed to life, throbbing in her hand like something alive.

She felt the muscles between her legs contract at the possibilities. She'd never once used a vibrator, but ever since Tina from marketing had invited her friend Dot to give that sex toy party, all the girls had been giving them as gifts.

Beth wondered if anyone had actually used the damned things.

Filling her glass with the last of the champagne, she wobbled across the plush carpeting with the purple penis buzzing in her hand. It felt alive, the covering warm and sleek. Slipping her panties off, she hiked up her long skirt and sprawled on the pillows in front of the fire, the same pillows where she had intended to seduce Steve.

Sipping at her champagne, Beth stared long and hard at the softly humming dildo, then took an experimental swipe with the vibrating tip across her clit.

She jumped and giggled. Champagne splashed down the front of her burgundy velvet dress, so she slipped the gown over her head and tossed it aside. Her brassiere went next.

Beth decided there was something wonderfully decadent about lying naked on a pile of pillows in front of a dying fire, sipping good champagne and fucking herself with a huge vibrating purple penis. She stroked between her legs, parting the wet folds with the throbbing head. It practically crawled in deeper on its own.

Who was she to fight the power of two D-cell batteries?

Damn it felt good. She spread her legs wide and ran the dildo all the way inside. She was wet and ready, something that usually took forever when she had sex with Steve. The pulsating vibrations reached all the way to her bones.

She slipped it in and out, sighing with the pure pleasure of being completely filled by something hot and *almost* alive. She let it touch her clit on every other pass, then realized she was spending just as much time on that needy little bit of flesh as anywhere else. She thought about pinching her breasts, but she was holding the champagne with one hand and the dildo with the other, and she'd just flat run out of hands.

It didn't matter. Not one bit, because suddenly her orgasm slammed into her out of the blue, a deep, throbbing, needy crush of nerves and muscles and ripe sensation. Gasping, sighing, Beth slowed her new favorite toy to a steady rhythm, catching each tiny quiver and clench, riding her climax to the very last shiver. Finally, with a long, shuddering sigh, she flipped the *off* switch.

She lay there a moment, staring at the huge purple monster still deeply imbedded between her thighs. It felt good, filling her completely while her pussy spasmed and rippled against the ribbed surface. Gazing thoughtfully at the vibrator, Beth finished off her last swallow of champagne and set the glass aside.

After a few minutes, she giggled. They'd all made silly jokes about women needing toys for sex, embarrassed to admit they even knew about the blasted things, but this was the best orgasm she'd had in her life.

Great sex without the complications. D-cell batteries and a purple plastic penis were certainly a lot cheaper and easier to handle than a selfish, thickheaded ex-boyfriend.

Chapter Two

ဆာ

Ouch! Beth awoke out of a sound sleep, stabbed in the crotch with the purple penis when she tried to roll over. Blinking herself awake, she removed the plastic toy from between her legs. Naked, the dildo hanging from her limp fingers, Beth headed toward her bedroom.

Her lonely bedroom. Damn. She'd really expected to spend the night with Steve, wearing a new diamond engagement ring and nothing else. Somehow, she didn't picture herself wearing a satellite receiver…

The little egg glistened on the dining room table. Beth picked it up and carried it into her room. She'd find the remote in the morning and put them away. Until she found another significant other, the egg would just have to wait.

She hoped it wouldn't be too long. The concept of wearing a vibrator that someone else controlled made her hot just thinking about it.

Still half asleep, she left the purple dildo on the nightstand by her bed. She stared at the little egg for a long moment, until curiosity won out, then with great care, inserted it way inside between her legs. Just knowing it was in there was a turn on.

Feeling more than a little bit decadent, Beth floated off to sleep.

* * * * *

Thump. Thump. Thump.

Beth jerked awake. *What the hell?*

A loud clatter followed the thumps. A bang, what sounded suspiciously like a curse, then another thump.

Steve! Damn him… The idiot must think that if he installed the stupid satellite dish, he'd get back in her good graces.

And her bed.

"Fat chance, you bastard." Beth jumped out of bed and grabbed her robe and slippers. Thank goodness she'd finally seen the light. Tina and Margaret had been telling her what a jerk Steve was, but she just hadn't been able to see it.

"Well, my eyes are wide open tonight, kiddo."

Like an avenging angel, Beth stormed out the front door.

How odd. There was no ladder in sight.

She heard it again. A thump and a muffled curse.

"Steve, *get off* my roof. I told you, I do *not* want a satellite dish."

"Huh? Wha…?" A startled shout, another curse. Suddenly a body slid over the edge of the roof, past the rain gutters, missed Beth by mere inches and landed in the snowdrift beside the front porch.

Not Steve. Definitely not Steve. Caught in the glow of the porch light, the figure was dressed all in red and buried face first in the snow. Cautiously, Beth leaned over to see if he was all right.

The figure moaned, grunted, said, "Aw, fuck," in a soft, dejected voice, and Beth heard a loud sigh. After a moment, he turned himself right side up and shook his head.

White hair, a long white beard…red suit and black boots.

It had to be… *Nah.* No way.

"I don't think so." Beth crossed her arms over her large breasts, suddenly feeling nearly naked and a whole lot vulnerable, standing in her front yard in her robe, talking to a strange man.

A *very* strange man. "Who the hell are you?"

"I was supposed to be the new Kris Kringle. They pink slipped me." He sighed, then held up his right hand. Without thinking, Beth reached out and helped pull him to his feet.

Just as quickly, she dropped his hand and rubbed hers against her thigh. Even beneath the black leather gloves he wore, his grip was warm and alive. She felt a shiver race from her fingertips to the spot where she suddenly remembered the little remote control egg was waiting for instructions.

Her vaginal muscles tightened involuntarily around the egg. Beth grabbed the porch railing for support.

Obviously favoring his right ankle, the man still towered over her, no great feat since she was barely over five feet tall. Beth fought the impulse to step back. "I'm still waiting to know who you are and what you were doing on my roof."

She thought of tapping her foot, realized her toes were numb from the cold, and stepped up on the porch. At least now she was closer to eye level with the man.

He grabbed the railing, as if for support. She wondered just how badly he'd hurt himself in his tumble from the roof.

"I'm Dominic. Dominic Claus." He reached up and swept the red hat off his head, taking the heavy white wig with it. The fake beard joined the wig. The two pieces dangled like dead white rabbits from his left hand. Beth shuddered and took another step back.

With his overly long coal-black hair and clean-shaven face, Nick Whoever-he-was suddenly looked a lot more threatening...and terribly appealing.

Once more, Beth was almost preternaturally aware of the little egg resting snug and warm inside her. She fought an impulse to glance toward the dining room table where she'd left the remote.

Then he shivered, and gave her a pleading look. "I'm freezing and my ankle hurts like a son of a gun. This has been one helluva night, and I could really use a drink. May I come in?"

Nonplussed, Beth realized she was already holding the door open for a complete stranger. Limping heavily, Dominic crossed over her threshold and entered Beth's little home.

* * * * *

Beth decided there was definitely something surrealistic about sipping brandy in front of a glowing fire in the wee hours of Christmas morning with the sexiest man she'd ever seen in her life—a sexy man dressed in a bright red Santa suit.

"So you're telling me there really *is* a Santa Claus, but he's not just one man, he's a succession of men, all related?"

"Right. Each generation, a new Santa is chosen by the Santa Committee of elders to carry on the family tradition." A look that might have been relief crossed his face. "I honestly didn't want the job, but I must admit to a sense of loss when I realized my cousin Nick made the cut." His smile was rueful, self-deprecating. "We've always been competitive. I hate losing, but I know Nick'll make a better Santa than I ever could. I'm more into research and development."

He was either totally bonkers, or one of the most sincere liars Beth had ever known. He was also making her think deliciously naughty things. "Research and development?" she asked, forcing her thoughts out of the bedroom. "Research and development of what?"

"Well, toys, of course. It's a big job." He spread his long fingers out as he spoke. Beth listened with only a fragment of her mind. The rest of it was concentrating on those long, almost elegant fingers, imagining them touching, pinching…probing…

"…world population isn't shrinking, you know. I got my business degree at Harvard and finished up the MBA at Stanford, but I've always been more interested in research and development of new toys than the actual distribution."

What did he say? Beth's gaze flew from his fingers to his face. "Harvard? Stanford?" At least when he told a story, it was a good one. "So, do you actually do all this research and development at the North Pole?" He couldn't be serious... She glanced around the room, wondering if she might need to defend herself from a complete nutcase.

Of course, depending on his intentions, she wasn't all that certain she'd defend too hard. She blinked, suddenly aware she hadn't thought of what's-his-name in ages.

Dominic laughed, a deep, mellow, sexy laugh that sent shivers along Beth's spine. "Of course not, silly. All that North Pole stuff is just to keep the fantasy alive for the kids, though I must admit, children appear to be a lot more cynical than when I was young. I own the Rudolph Toys chain. We're international, you know." The pride in his voice was typical male. Beth found it endearing.

She was also completely familiar with Rudolph Toys. She even had stock in the company—one of the few stocks she owned that actually made money.

"Of course, we sell a lot of our product, but most of it is funneled through the Santa Claus franchise for Christmas deliveries. Commercial sales cover the costs of answering all the requests we get on the letters to Santa. Tonight was a test run for the seven of us in this generation who had a shot at the Santa Claus title and position. Usually, if you aren't selected, the reindeer immediately take you back to headquarters. It's all done by very old magic, but unfortunately, I'd gotten out of the sleigh to pick up a bell that fell off the harness. I made a consummate error by not keeping contact with the sleigh, so when it was called back, it went without me. That's how I ended up stranded on your roof."

"Reindeer?" Beth swallowed. "Magic?"

Dominic yawned. "You know, little flying beasts that carry Santa's sleigh?" He yawned again and smiled at her. "Would it be asking too much to let me spend a few hours on your couch? I'm beat, and it's going to take a call into headquarters to see if they can arrange transportation home for me." He shook his head, his expression rueful. "I feel like such an idiot. This is a terrible time to screw up. I doubt anyone's even answering the phones."

"At the North Pole?" *No,* Beth thought. *I am not having this conversation.*

Dominic smiled. His lips were full, his teeth perfect. Everything about him was perfect, except for the fact he was nuts. "Actually, no," he said. "I live in Akron. That's where Reindeer Toys is headquartered."

"Right." Beth wanted to rely on her gut. She really wanted him to be telling the truth, but of course that was impossible. Still, he didn't appear dangerous. He'd been more than sympathetic when she'd explained her break-up with Steve. He'd agreed completely with Beth's decision to end the relationship.

He might be absolutely nuts, but he was also sincere and warm and funny. Beth nodded, wondering if she was preparing to make the biggest mistake of her life. "You can stay," she said. "No funny business."

Head spinning, heart pounding, she went directly to her bedroom and locked the door behind her.

Chapter Three

જી

It was the most delicious dream she'd ever had. Dom was there, his dark hair mussed as if from sleep, that serious half-smile on his face that somehow felt achingly familiar. He leaned over her, his big hands splayed out on either side of her head, his long fingers tangled in her hair. He was naked, his body taut with barely contained passion, the huge head of his cock barely pressing between her legs, teasing her, sweeping through the tangle of auburn curls.

He practically vibrated against her and she felt him deep inside.

Impossible. Her door was locked and the man in her bed was pure fantasy.

Writhing against her tangled bedding, Beth felt her climax building, felt the deep vibrations against her womb, the low thrum of passion climbing to a crescendo, an earth-shattering, mind-numbing, toe-tingling…

Nothing.

The vibrations stopped. Beth hung there, suspended between lust and incredulity.

The egg! The damned egg was still inside her!

But that meant…

A tentative knock on her bedroom door snapped her fully awake.

"Beth? Are you awake yet?"

Dominic!

"Um, yes. I'm awake." Brushing her tangled hair back from her eyes, Beth grabbed her bathrobe off the floor. "Just a minute."

She opened the door just enough to peek around the edge. Dom waited on the other side, hair slightly mussed, his dark eyes looking warm and seductive, the red velvet Santa pants riding low on his hips. His chest was bare, the dark whorl of hair spinning over taut muscles and arrowing down a narrow trail to disappear beneath the waistband of his pants. He held a steaming cup of coffee in one hand, the damned control for the vibrating egg in the other.

"Merry Christmas and good morning, sleepyhead. I wondered if you were ever going to wake up." He chuckled, the sound deep and as seductive as the aroma of freshly brewed coffee. "I hope you don't mind my snooping around your kitchen, but I saw the coffee grinder on the counter and figured you liked your cup in the morning as much as I do. Here." He held the steaming mug out to her. "I hope you like it black."

Beth opened the door just enough to grab the coffee. She couldn't take her eyes off the little plastic remote he held in his left hand. "What are you doing with that?"

Dom looked down at the remote. "Oh, I was trying to get the TV to work. Battery must be dead." He negligently flipped the switch.

The egg went back to vibrating against Beth's already sensitive womb. She gritted her teeth and clutched the handle of her coffee cup so hard her knuckles turned white.

"Uh, Dom...that's not actually the remote for the TV."

Dom continued to fiddle with the controls for a moment. The vibrations revved up a few notches. Beth felt the first stirrings of her delayed climax, the shivers and rhythmic clenching deep inside. She stared helplessly at Dom's big hands, the long fingers playing with the buttons on the remote. The egg vibrated faster.

Dom turned his attention from the remote in his hand to smile directly at Beth.

"I know it's not the TV remote," he said, grinning devilishly. "This is one of my creations. We make these at Rudolph Toys." He brushed a wisp of hair back from Beth's forehead. His voice was low, conspiratorial. "They're very popular in our adult toys section. One of our best sellers." He held the remote up for her inspection. "See this little button? The red one? Heat."

He pressed it with his thumb. Within seconds, the vibrating egg began to grow warmer inside Beth. Helplessly, she watched him work his fingers across the buttons, as if he played a computer game.

"This one increases vibrations…"

The egg practically buzzed inside her. She felt her teeth start to vibrate.

"But this is the most popular feature." Grinning even wider, Dom pressed another little button.

The hot little egg began to slowly tumble back and forth, vibrating and moving about inside Beth's pussy like a thing alive.

Her lungs expanded but she couldn't draw enough air. She grabbed the door frame as lights danced behind her eyes, her field of vision narrowed to Dom's eyes, his lips, no longer smiling now, but slightly parted as if he, too, shared her building climax.

The cup of hot coffee would have tipped from her fingers but Dom caught the cup and deftly set it on a table in the hallway. Beth screamed, her knees buckled and Dom caught her up in his strong embrace, his mouth finding hers, his tongue thrusting deep between her lips as she shuddered and pulsed with the rhythmic vibrations deep inside.

Dom fingered the controls and the egg slowed to a gentle vibration, just enough to ease Beth down from a mind numbing orgasm. He kissed her once more, gently, then carried her into her room, laying her out on her bed. He leaned over her and brushed her sweat-dampened hair back from her eyes and kissed her once more on the mouth.

Waves of pure pleasure gave way to the hot and cold wash of absolute humiliation. Turning away from Dom's sweet smile, Beth tried to decide the best way out of what had to be the most embarrassing thing that had ever happened to her in her life.

She had no control over the tears that squeezed from beneath her tightly closed eyelids. *Just go away,* she begged silently. *Just go away so I can pretend this never happened.*

"My God. That was the most beautiful thing I've ever seen in my life."

Dom's voice sounded reverent, almost awestruck.

Beth opened her eyes just enough to see through tear-clumped lashes. His face was mere inches from hers. She hadn't really noticed the color of his eyes last night. Now she saw they were a deep gray, lost somewhere between green and blue. "What?"

"Your climax." His voice was barely a whisper, rough around the edges, emotional. "That was the most amazing... I mean, when I created the egg, I thought of it as a great thing for couples to play with at parties and such. I never thought beyond the social aspects of it as a silly sex toy. Watching you come just now, knowing I had control over you, knowing what was happening inside you with each button I pushed... We don't know each other, Beth, but I have never, not in my entire life, felt such a connection to another person. I don't think I've ever wanted a woman as much as I want you right now."

He sat back and held his hand up. "No. Please. Don't be frightened. I would never do anything you don't want." He shook his head, apologetically. "Well, beyond pushing your buttons." He reached playfully for the remote.

Beth giggled and swatted his hand away.

"I should probably call a cab," he said, turning to sit on the edge of the bed. "I doubt anyone's at the office this morning, and I've imposed on you more than enough."

"It's Christmas Day." Beth scooted back and leaned against her headboard. "What will you do?"

"Go back to work. In a way, I'm glad the Santa selection process is over for this generation. It means I can concentrate on what I do best."

"Thinking up sex toys?" She giggled again, aware on a visceral level of the little egg, still now, that was resting inside her pussy.

"Among other things." He smiled, touched the side of her face. "What are your plans?"

Beth sighed. "I don't know. Like I told you last night, I expected to be planning my wedding. I don't know what I'm going to do today."

"Wanna do whatever it is, together?"

Dom glanced sideways at her out of hooded eyes. His look conjured up all kinds of thoughts in Beth, most of the carnal variety.

She didn't know him. Didn't believe half of what he said.

She wanted to know him. Wanted to believe.

"Yeah," she said, putting her heart in his hands. "Let's do it together."

Chapter Four

80

Beth wasn't quite sure what she'd expected, but ice skating in the park wasn't on her list, at least not until Dominic suggested it. She noticed there was no sign of the limp that had convinced her to let him in the night before. He wore the Santa suit, along with the flowing white wig and beard, and stayed in character throughout the day. The children trying out their new ice skates loved it.

Not nearly as much as Beth, though. She kept looking for flaws. There weren't any, once you got past the fact Dom still believed in Santa, in fact believed he could have been Santa. Dom was funny and sweet, he loved little kids and was polite to their mothers. He found candy canes in his pockets for each child he saw, and helped one little girl learn to skate when her very pregnant mother begged off.

They found a hot dog stand under a snow covered cedar and ate polish sausages and sipped hot chocolate. Dom held her hand as if he'd known her forever, twirled her on the ice like a ballerina and kissed her nose to warm her up.

She wanted him to kiss even more, but he was the perfect gentleman. They walked hand in hand down Main Street as the short day turned to night, gazing at the lighted displays in each store window. At dinnertime they ate the roast dinner Beth had fixed the night before, sitting in front of the fire in their stocking feet, toes pointed toward the warming flames.

She could hardly recall the reason she'd prepared such a feast.

Later, they cleaned up the kitchen, the conversation between them light and fun, the tension simmering between them hot enough to steam the windows.

"I don't want to leave, but I've imposed on you long enough." Dom dried his hands on the dishtowel and wiped down the counters as Beth put the last of the dishes away. "It's been an amazing day, Beth. Absolutely amazing."

He hadn't kissed her all day. Hadn't made a move of any kind. Still, Beth knew he felt the same desire shimmering and pulsing just beneath the surface. The tension between them had about it a lovely, expectant sort of feeling.

One she wasn't about to waste.

She opened her mouth, closed it, swallowed and tried again. "It could be an amazing night, I think. Dom, will you stay with me tonight?"

He didn't say a word, just smiled at her with that half-expectant smile she'd grown to love over the course of one day. Smiled and touched the side of her face, then slowly leaned over and kissed her.

This was the kind of kiss Beth had dreamed of, the searching, touching, tasting kind of kiss that parted her lips and drew her tongue into play, a dance of the senses as they slowly but thoroughly explored each other's mouths. Dom cupped her shoulders with his big hands, drawing her closer, molding her body to his.

"Mmpf!" Beth tilted her hips away from the heavy brass buckle on Dom's Santa suit belt. Without breaking the kiss, Dom unbuttoned the red velvet jacket, undid the belt and slipped out of the Santa coat.

Beth traced the heavy pectoral muscles across his chest with her fingernails, dragging them across Dom's nipples. He moaned into her mouth, his fingers searching for the hem of her sweater.

Gasping, he stepped back just far enough to tug the sweater over her head. Her long braid caught in the knit. Dom pulled the band off the end of her thick rope of hair, slipped the sweater off of her and flung it across the room. Then he stepped back, gazing at her breasts with frank admiration.

"Oh my." His hands came up to cup them on either side, tracing the pale lavender colored lace on her bra. He reached for the front closure and carefully released the snap, then eased the straps over Beth's shoulders.

Her breasts spilled free, large enough to fill his large hands, the rosy tips already puckering with need. Dominick stared at them transfixed, holding the smooth globes in his palms, running his thumbs over the sensitive tips.

This time Beth moaned, arching her back into his touch. Reverently, Dom leaned over and drew one taut nipple between his lips, biting down just hard enough to send a piercing stab of need arrowing straight between her legs.

Her knees almost buckled. Dom caught her up in his arms and carried Beth into her bedroom where he lay her down on the bed. Standing over her, he slipped out of the red velvet pants, pushing his socks off at the same time.

Beth watched, fascinated, as the pants slid down past his thighs, uncovering a pair of very brief, bright red silk underwear.

Tented underwear. Dom's cock stretched the fabric to its max.

She giggled. "Wow, to think I never imagined what Santa wore beneath his suit!" She reached out and stroked him through the smooth silk. Dom closed his eyes and groaned, thrusting his hips forward, forcing his ready cock into her hand.

She stroked him again, then leaned over and tasted him through the silk. A drop of fluid darkened the red silk at the very tip. Suddenly, Dom pulled away and leaned over Beth, tugging her jeans and panties quickly down over her knees. She raised up to help him, parting her knees and lifting her hips to give him a better view of the secrets between her legs.

He paused, swallowed deeply, then reached down and ran his finger through the juices spilling from her pussy. Beth sighed and pressed herself against his hand.

She had no shame with this man. None. No worries that he might find her too big, too short, too round, too anything. The look of pure adoration in his eyes removed any inhibitions she might have found.

She lay in front of him, completely naked, her unbound hair spilling over her chest in an auburn mass of shining silk. Her breasts practically tingled with desire. She felt the thick fluid between her legs, felt the pressure building as she waited for Dom to touch her, to fill her with the hot, hard thrusts she needed.

Instead, he worshipped her. Kneeling between her legs, still covered in the red silk briefs, he touched her belly, her mons, ran his fingers through the tight curls between her legs. Almost hesitantly he leaned over and kissed her stomach, running his tongue around her navel, dipping lower to lick at the tuft of auburn hair between her legs.

Sighing, she let him part her knees, opening her secrets to his curious eyes. He knelt there for a moment, watching her, then leaned over and gently suckled her clit between his lips. Beth felt the shock of contact, the bone shuddering current when Dom scraped the sensitive nub oh, so gently, with his teeth, then laved her with his tongue.

He spread her legs wide, giving himself access to her heat. Nibbling at the fleshy lips, he drew first one and then the other into his mouth, sucking and licking at the sensitive flesh until Beth squirmed beneath his touch. She raised her hips and he speared her with his tongue, licking and suckling at the juices flowing freely between her legs.

She was helpless, caught there in the sensual caress of his mouth, hanging on the very edge of ecstasy. Dom grasped her buttocks in his hands, lifting her to his mouth, filling her with his tongue while his fingers made furtive explorations over her flesh, tickling her ass, pressing at the sensitive ring of flesh as his tongue probed her pussy deeper, hotter.

Suddenly his finger gained entrance to her ass just as his tongue flicked quickly over her clit. Without warning, Beth exploded, clamping her legs tightly against his head, arching into his mouth, screaming out in wanton ecstasy. His finger probed deeper, harder, finding nerves and sensations Beth had never even suspected.

Slowly, so slowly she felt herself coming down from her climax when Dom suddenly found her clit once more, drawing it between his lips, tonguing it with rapid flicks as his finger moved in delicious circles within her ass.

Barely able to breathe, Beth screamed again, riding this climax to the very end as her body finally subsided in shuddering, shivering release.

Dom sat back on his heels, a big grin on his handsome face. His chin was shiny with the fluids from her climax, his cock was rock hard and jutting forth in red silken splendor.

Beth struggled for breath, her mind working at a feverish rate. Dom looked much too self-satisfied for a man who still hadn't had his turn. The least she could do was make his wait worthwhile.

Sitting up, she gently pushed Dom to the bed. He offered absolutely no resistance. She spread his legs out, then his arms, so that he lay there in a most helpless position. "Close your eyes," she whispered.

He did.

"Keep them closed," she said, reaching for the silk scarves she kept in the bedside table. She'd never once used them on Steve, but there was no hesitation with Dom. She tied one around his eyes, effectively blindfolding him. "You'll like this," she promised, mentally crossing her fingers. Quickly, Beth secured his hands to the bedposts, then slipped his red silk underwear down his long legs.

Dom played along, blissfully unaware of what was going on in Beth's mind. She was absolutely certain he didn't have a clue.

Damn but he was gorgeous! His cock waved unfettered, finally free of the restraining briefs. It bobbed in the cool air, surrounded by a nest of dark hair. Beth paused a moment, hoping her plan would work. Dom was huge, his penis almost twice the size of Steve's, and Steve was the only lover Beth had ever had.

She swallowed back a momentary stab of fear, leaned over and kissed the purple tip, then backed off when Dom thrust his hips forward.

"Not yet," she said. Quickly she tied his feet to the bedposts, spreading his legs wide and securing him so he couldn't free himself.

Dom tugged lightly at the restraints, then grinned. "Have you been reading my mind?" he asked. "This is my ultimate fantasy…a beautiful woman tying me to the bed and having her way with me."

Beth sat back on her heels and laughed. "No, haven't read your mind, but we're doing my fantasy, not yours. It's merely your luck that we share this one." She leaned over and kissed Dom on the lips. He kissed her back, raising his head to follow her as she pulled back.

Beth got up from the bed and found the little electronic egg. She'd carefully washed it and checked to make sure the batteries were good. Now she covered it with a lubricant before crawling back on the bed and kneeling between Dom's legs. "I've always wanted to take a man in my mouth and make him come," she said, softly stroking Dom's huge erection. "I've never done it before. Is that okay with you?"

Dom's laughter ended in a choking sound. "Okay? You think I'd complain about that? Is that why you tied me up?"

"Partially." Beth leaned over and drew his cock into her mouth. The flesh was smooth, hot, the taste a little salty. It made her blood run hot, her heart beat fast. She fondled Dom's balls between her fingers and he thrust himself forward as if reaching for her touch. Beth took the egg and rubbed it over his cock, along the length of the shaft, up and down as she traced the same movements with her tongue. After a few moments, she turned on the remote so that the egg vibrated against Dom's erection.

He moaned, lifting his hips as he thrust against the vibrations, against Beth's lapping tongue.

She ran her fingers along his balls, rolling each round sac between her fingers, and heard Dom's breath catch in his throat. With one finger, she traced the crease from his scrotum to his ass, rubbing the sensitive flesh back and forth, over and over.

Dom twisted against the restraints, his breath huffing out in short gasps. Beth found the little tube of lubricant and quickly massaged the opening around his ass, rimming the puckered flesh, occasionally breaching the opening. Dom moaned, but he didn't say a word.

She penetrated him again and again with her finger, each time finding the entrance easier, the muscles relaxing.

Quickly, before Dom could figure out her intentions, Beth shoved the mechanical egg up his ass. Only the little removal string remained outside. The minute she inserted it, Dom went still.

Too still.

"What the hell are you doing?" He didn't sound particularly happy.

"What do you think?"

"Did you just shove that egg up my ass?"

"Maybe."

"Why?"

"You'll see." Beth leaned over and drew his cock between her lips, suckling him deep and hard. At the same time, she hit the little button on the remote control.

Dom jumped. Beth bit down, then settled into a slow, sensual rhythm. She raised the vibrations on the egg. Dom's cock got bigger, harder. He moaned, tugging at the restraints.

She heard him muttering under his breath. "Oh shit, oh shit, oh shit…"

Beth hit the "tumble" button.

Dom cried out, arched his back and his cock convulsed. Beth caught the spurting semen, suckling him hard, her mouth covering him and taking everything he could give her.

She reduced the rate of vibration, finally easing the egg to the off position. Dom lay gasping on the bed, his cock still rock hard between her lips, his balls drawn up tight to his body. His trembling body. The body that was still tied tightly to the bedposts.

Beth slowly suckled along the length of his softening cock, then turned the remote back on low. Dom immediately got hard again.

"Ohmygod." He raised his head, his eyes still covered by the blindfold. "What the fuck are you doing to me?"

"Do you like it?" Beth sat back on her heels and grinned. She slowly raised the vibration level on the egg. Dom's cock twitched, expanded, then bobbed in a lonely circle.

"Hell, yes." He tugged once more at the restraints. "I really, really want to fuck you, though. Is that in your plan?"

"Oh yeah…" Beth scooted forward along Dom's chest, finally reaching a point where her pussy was at lip level. Without any instruction, Dominic leaned forward and began suckling at her needy clit. His tongue gained entrance and he lapped at the juices flowing freely from her pussy. It felt so fantastic Beth pushed the next button on the remote.

"Oh shit, oh shit, oh shit…" Dom bucked beneath her and bit down on her clit. Beth bit back a scream, scooted back down his body and hovered over his straining cock. She grabbed a condom out of the table by her bed and carefully sheathed him, spending an inordinate amount of time smoothing the latex down over his swollen cock.

Slowly, so very slowly, she eased herself down over him. She felt his hard shaft enter, stretching and throbbing against her vaginal walls, slipping into the wet and ready place she kept for him.

Raising and lowering herself over his huge cock, Beth felt her climax growing. Unwilling to go alone, she increased the speed on the egg, sending it into that tumbling mode Dom was so proud of.

He thrust into her, hard and solid and hot, so very hot, his cry echoing in her small room. Beth took him deep inside herself, crying out as he did, her thighs clamping down on his hips, her mouth latching on to the taut nipple on the left side of his chest, just over his rapidly beating heart.

He came into her over and over again, each thrust of his hips claiming another piece of her heart. Finally, long moments later, Beth turned off the remote and Dom stilled within her embrace.

"Payback?" he whispered, his voice breaking with each gasping breath.

"Not really." Beth quietly untied the restraints holding his hands and feet and removed the blindfold. "I wanted you to experience what I did, that sense of no control, of pure physical sensation." She looked into his dark eyes. "Did you feel it?"

"Oh yeah." Dom reached up and kissed her, hard on the lips. "Oh yeah, my love. I felt it. Shit. Did I ever."

Chapter Five

ல

They showered together. Sex while standing under a cascade of steaming water was something Beth figured she could become addicted to. Dom lifted her so easily, wrapping her legs around his waist, filling her with his huge cock and never missing a beat, even when she accidentally kicked the faucet with her left foot and turned off the hot water.

Contrary to common belief, the icy blast had absolutely no effect on Dom's libido. Of course, he got the temperature adjusted in record time without missing a stroke.

He caressed her thighs, grabbing her round cheeks in both hands and holding her close, thrusting with long, smooth strokes that filled her with heat and fire and need. Sobbing, she broke in his arms, her climax tearing out a little piece of her heart with each pulsing contraction.

Dom cried out as well, a shout of triumph, of pure masculine joy. He wrapped his arms tightly around Beth and slowly slid down the wall until they sat together on the floor of the big shower, steaming water cascading over the two of them.

She could still feel him inside her, erect and filling her more completely than she'd ever been.

Dom kissed her ear, the sensitive line of her jaw. "My God, Beth. I am one lucky elf. You're magic...who you are, what you do to me. I felt it the first time I saw you, standing out there in the snow with a look of total disbelief on your face." He chuckled. Beth felt his stomach move beneath her clasping thighs. "I've heard it can happen like this, heard about guys who found *the one* they were meant to find. I never dreamed I'd find you."

He hugged her close, his lips buried in her wet hair.

Beth kissed Dom's neck as the water sluiced over her back and shoulders, thankful it disguised her flowing tears. There'd been no warning, no wake-up call, no sign that this Christmas Day would be the most bittersweet of her life.

She'd gone and fallen in love with a man with delusions of Santa, a man who thought he was a Christmas elf, who believed in magic and flying reindeer and Santa Claus. A man who, despite his peculiar beliefs, was perfect in every way.

Dom tilted her chin up and kissed her. His dark hair was slicked down around his face and his eyes sparkled with laughter, as if they shared a most beguiling secret. "Have I told you lately how beautiful you are? How much I love what we are together?" He kissed her again, then trailed tiny kisses across her jaw. His tongue touched the side of her mouth, then followed the trail of her tears.

Gently, he kissed the corner of her eye, then her temple. "Tears? Either you're crying, or the water in this town has way too high a salt content."

"It's nothing." Beth ducked her head, unwilling to look at him. How could she tell him it was everything? She untangled herself from his embrace and clambered awkwardly to her feet and turned off the water.

"C'mon." She held her hand out and Dom grabbed it. Looking down at their entwined fingers made her want to cry again. Beth took a deep breath instead and led Dom into the bedroom.

* * * * *

The pale winter sunlight barely lighted the dark corners of Beth's bedroom. She lay there, naked, caught in a tangle of sheets, the room awash in the sweet/pungent scent of sex and sweat. Dom slept, one arm thrown over his head, stretching toward the headboard. The other was curled close to his chest.

Beth watched him, wondering how she could possibly let this man go. He wanted her to come with him, to see the plant in Akron, to meet the members of the Santa Committee, the board of elders.

They were elves, he said. Elves just like him. He'd swept his hair back and, though she had to admit his ears did have a bit of a point to them, it certainly wasn't enough to convince her.

She thought of her job, the daily grind she truly loved, the fact that her ability for organizing kept her boss on time for his meetings and in good graces with both his wife and his mistress. Then she compared it to the last twenty-four hours she'd spent with a madman.

There was no other way to describe him. Dom made her laugh, made her forget her pragmatic, organized world, and he made sweet, wonderful love to her. He took her to heights she'd only imagined, tasting and touching her in places she'd barely known existed on her own body.

He'd managed to put that purple penis to shame, but not until he'd put it to lots of good use.

It was also one of his products — at least he said it was.

And that was the problem. Could she really trust a man who believed in Santa Claus? Who said he was an elf, explained how he took his directions from a governing board of elves? Could she tie her future to a stranger who believed in magic, who waited for the flying reindeer to come back and rescue him?

It made Beth want to weep. Damn it, how could she have fallen in love with a nut?

* * * * *

Beth awoke early the morning after Christmas. The room was a dismal gray, awash in the thin sunlight of an early winter's morning. She ached in places she'd hardly noticed before and was decidedly aware of a tenderness between her legs that was definitely new.

The place beside her was empty, the indention on the pillow the only proof anyone had shared her bed. Aware of a hollowness deep inside, a premonition of utter dread, Beth grabbed her robe and headed for the kitchen.

Dom sat at the kitchen table, nursing a cup of coffee. He wore dark slacks and a white dress shirt. A coat and tie hung neatly over the back of one of her kitchen chairs. The black hairs on the back of his hands and the day's growth of beard shadowing his hollow cheeks gave him a ruthless appearance, even dressed as he was.

Dom looked up as she hovered there in the doorway. His eyes were dark, hidden beneath sooty lashes. He stared solemnly at Beth for a long moment, then sighed. "Are you sure you won't come with me? I contacted headquarters. My ride will be here in about fifteen minutes."

"What? Eight tiny reindeer and a little bell-covered sleigh?" She couldn't even hide the bitterness in her voice, didn't try. Without giving Dom a chance to answer her sarcastic question, she demanded, "Where did the clothes come from? All you had was the Santa suit."

Dom blinked, as if suddenly aware, for the first time, he was wearing something entirely different. "I can't wear a Santa suit today. Christmas is over. It reverted."

"Reverted?" Beth swallowed back the little squeak that threatened to escape. "What do you mean, 'reverted?'"

"The red suit is Santa's business suit. This is mine. It was red velvet when I needed red velvet. Now I need a dark suit, so that's what it is. It's just a small magic, but really handy. You can't expect me to go back to Akron dressed like Santa. People would think I was nuts." He spread his hands wide, as if his explanation made perfect sense.

Beth felt the tears threatening again. "I can't go to Akron with you, Dom. I have a life here, a job I need and love." *I can't tie my future to a madman.* She folded her hands across her chest in what she knew was a purely defensive position. It would be so easy to go with him, so easy to throw away everything she had worked for, just throw it all away for love.

Dom sighed. His big shoulders drooped. He folded his hands together on the table in front of him, but for all the vulnerability in his pose, his voice was pure, masculine intransigence. "I wish you'd tell me why. Why can't you believe? We may have only known each other a couple days, but we have something so special we'd be fools to let it go. I recognized it the moment I saw you. You can't possibly deny that you feel it too! Beth, you complete me. You make me feel like the man I should be. I woke up this morning thinking how depressed I should have been, knowing the Santa job didn't go to me, and then I looked at you sleeping beside me and realized I didn't care a bit about being Santa. I was relieved I wouldn't have that hanging over my head, wouldn't have to worry about having my wife approved by the Santa Committee."

"What?" Beth took a step forward, into the kitchen. She wasn't sure which statement affected her more—the fact he was still talking about that dumb Santa Committee or the fact they wouldn't have to approve his wife.

"What do you mean, the committee has to approve your wife?"

"If I had been selected as Santa, my choice for Mrs. Claus would have to meet certain requirements. She'd have to be jolly and sweet and love to bake cookies, she'd have to love children and be willing to help care for the reindeer and accept the fact that her husband will be away every Christmas. Some women just aren't cut out for the job."

"Oh." What else could she say? Obviously the delusion was a major part of Dom's existence. "I guess it doesn't matter who you marry, now you're out of contention for the job, then.

That should be a relief." Beth bit her lower lip, ashamed at the sarcasm in her reply.

"It matters to me." Dom stood up, suddenly filling the small kitchen with barely restrained emotion. "I hardly know you, but I can honestly say I love you, Beth. I want you to come to Akron as my wife, dammit, but I can see that you're just humoring me. Until you can believe that what I say is true, there's no chance for us. No chance at all."

Suddenly he raised his head. "My ride is here." He flipped a red business card down on her table. "If you change your mind, if you realize you have it in you to accept the magic, to *believe,* call me." He looked down at the little card, then back at Beth. "You, me…we're magic. Can't you see that? Call me, Beth. I'll be waiting."

He grabbed his coat and tie, slung them over his arm and headed for the door. As he passed Beth, Dom leaned over and kissed her. She knew it was meant to be a punishing, angry kiss, but her heart practically broke under the love she felt in Dom's touch.

Still, it was too soon, too much, too unbelievable.

Dom broke the kiss and stepped back. He stared at Beth for a long, tension-filled moment, then opened the front door and practically ran down the front steps.

A long, black limo waited in front of Beth's house. Steam billowed from the exhaust though she couldn't hear a motor running. The windows were dark, but tiny bells hung from the radio antennae. The front door opened and a little man dressed all in green climbed out of the car. He bowed deeply to Dom, sweeping his pointed cap off his head as he opened the door to the back seat.

His ears were just as pointed as his cap. Beth could practically see the twinkle in his eyes from her doorway. He closed the door behind Dom, jumped into the front seat and the limo pulled silently out into the snow-covered street. As

Beth watched, the back of the limo seemed to sparkle as if it were lost in a storm of fairy dust.

Then it simply disappeared.

Chapter Six

ஐ

By ten A.M. Beth had quit her job and arranged for a real estate agent to give an appraisal on her house. By airplane, it should have taken Dom about four hours to reach his office. Beth wasn't sure how long it took by magic limo.

Still, her hand was shaking when she picked up the phone. Her mouth was so dry she could barely make herself heard when Dom's warm baritone sounded on the line.

"I love you, Dom. How do I find you? There's only a phone number on the card, no address. Will you forgive me? Do you really love me?"

She hadn't meant to sound so desperate, hadn't meant to beg...hadn't realized how empty her house would feel with Dom not in it.

How empty her life could be after knowing him. She couldn't face another day without him, couldn't face her life without Dom in it. How could he have burrowed so deeply into her heart in a mere matter of hours?

It had to be magic.

"I love you more than life itself. Can you be packed and ready to go in half an hour? It'll take me that long to arrange for transportation."

Beth giggled, imagining the magic limo landing in her neighborhood. "What do I need?"

There was a slow, sexy chuckle from Dom's end of the line. "That negligee you had on last night might be good for starters."

Beth laughed out loud. "Clothes, Dom. What kind of clothes?"

"What you're wearing. I carry a line of women's clothes. You'll be the perfect model." He laughed again, as if he felt the same relief at Beth's decision as she did. "Don't worry about a thing. We can come back to your place later and get whatever's important to you."

"Dom?" Beth gripped the phone in both hands. "I realized the moment you left...you're important to me. Without you, nothing else matters. I love you."

"I love you, too. Make that fifteen minutes."

* * * * *

Beth tugged lightly at the handcuffs securing her wrists to the headboard and tried, unsuccessfully, to move her feet, which were secured to the other end of the bed. She grinned in anticipation, almost certain Dom was in the room, though everything remained dark behind the silk blindfold covering her eyes.

All Dom had told her was that they were going to be testing some new products for the adult section of Rudolph Toys. After a little over a year of marriage to her favorite elf, Beth figured product testing was just about her favorite part of her job at Rudolph Toys.

Occasionally she thought of life before Dom, but not nearly so much anymore. His was a world on the cusp, hovering between magic and reality. Beth never would have dreamed how much she loved the magic.

She sensed him, almost preternaturally aware of his presence close by. His hand cupped her left breast, rubbing, caressing and then gently pinching the nipple. She arched into his touch, only to feel him clamp something over her nipple. It didn't hurt—the pressure wasn't that great—but it was getting hot and she was almost sure it was beginning to vibrate.

Before her other breast had a chance to feel ignored, Dom repeated the procedure. The heat and vibration seemed to send a shock directly between Beth's legs. She arched her back, hoping Dom would take her up on the invitation.

His fingers found the damp folds between her legs. Beth sighed with a sense of pure carnal anticipation. Dom was amazingly good with those long fingers of his! She felt him slide the tiny hood of flesh back from her sensitive clit, knew he spread the moisture gathering between her legs to lubricate her. Expecting his fingers, she jerked in surprise when a third little vibrator suddenly clamped down on her clit.

"That doesn't hurt, does it?" Dom's voice was right next to her ear. So close, she wasn't surprised when his tongue traced its contours.

"No," she gasped, suddenly overwhelmed by tiny little hot vibrations on her most sensitive parts. "Doesn't hurt." She took a shuddering breath. "Surprised. Just surprised." She gasped again when his tongue traveled a little deeper into her ear. "Ohhhhh, Dom. What are you doing?"

"Testing our mini-vibrating clamps. What do you think?"

"I think you're trying to drive me insane!" The vibrations increased, taking her just to the edge of ecstasy but not letting her go beyond. Her pussy clenched in frustration but the sensations merely kept her on the edge of climax.

The bed dipped from Dom's weight. Beth knew he knelt over her now, but he didn't touch any part of her body. He did, however, lightly touch each vibrator. The level of sensation increased even more. Still, it wasn't enough! Beth squirmed and thrashed against her restraints, lost in a frustrating maelstrom of sensation, reaching for an orgasm that wouldn't come. Her breasts ached with as much need as her pussy. How long did Dom intend to leave her like this — her body needing, wanting, demanding release?

Crying out, Beth arched her back and raised her hips off the bed.

Dom's huge cock slipped into her, filling her needy pussy with heat and hard muscle. She laughed and thrust her hips against him. "You creep! You were waiting for me, weren't you?"

His laughter echoed off the walls. "Ready and waiting. I didn't think you'd be able to last very long." He kissed her, hard, on the mouth, driving into her with enough force to stretch her ankles against their restraints. She grasped the chains to the handcuffs, holding herself against his onslaught.

The tiny vibrators buzzed over her sensitive flesh, Dom's cock pounded between her legs. It was all Beth needed.

Gasping, writhing against her restraints, she screamed. Dom groaned, pumping into her, flooding her with heat and something more—Beth smiled, even in the throes of climax. It was time to think about bringing a new generation of potential little Santas into the family.

* * * * *

Christmas morning, nine months later…

"He has his father's eyes." Tired, elated, fulfilled, Beth stared into the dark eyes of her newborn son as he suckled at her full breast. Dom stood next to the bed looking haggard, concerned, and very much in love.

"And his mother's smile." Dom leaned over and kissed her, then placed a gentle kiss on his newborn son. "This is the real magic, my love."

The snow was falling softly, just outside the window. Beth glanced at the myriad flakes, then back at her husband and son. To think she hadn't believed. She shook her head, smiling at her own lack of faith, then stroked her son's perfect little pointed ear.

Also by Kate Douglas

ఔ

About the Author

❦

For over thirty years Kate Douglas has been lucky enough to call writing her profession. She has won three EPPIES, two for Best Contemporary Romance in 2001 and 2002, and a third for Best Romantic Suspense in 2001. Kate also creates cover art and is the winner of EPIC's Quasar Award for outstanding bookcover graphics.

She is multi-published in contemporary romance, both print and electronic formats, as well as her popular futuristic Romantica StarQuest. She and her husband of over thirty years live in the northern California wine country where they find more than enough subject material for their shared passion for photography, though their new grandson is most often in front of the lens. Kate is currently working on the screenplay adaptation for one of her contemporary romances.

Kate welcomes comments from readers. You can find her website and email address on her author bio page at www.ellorascave.com.

Tell Us What You Think

We appreciate hearing reader opinions about our books. You can email us at Comments@EllorasCave.com.

RINGING IN THE SEASON
Rachel Bo

ഔ

Chapter One
Appetite

ॐ

Red taillights flashed, and Traci's heart pounded as she slammed down the brake pedal, stopping just short of the bumper in front of her. God, how she hated holiday traffic! *Stop thinking about Rick and concentrate on your driving*, she admonished herself.

Easier said than done. Traci frowned, blinking back the tears that welled unexpectedly. She had tried so hard the last few weeks. After seventeen years of marriage she couldn't bear the thought of losing her husband, but she was nearly to the point of giving up.

She *still* couldn't believe that he had gone to work on Thanksgiving. *The security system's down at the county hospital*, he'd said. *It's one of our biggest accounts. I have to be there, Trace.* Traci shook her head. *Bullshit.* He had worked his way to the top in that company, from a residential system installer to the small business systems coordinator, all the way to Senior VP of Corporate Accounts. He now directed several technologists, who in turn directed teams of technicians. They were perfectly capable of handling any problems without his intervention. It hadn't been necessary for him to go. But he'd gone anyway.

Traci turned into their driveway, thumbed the remote to open the security gate and drove through the gap, watching in her rear-view mirror as the wrought-iron gates swung shut behind her. Closing out the world almost as effectively as Rick had shut her out for the last few years. She pulled up in front of the garage and turned off the ignition, then rested her forehead on the backs of the hands still gripping the steering wheel tightly.

He hadn't come home until after midnight that night—another missed family gathering, another lame promise (*I won't be late, Trace*) broken. She'd waited for him. Sitting on the bed, a bag packed, fully intending to leave him if she didn't get satisfactory answers.

He had listened to her tirade, the anguish she'd been burying for…oh, it must be three years at least, since she had first sensed him drawing away. Laughed when she accused him of cheating. *I don't look at other women, Traci. I never have.* Seemed truly wounded by her bitterness, her sense of loss. *I DO love you Trace. I don't know why I don't say it.* Defended his absences forcefully. *I don't see how you can object to work, Trace. I'm doing this for US!* But in the end, he'd apologized. *I'm sorry. I'll spend more time at home. I'll try to do better.*

Traci hadn't believed him, but she'd given in. Even promised to try harder herself. He had pointed out some things she found herself admitting were true. Said it had been ages since she welcomed him home with a kiss rather than a lecture. Said he couldn't remember the last time she'd cooked a homemade meal; *truly* homemade, not just Pan Helper or frozen family-sized entrees and a couple of canned veggies. So she'd tried. She'd come home every night for the past month and cooked like she used to. Met Rick at the door and kissed him the way she had when they were newlyweds, even when he'd come home late after promising not to. Warmed up his meal for him instead of making him do it himself, and sat in the kitchen making small talk while he ate. Waiting for some sign. Waiting for him to say *I love you*. Longing for him to turn to her in bed and draw her into his arms…*touch* her.

Traci lifted her head and rubbed at her damp eyes angrily. But, no. Nothing. He was still spending more time at work than home. Still seeing next to nothing of the kids. Still turning his back to her every evening in bed, with a firm and final goodnight. Leaving her body aching with need. It had been four months since they last made love. Actually, she couldn't even call it *making love*. He'd been horny, and she'd relieved him. He had barely even acknowledged her participation.

Abruptly, she reached for her purse and opened the car door. *No more*, she decided. Tomorrow was Christmas Eve, and Friday was Christmas Day. She wouldn't ruin those days for the kids, but on Saturday…on Saturday, she would send Chase and Amy to her parents' house to spend the night, and she and Rick were settling this once and for all. She loved him with all her being and couldn't imagine her life without him, but if she had to let him go to make him happy and end this slow torment, she would.

She stepped out of the car and slammed the door. Snow had begun to fall, and Traci tilted her face up and stood there for a moment, the soft, cool flakes melting on her brow. Making her way to the portico, she felt a heavy knot of dread settling in the pit of her stomach; but there was relief, as well. It felt good to have finally made a decision.

Chapter Two
Memory

ဢ

She unlocked the front door and stepped inside. Every light in the house seemed to be on. She shook her head in exasperation and dropped her purse onto the entry hall table, stepping into the living room. Uncharacteristically, the television was off, the floor was spotless, and the coffee table showed no trace of the usual after-school snack trash build-up. Amy must want something. The only time their fifteen-year-old daughter cleaned now was when she wanted something.

"Amy?" Traci walked through the living room and into the kitchen. "Chase?" She listened carefully. It was too quiet. Where were her kids? Every light in the house on; but no TV, no music blaring, no kids arguing? Heart pounding, Traci picked up the portable phone from its receiver. What if someone had broken in? Hurt her babies? Traci depressed the Call button and reached for the '9' with her thumb as she tiptoed over to peek cautiously around the door jamb, into the dining room.

A wonderful aroma assailed her nostrils. There on the table was her favorite meal. Rick's famous onion-cheddar chicken, steamed broccoli, and…Traci sniffed. Yes, garlic mashed potatoes. She hesitated, then hung up the phone and set it on the buffet to the left of the door. She walked up to the table and held her hand over the plate. Warm. Steaming, actually, as though it had just been taken from the oven.

Traci glanced around the room, wondering what was going on. Finally, she pulled out the chair. Resting across the seat was a long florist's box, with a large manila envelope attached bearing her name. Her heart skipped a beat. She picked up the box and set it on the table, then pulled off the envelope and opened the lid. Surrounded by red and green tissue paper were five white roses, the petals blushing to red around their edges. Traci picked up the card nestled in the foliage and read:

The red rose whispers of passion
and the white rose breathes of love.
Oh, the red rose is a falcon
and the white rose a dove.

But I send you a cream-white rosebud,
with a flush on its petal-tip;
For the love that is purest and sweetest
has a kiss of desire on the lips.

by John Boyle O'Reilly

It was signed, "Rick". Traci brushed away a tear that escaped her trembling lashes and brought one of the roses to her nose, breathing deeply of its heady scent. Her legs suddenly weak, she settled into the chair and replaced the rose carefully. Picking up her dinner knife, she slit open the manila envelope and tilted it. The contents spilled onto the table—a note, a tiny white box tied with silver ribbon, and a small, cream-colored envelope the size of a business card. She picked up the note. Rick had written: *I've already trimmed the stems, the vase is ready. The kids are taken care of.* Traci glanced up, noticing for the first time the tall crystal vase gracing the table's center. She looked back at the note. *I remember our first night in this house. It was also the first time I cooked for you. This exact meal. You've always said it's your favorite. Mine, too, because it makes me think of that day. We ate; we laughed; we talked about having children; and then we made love on this very table. Do you remember?*

215

Traci swallowed and nodded to herself. She remembered. His firm lips on hers. His tongue lapping white wine from her belly. The heat of his cock as it slid into her pussy...Traci gasped, her pelvis flooded with hot desire. The next line read: *I knew you would.* Traci licked her lips and tried to slow her racing pulse. *Eat, drink, then open the second envelope.*

Traci laid the note aside. Her gaze took in her dinner, the vase, the roses. She stood and removed the flowers from their box, placing them reverently in the tall, fluted crystal. *Five. Why five?* she wondered. Traci resumed her seat. Her stomach rumbled; she was starving. She wasn't sure just what was going on, but she might as well eat. Rick hadn't cooked for her in a long time. She cut her first bite and placed it in her mouth. "Mmmmm." It melted on her tongue, every bit as good as she remembered. As she ate, she kept expecting him to appear. Hoping, really, because the memory of that first night in this house kept running through her brain, filling her with a different kind of hunger. One that only Rick could satisfy. What kind of game was he playing?

Her gaze strayed to the box and the small, white envelope, her hands itching to open them. She even reached out; but no, he'd said to eat first. If this was Rick's attempt at re-kindling their romance, Traci would do nothing to jeopardize that. She turned back to her meal.

When she had finished—eaten every bite and drained the last sparkling drop from her wine glass—she reached for the envelope and opened it. Inside were numbered cards. Removing the first one, Traci read: *There are more memories to be discovered, but first, take off your shirt.* Shocked, Traci placed the card on the table and leaned forward on her elbows, rubbing her temples with her fingertips. Her crotch was throbbing and her nipples tingled. Quite an erotic game Rick was playing. But what if it was a trick? What if he was just trying to see how far she would go to keep him? Did she want to humiliate herself?

Traci suddenly sat up, eyes wide as she realized that she didn't care. If loving Rick so much that she would do anything he wanted made her look pathetic, so be it. Because it was true. She realized that now. She would do anything—*anything*—to keep him. With fumbling fingers, she undid her buttons and let the shirt slide off her arms onto the chair. Reaching into the envelope, she pulled out the next card. Her breath caught as she read the next message. *Thank you. Now, take off your bra.* Traci bit her lip, but reached back and unfastened her bra, pulling it off and letting it fall to the floor. The next line read, *Open the white box and follow the instructions.*

Traci pulled one end of the silver ribbon and the bow came undone. Lifting off the tiny lid, she peeked inside. Nestled on a bed of cotton was a golden ring, about the circumference of a nickel. She picked it up and studied it. The ring was not continuous; instead, there were two gold balls, a trifle smaller than peas, at each end of an almost-complete circle. On the cotton beneath it lay a small booklet.

Picking up the booklet, Traci found that it was actually a piece of paper folded in quarters. Opening it, she discovered simple pictorial instructions. A line drawing of a breast with a distended nipple, another of fingers holding the golden circle open. Arrows indicated that the golden balls should be positioned to either side of the nipple, then pinched shut, so that the circle dangled from the bud. It was a nipple ring, only without the pain of a piercing. Rick had penciled in at the bottom of the sheet *Place on right nipple.*

Traci stared at the item for several minutes. She could see, now, the spring located inside the circle's arc. This seemed…a little kinky, but she had to admit her blood was racing as it hadn't for a long time. She opened the ring. Looking down, she saw that her nipples were swollen already, standing erect quite nicely. She positioned the golden balls to either side of the now-throbbing peak of her right breast and snapped it shut. "Oh, Lord!" she exclaimed involuntarily. She gripped the edge of the table and breathed slowly.

So…not totally without pain. The ring had *quite* a grip. As she waited, though, wanting to see this through, the discomfort began to fade, replaced by a tingling, buzzing heat. Traci moaned. It felt *good*. *What is Rick doing to me?* Traci cupped her breast in her hands. She couldn't help herself. The nipple was so *feverish*. She tilted her breast up until she could lick its tip. "Mmmm." She lapped at the swollen pyramid, finding that the soft flesh on the back of her tongue was very soothing. She slipped her tongue through the ring, began tugging experimentally. Pleasure blossomed in her breast. *Oh, God!* She withdrew and blew on her moist flesh, cooling the fiery tip just enough to quell her desire so that she could read the next card.

July 4, 1981. Traci frowned. A *date*? She shook her head. What did *this* mean? She rifled through the other cards, pausing when she read again *There are more memories to be found*. Her brain finally clicked. The Independence Day Picnic—their first official date. She closed her eyes. Rick had been so full of life, so romantic, back then. He had picked her up in that crazy old blue Duster of his, boyishly gleeful. Traci had climbed in, and Rick drove them to the park. He jumped out of the car and pulled an honest-to-goodness picnic basket from the back seat, and a pink and blue checkered blanket.

Traci stared at the card. Was that what Rick wanted? Just for her to remember? No. More memories to be found. She had the feeling this was a treasure hunt. But where to look? Wait—the picnic basket was long gone, but the blanket was in a trunk in the attic. Traci stood slowly and walked to the stairs, her excitement mounting as she climbed. Traci had been convinced Rick never gave the old days a moment's thought. She never dreamed he remembered these things.

Chapter Three
Desire

 හ

She paused at the attic door to catch her breath, then opened it and climbed up the narrow stairwell. Here, too, the lights gleamed. Chase and Amy loved to come up here—to sit in the rocker and read, to investigate the trunks, and to reminisce over childhood toys—so she kept the room well-lit, dusted and swept. Tinsel glittered on the miniature Christmas tree that she and the kids had bought and decorated specifically for this room. It didn't look like a typical attic. It was more of a cozy, albeit cluttered, sitting room. Traci strode over to the leather trunk beside the frame of Amy and Chase's old bunk beds and knelt in front of it. Lifting the lid, she found the blanket. Resting at its center was a crystal bowl with a lid, another small white box, and another envelope. Traci tore open the envelope.

Open the box and follow the instructions. Traci opened the box and found another nipple ring, identical to the first, with 'left breast' scrawled across the bottom of the directions. Traci licked her lips and mimicked her earlier movements, locking the ring into place on her left nipple. "Oh!" She closed her eyes as the pleasure/pain enveloped her again. Arching her back, Traci opened her eyes and caught a glimpse of herself in her grandmother's oak-framed dressing mirror. She studied herself. Her hair was drawn back into a tight bun, every wayward strand tamed by a bobby pin. The look was too severe for her.

When did I start wearing my hair like that? she thought. Standing up, she approached the mirror. She removed all the pins and unwound her hair from the band confining it. Her fine, dark locks draped over her shoulders, the smooth, shiny strands nearly touching her two golden rings. She marveled at her image. Cheeks flushed with desire, hair loose and flowing, and her body…well, she'd always been a little plump, but Rick *liked* that. She smiled at herself. For the first time in a while, she admired what she saw, as well.

Returning to the trunk, she pulled out the next item in the envelope, a folded sheet of notebook paper. *I remember that date – our first 'real' one. I was so proud to have you on my arm. I wanted to picnic right in front of the bandstand, so everyone would see us together, but you insisted on a spot further away, hidden in the trees.* Traci did remember. They had been interested in each other for two years. They'd stolen kisses beneath the bleachers at football games, and spent time talking and engaging in light petting in dark corners at group functions and whenever their families got together for backyard barbecues or cards. But her father wouldn't let her date until she was seventeen. So on the very day she turned seventeen, July 1, 1981, Rick asked her father if she could go to the Independence Day Picnic with him, and her father had said yes.

She smiled. *I couldn't believe how beautiful you were. How smart. I felt like the luckiest guy in the world. And, I couldn't believe how much I wanted you. How just looking at you was enough to make my cock hard. I can't tell you how many times I masturbated to fantasies of you before we went out on that first date.* Traci trembled as a trickle of moisture made its way down the inside of her thigh. Her panties were soaked! She glanced around the room, wishing Rick were there, to bury that hot cock she remembered in her tight, neglected pussy. Sighing, she returned her attention to the note. *After it got dark, you sat beside me, and took my hand and put it under your skirt. I almost swallowed my tongue when I realized you weren't wearing anything beneath, and then you pushed my finger inside your pussy, and yours with it.*

Rick's handwriting wavered, here, the letters awkwardly formed. Traci wondered if he'd been horny. If he had to stop and jack off before he continued, because his writing improved again on the next line. *I nearly exploded right then, but I wouldn't let myself, because I wanted to bury my cock inside your wet pussy so bad.* Rick's note became difficult to read again, and Traci wasn't sure if it was his handwriting, or the way her hand was shaking. God, she wanted him. Desperately.

And then you hiked up your skirt and spread your legs. Right there, not fifteen feet from the couples around us, and said "I'm yours, Rick. I've been waiting for you." Traci swallowed hard. The screen of trees and bushes around them had made her bold. She'd been wanting him for so long. But he'd always been shy, and she had known she would have to make her desire obvious. Be the aggressor. She shivered, remembering the mixture of loving wonder and savage desire she had witnessed on Rick's features. *I was too horny. I'd been wanting you, fantasizing about you, for so long, I forgot to be careful. I rammed myself into you, over and over, and then you were whimpering — I know you didn't want me to hear — and I realized. Your pussy was so TIGHT. So RESISTANT. A virgin. So I pulled out. I was so afraid I had hurt you. So afraid I'd gone and lost you. But then you begged me. Begged me to fuck you. And I did. Five times, before the fireworks had finished. And no one ever knew. Do you remember?*

"Yes, Rick," Traci whispered. "I remember." She pulled out the next item, a small card. *Take the lid off the bowl.* Traci removed the lid. Cradled inside were five cherries. *Take off your pants and panties.* Traci's legs were like gelatin as she stepped out of the garments. *Place the cherries inside your pussy, stems out.* Traci took a deep breath, her crotch flooding as she read these words. A fresh rivulet of moisture trickled its way down her thigh. She hesitated only a moment before sitting cross-legged on the floor. Taking up each small fruit, she pushed it deep inside with her finger. "Oh, God. Rick," she whispered, even though he wasn't there. It was too much. Especially after Rick's note. She *had* to have some relief. Traci lay back on the floor, crossing her legs, pressing her thighs tight against her clitoris. Squeezing the cherries buried in her cunt, she came, crying out Rick's name.

When she had recovered, she crawled back to the trunk on all fours. Pink juice from her fingers stained the next card when she picked it up. *Christmas, 1990.* Traci knew immediately where to go. She stood and raced to the stairway, pausing just long enough to remove the shoes and stockings from her feet. As she jogged down the steps, heat flooded her groin again and she had to stop at the foot of the stairs and hold on to the banister as another orgasm ripped through her. Breathing hard, she continued on, crossing the second floor landing and opening the door to her sewing room. She stopped short when she saw the pile of wrapped packages in the corner of the big room. Rick had wrapped all the gifts. Funny, how something so simple made her feel like crying. She had been thinking she was going to have to stay up until three or four o'clock on Christmas Eve, probably by herself, finishing up the wrapping. Somehow, this one gesture meant more at the moment than anything else she had encountered this night.

On the craft table in the center of the room were the expected items, plus one. Eying the extra box curiously, Traci opened the envelope and read the first note. *Thirteen years ago, you and I were wrapping presents together. We had so much fun that night. Amy was two years old, finally old enough to really take an interest in Christmas, and we had gone way overboard with the gifts. We were laughing, teasing each other. You looked so happy. You haven't looked that happy for a long time now. Maybe because you were right, I don't make enough time for you. But I made time that night, and you glowed. And after the last package was wrapped, you were sitting in my lap, and you asked me if there was anything I had ever wanted to do, sexually, that I was afraid to ask.* Traci's cheeks burned. Yes, she remembered. She still couldn't believe she had even asked. But, that night, her love for him had been a raging fire inside her. She had wanted to be his fantasy. Give him everything he wanted. *I don't know what made me answer. I had promised myself I would never ask you for that, but…you were very persuasive. I admitted that I had always wanted to fuck you in the ass.*

Traci nodded. Yes, he had. And she had been scared to death; but again, willing to do anything. And God, it was good. *I expected you to be shocked, but you smiled at me and left the room, and then you came back naked, carrying a bottle of lotion. You locked the door and climbed up onto this table, and scooted to the edge. You rubbed lotion all over my cock, and then squirted it into your crack. God, Trace! Writing this, I'm hard as a rock!* Traci bit her lip, wishing she had been there, to crawl onto his lap and take him inside her...she shook her head, returning her attention to his note. *You were hesitant, at first, but then...God, I couldn't believe how much we both wanted it. Your ass, then your pussy, then your ass again. All night long. We almost didn't get the presents out before Amy came down Christmas morning, remember? And Chase was born nine months later.* The writing ended there. God, did she remember! Reaching back into the envelope, she fished out several cards.

Open the SMALL box. Follow the instructions. Traci removed a third golden ring from a third silver-bowed box. This time, there was a different diagram, showing how to place the device on one's labium. The word 'Right' was written on the bottom. Traci immediately sat down in her sewing chair, no longer hesitant about fulfilling Rick's erotic demands. She splayed her legs and fastened the ring onto her right labium. *Mmmm.* She stood carefully and grabbed up the next card. *Now, open the BIG box.* Traci removed the lid from the bigger box. Inside were a long, narrow dildo and a small bottle of lotion. Traci breathed hard as she took them out and set them on the table. The third card read, *You know what I want.*

Traci closed her eyes. Why was Rick doing this? He was going to drive her crazy. She didn't want a *dildo*, she wanted *him*! She opened her eyes and stared at the toy on the table. A muted, insistent throbbing had developed in her anus. Some women didn't like anal penetration; but once she and Rick had tried it, Traci had enjoyed it immensely. And Rick had been very, very good; but they hadn't done that in a long time. She licked her lips. She glanced around, then laughed at herself.

There was no one here to see. Turning, she hopped up onto the side of the table. She squirted the lotion onto her hands and between her buttocks, then began massaging herself. She slipped one finger inside her anal rim, then two. Spread them gently to loosen the tight orifice. *Aaah.* Tendrils of arousal suffused her abdomen. She definitely missed this.

Taking up her new toy, she covered it with lotion and pushed against the opening. Gently at first, then more firmly as the tight hole stretched. *Mmmm.* Her present was slender and long. Very nice. *I wish Rick were here.* The throbbing wasn't muted anymore; it was a demanding, thunderous roar. Traci gasped and began thrusting the dildo in and out, taking it deeper and deeper each time. *So LONG!* Traci pumped quickly, furiously, as need swelled inside her. Relief came in the form of a massive orgasm, her anal muscles compressing convulsively on the hard length sheathed inside her. Traci lay panting on the table for a long time, sweat beading on her brow. Man, even without Rick, that had been *good.* She slipped the dildo out and sat up shakily, replacing it in the box. She'd have to remember to come back later and get it—she didn't want the kids coming across it.

She reached for the last card. *Maine, October, 1988.* Again, Traci didn't even have to think twice about what the card meant. She stood. The air was cool on her sweat-dampened skin as she left the room on weak legs and crossed the landing, padding down the stairs to the first floor. The fruit still nestled in her vagina created some very intriguing sensations as it shifted slightly with her movements. She crossed the kitchen and flung open the cellar door, making her way to the bottom of yet another flight of steps. There, on a round wooden table, was an open bottle of wine, nestled in a bucket of crushed ice. A wineglass etched with two hearts, entwined, stood beside it.

Traci knelt and picked up the bottle, reading the label. Just as she'd thought. She poured herself a drink (apparently Rick had tasted as well, because there was *only* enough left for one glass) and drank it down quickly, eager to move on to the next part of this wildly intoxicating night. She opened the usual envelope and pulled out a note and several cards. *I remember the night we conceived our first child.* Traci 's heart swelled as her eyes filled with tears. *We let that travel agent talk us into booking a week at that ancient inn in Maine, instead of the cruise we'd been considering. That cold front came through and we were trapped with a houseful of couples three times our age, sitting around playing cribbage and drinking hot chocolate. It was torture. Our last night there, we snuck down into the inn's cellar with two wine glasses and opened five bottles of wine, until we found one we liked. This one.*

We drank the entire bottle, and then I pulled off your gown. You knelt in front of me and wrapped your gorgeous big breasts around my cock. I grabbed one of the other bottles and poured some of the wine over us both. You teased the tip of my penis with your tongue every time I thrust into that valley, and my seed started spurting, and you drank every drop. You were so horny, I wanted to make you come. Right then. I didn't want to wait for my cock to recover, so I grabbed the empty wine bottle.

Traci's entire body burned with desire, every nerve ending buzzing with need. *I didn't know what you would think, but you lay down on the dirt floor, and I put the bottle between your legs. "Yes, Rick," you said. "Oh, God. Yes." Mmmm. I'm touching myself now, Traci, wishing you were here.* The note shook in Traci's hand. God, where was he? Why was he making them both wait? He should be here, with her. *I knelt between your legs, watching the bottle slide in and out of your pussy, my cock getting harder and harder until you came. I love watching your pussy when you come. Watching the way your juicy lips expand and contract, like a kiss. I wanted those lips to kiss ME, so I pulled out the bottle and my cock exploded inside you before you even finished climaxing.*

Traci's eyes blurred. How could Rick forget her birthday and their anniversary, but remember every word, every tiny detail, of these moments? The note ended there, and Traci picked up the first card. *Because I only remember what's really important.* Traci nearly dropped the card. He knew her *so* well. Knew what she would be thinking. She considered what he had written. Decided he was right. Remembering her birthday wasn't important; *forgetting* her birthday wasn't important. Cherishing the moments they had shared, cultivating those memories—*that* was important. Not wallowing in what was *missing*, but remembering what they *had*. After seventeen years, she was discovering that her husband had hidden depths. She had never suspected Rick still carried all this inside him—the love *or* the lust.

Traci wiped the tears from her cheeks and reached for the third card. *Use the bottle for me, baby.* Traci took a deep breath. She reached out and pulled the wine bottle from where she had stuck it back in the bucket. She lay back on the cold tile floor, legs splayed, and shivered as she placed the chilled glass rim inside her pussy. Tremors shook her body, and primal need reverberated through her core. Closing her eyes, she pumped the bottle in and out with one hand, rubbing her clit with the other. Her thrusts were quick and shallow to avoid damaging the cherries. Fierce heat burned in her abdomen, finally swamping her with another fiery orgasm. Traci lay on the floor, moaning as the aftershocks rippled through her.

She removed the bottle and sat up. Read the next card. *Open the box. Follow instructions.* Traci opened the box. When she had the fourth gold ring in its proper place on her left labium, she reached for the last card. *I'm watching you.* Was this her clue? Traci looked for another card, found none. Her cheeks flooded with heat. She surveyed the cellar, looking for Rick. She stood and walked between the shelves, hunting. He was nowhere to be found. What could he mean? She wracked her brain for some kind of idea, but came up empty. She turned and climbed up the stairs on legs like jelly, her body screaming "More!"

Chapter Four
Seduction

ဢ

Traci wandered through the house, searching for Rick, or for something that might stimulate her mind into recognizing the solution. She peered into the den, her gaze coming to rest on the television. Sudden inspiration hit. The people who had lived here before them had had a couple of on-site security guards, and there was a guardroom where they had monitored the cameras on the gate and the outside of the house. But it was at the bottom of the drive, just inside the gates.

Traci was too eager to take the time to put on something warm. Instead, she went out the front door and ran across the snowy lawn to the gatehouse. Teeth chattering, she opened the door and stood in the doorway, gaping. The room had been transformed. Banks of television screens covered the wall to her left and across from the door. A king-size bed snugged up against the wall to her right. In the flickering blue illumination from the screens, she could see a small, rectangular box on a desk in front of the consoles to her left. Traci walked over to the desk. The white envelope gleamed in the blue light. Traci tore it open. *Close the door.*

Traci's cheeks blazed. *Damn it, he DOES know me!* She definitely had a one-track mind, and the only thing on it when she had walked in was their little game. She hurried over and shut the door, then returned to the desk. *Press the green button on the remote.* Traci picked up the remote sitting next to a fifth small, white box and pressed the button that was flashing green.

The screens around her brightened, flashing images of her life. Pictures of her and Rick with their arms around each other, looking into each other's eyes, lost to the world around them. Rick, blinking back tears of joy, holding their babies in his arms. Video from parties, family gatherings, holidays, Chase's baseball games, Amy's ballet recitals. And Rick was present in far more of them than she would have imagined. Just a few years of neglect, and she had managed to forget all the times he *was* there. There were shots she'd never seen before, as well. Pictures of her asleep, a disembodied hand — Rick's hand — reaching into the frame to caress her cheek. Shots of Rick sitting beside her on the couch, watching her while she read, love and tenderness radiating from him. Amy must have taken those. She'd caught the shutterbug when she was ten and was constantly sneaking around, shooting candid shots.

They were images of love, every one, and Traci collapsed into the desk chair, crying. The images disappeared, leaving blue screens once more. Traci picked up the second card. *Do you remember how much I love you?* Traci smiled through the tears. "Yes," she said, her voice firm and loud. She picked up the third card. *Carry the box over to the bed. Set the box on the bed, lie down, and close your eyes. Do NOT open your eyes until I tell you to.*

Traci carried the box to the bed. Setting it to one side, she lay back and closed her eyes. Within moments, a strong hand gripped her right arm, pulling it up and back toward the headboard. She felt something being wrapped around her wrist, and tied securely to the headboard. Traci swallowed nervously. *God, I hope this is Rick.* The process was repeated, three times. When her arms and legs were bound, she felt a weight settle at the foot of the bed. She heard faint whispers of movement. A moment later, Traci bucked as cold metal captured her clit in an inexorable grip. Traci whimpered.

"Does it hurt?" Rick's voice, thank God.

She nodded, not trusting herself to speak, hoping he could see her in the pale illumination. A fingertip flicked across the tip of her throbbing nub, and Traci gasped. Several minutes passed, and Traci couldn't hold back a sob.

"Still hurting?"

"Yes," Traci whispered.

"Maybe this will help." Traci felt Rick's knuckle brush across her clit as he hooked his finger in the ring and pulled it away from her body, its tight grip drawing her clitoris with it. "Oh, God!" Traci clenched her fingers around the ties that bound her hands. Her clit moved up and down, back and forth, then in slow circles, as Rick pulled on the ring. Pain transformed into pleasure, and Traci moaned. "Oh, God, Rick. Yes."

His finger circled faster and faster. "Yes, Rick. Yes!" Just when Traci felt she couldn't take any more, he pushed the ring into her, grinding her clit against her pubic bone. "Oh!" she cried. "Rick!"

Traci arched her back, and Rick let go of the ring as he watched her cunt spasm repeatedly, glistening wetly in the flickering light. He licked his lips and leaned in. Grasping the rings on her labia, he pulled them aside, exposing her pulsing, velvet folds. Hungrily, he plunged his tongue into her pussy.

Before the last echoes of the first climax had faded, Traci came again. Rick smiled to himself as her pussy milked his tongue. When the spasms had passed, he used the rings to pull her lips as far apart as possible. Searching her warm wet cunt, he found a cherry stem and grasped it with his teeth. He pulled it from her, dropping it on the bed, then immersed himself again—finding each stem, slowly pulling the slightly crushed fruits from Traci's feverish cavern, to the music of her breathless cries. He ate each one, savoring their salty-sweet flavor; then dove into her pussy again, drinking her juice, nipping her exposed flesh, until she screamed. Her pussy clenched, juices gushing into his eager, questing mouth. Licking her taste from his lips, he inhaled the scent of her sex deeply. "Aaaah, you smell so good."

He sat up. "Open your eyes," he commanded. Traci opened her eyes and found herself staring into the ravenous gaze of a man she thought she'd lost. He picked up something from the bed, and lights came on, though he kept them somewhat dim. Traci watched as he set aside the remote and rummaged in a bag hanging from the bedpost. He crawled over her, straddling her stomach. Holding out his hand, he let a strand of gold cascade through his fingers.

Traci watched raptly as he slipped the end of one strand through the nipple ring on her right breast and fastened it to a band around the middle finger of his left hand, then did the same with her left breast, fastening the chain to his right middle finger.

He rocked his hands back and forth, allowing the gold links to ripple over the ultra-sensitive peaks of her nipples. Traci sighed contentedly. Rick raised his hands, pulling Traci's peaks up with the golden strands. The rings gleamed in the soft light—stretching, pinching, until she moaned.

"Shall I stop?" Rick asked.

Traci shook her head, beads of sweat appearing on her brow. Rick jiggled the golden links, making her nipples dance like marionettes. Traci cried out in pleasure. Rick stretched her nipples out over and over again, releasing the tension each time he felt her approaching a climax, until her body was covered in a fine sheen of sweat and she begged for release. "Please, Rick. Please. Let me come," she whispered brokenly. He locked her gaze with his, pulling and stretching, moving her nipples in slow figure eights, his own excitement growing as her eyes darkened with sultry heat. Traci bit her lip as the orgasm hit, but didn't look away, and Rick watched a storm of passion raging in her eyes. He groaned as he felt her stomach muscles clenching beneath his buttocks, and his semen fountained over her chest.

He climbed off of her, hands shaking as he unfastened the chains from his fingers, withdrawing them from the golden loops. He licked shimmering droplets from Traci's chin, her neck, her chest. Her ripe nipples beckoned, and he sucked them, teasing their tips with his lips, tugging gently on the rings with his tongue. Traci breathed faster, and Rick sat up, absorbing the sight of her arousal. Her nipples gleamed wetly, like shiny, dark pearls.

Groaning, Rick moved back between her legs. He untied the restraints from the bedposts and pushed Traci's knees out and back. Reaching into his bag of tricks, he removed a large plastic bottle. He squirted lubricant onto her buttocks. "Oh, yes," Traci exclaimed, as her anus began throbbing insistently again. "Yes, Rick." Grinning lasciviously, Rick massaged the oil into her plump cheeks. Turning his hand sideways, he ran his finger rapidly up and down between them.

The warming friction drove Traci wild. She began clenching and relaxing her muscles, making her anus pucker and contract as Rick drew his finger across it. "Oho!" Rick exclaimed. He met her gaze and parted her cheeks. "Do it again," he said. "I want to see."

Traci complied, memorizing the look of wild lust that arose on Rick's face as he watched the pink pucker move, as if blowing him kisses. "God, Trace!" He couldn't wait any longer. He eased his cock into her, burying himself to the hilt in her luscious ass.

"Yes!" Traci screamed. His hot, hard flesh was so much better than a toy. "Yes, Rick. Yes!" She wiggled her hips. "Fuck my ass."

It had been a long time since Rick had taken her this way — *any* way, for that matter — and he couldn't imagine why. It felt so *good*. Despite the self-preparation he'd had her engage in earlier, her canal was narrow and tight, tugging on his cock as he backed out slowly. Oh, God. He'd forgotten how *fantastic* this felt. He had intended to take his time, savoring the experience, but Traci was yelling, "Fuck me, baby! Please. Fuck me!" Her screams ignited a fierce, carnal lust deep inside him. He cored her, grunting with each thrust. "Yes. Harder! Yes!"

A red haze blinded Rick as his cock gushed, his essence flowing into the only woman he had ever loved. Traci held her breath, pumping her anus as Rick's cock pulsed inside her, pouring his seed onto the fire of her need. Rick looped one finger through her clitoral ring, wanting; no, *needing*, to make her lose control. For him. He twisted the ring left, right, then left again.

Traci arched, her body spasming, her anal canal tightening like a vise on his deflated penis. Unbelievably, he felt himself firming again, his cock expanding inside her. Traci writhed on the bed. She could feel Rick's returning erection, his hot flesh filling her.

Rick didn't want to come again so soon, and knew he would if he stayed inside her. He pulled out, despite Traci's startled protest. He tied her legs to the bed again, then grabbed the remote and dimmed the lights. He lay beside her on the bed and whispered in her ear. "There's something I want you to see."

The bank of screens came to life again, each one displaying an image of Traci, licking her nipple, her tongue playing with a gold ring. "What—" Traci watched, open-mouthed, as the picture changed, to one of her carefully placing cherries in her crotch. The next frame was her, prone on the floor in front of her grandmother's mirror, legs tight and rigid as she climaxed. Another flicker, and she was holding onto the attic banister, legs trembling as she came again on her way to the sewing room. He had recorded *everything*. This explained all those lights. She turned her head. "I can't watch, Rick."

"Yes you can." He took her face in his hands and turned it back toward the monitors. "See how beautiful you are." He pushed sweat-soaked strands of dark hair back from her cheek, watching her carefully. Her breath quickened as the image of her reamed itself with Rick's toy. Then, an image of her pussy expanded to fill each screen, her hand plunging the bottle in and out of the dripping slit between her labial rings, her finger swirling frantically on her clit. "Oh, God," Traci moaned.

"See, Trace?" Rick whispered, kissing the rapidly beating pulse in her neck. "You even turn yourself on. How can you think I would even *look* at another woman, when I have *this* at home." The camera panned up to her face. "That look alone is enough to drive a man wild!"

Traci moaned again. His warm breath caressed her ear. She wanted to look away; but damn it, he was right. Watching herself — horny, gasping, thrashing on the cellar floor — incited incredible lust. She felt her juices running from her cunt, soaking the sheets beneath her. Rick watched as her breath came more and more rapidly. He slid his hand down her belly and slipped two of his fingers into her pussy, watching her face. Traci turned her head to look at him, her expression desperate. "Please, Rick. Take me." Rick's balls tingled. "Please. I need to feel your cock inside me." Her voice shook. "Please!"

Rick pressed a button, pausing the images, and removed the restraints from Traci's arms and legs. He coaxed her onto all fours on the bed, facing the longest wall and its bank of monitors. "So we can still watch," he murmured in her ear. He resumed the playback.

Rick's long, thick cock slowly inched its way into Traci's pussy. On the screens, she watched video of him eating her cunt, torturing her nipples, pounding himself into her ass. "Rick!" she cried out, her voice thick with need. Rick was fucking her shallowly, teasing her vagina with the tip of his cock. "Deeper," she pleaded, watching as the images on the screen flashed again. And then she was watching herself real-time, watching as Rick buried his cock in her pussy from behind. The images speeded up, cycling faster and faster. Flashes of nipple and pussy and cock and cum. "Faster, Rick!"

Rick's cock burned with need as he pumped in rhythm with the swiftly changing images. "Harder!" Traci screamed.

Rick pulled out and flipped her onto her back, hammering into her, hard and fast, gasping with the effort of holding back. He wanted to come when *she* came. Traci moaned and wrapped her legs around him. His pelvis pounded against her clit, the ring there flipping and pulling, twisting and rubbing between them. "Oh, God!" She dug her nails into his back. "Oh, God!"

Rick gasped. Traci's labial rings were hard and insistent, running up and down the sides of his cock as he fucked her. He didn't know if he could hold back much longer. Suddenly Traci arched, melding her hips to his. Rick speared her one final time and froze, limbs locked, as his seed spurted. They remained that way, drowning in forgotten sensations, swimming in an orgasm that seemed to last for hours. Finally, they collapsed against the bed.

Rick cupped Traci's face with his hands, kissing her lips tenderly.

"I love you so much," she whispered.

He traced the curve of her eyebrows, her cheekbone, her jawline with his fingertips. "I love you, too," he whispered hoarsely. "Do you believe me?" He stared into her eyes.

Traci nodded. "It's just that…it had been *months*, and—"

"I know." Rick spoke between quick kisses he was planting all over her face. "I'm sorry. I can't believe I let myself get so caught up in my work. I can't lose you, Trace."

Traci sighed and snuggled against his shoulder. "How did you film me?"

Rick pointed toward the ceiling and Traci noticed for the first time a series of tiny cameras mounted along the room's perimeter. "The house is wired, too."

"How did you do all this? When?"

"I've had a team working on it since the week after Thanksgiving. They've been coming in during the day, while you were at work, leaving before the kids get home from school."

Traci shook her head, amazed. Then another thought occurred to her. "How are we going to *afford* all this?"

Rick smiled. "You are looking at the new *President* of Corporate Accounts."

Instead of congratulating him, Traci grimaced. "What is it?" he asked.

"This means we'll see even less of you than before, doesn't it?"

Rick sat up, meeting her frown with an earnest expression. "No, Trace. I can send guys like me to placate the customers. And, I'm connected to the office from here now. I'm going to be doing a lot more work from *home*." He turned up the lights and waved toward the desktop, his gesture encompassing a computer monitor, keyboard, cable modem, fax, and other equipment Traci didn't recognize.

"Promise?" Traci asked in a skeptical voice.

"A promise I'm *not* going to break," he insisted. "And if I start slipping, just show me one of these rings." He gave her nipple rings a playful tug, and his voice deepened with passion. "I *guarantee* I won't be able to resist."

Traci inhaled deeply. The scent of sex hung heavily in the air. "We can't let the kids see this place."

"I know. As far as they're concerned, this is my office now. Locked, unless I'm in it." He ran his hand down Traci's abdomen, feathered his fingers along the inside of her thigh. "Let's go to bed," he murmured, dimming the lights again, and Traci shivered at the sensual promise in his voice.

Chapter Five
Fulfillment

෨

Several weeks later, Rick glanced up at the consoles above his desk and smiled to himself as he watched his wife. Sitting in the library, she was reading intently. He rested his chin on his hand and thought to himself once more how lucky he was to have a wife who had cared enough about their marriage to *talk* to him about their problems, rather than walking out. Their passion had come full circle, and he couldn't imagine how they had ever let it be otherwise.

Traci had taken to wearing her hair down again, sleek and shiny. It made her appear softer, more approachable. In the past few weeks, the tightness around her lips had disappeared, the laugh lines were back around her eyes. Rick's gaze followed the dark strands spilling across her chest down to the gentle rise of her breasts beneath a shirt unbuttoned far enough that he caught a tantalizing glimpse of one pale swell. As he watched, Traci set the book aside and looked up at the camera in the corner of the room. Her recliner was positioned so that she faced it squarely. Grinning wickedly, she stood and unbuttoned her shirt slowly, exposing her naked breasts. She unzipped her pants and let them fall to the floor. Sitting back, she elevated the recliner and spread her legs.

Rick's cock twitched. The kids had left earlier to visit with his brother's family. He and Traci would have the whole weekend to themselves. Fierce desire flickered within as he activated the zoom, centering on his lovely wife's crotch. To his pleasant surprise, she was wearing her rings. Her hand entered the frame, two slender fingers spreading her labia apart. Rick's breath caught as she displayed her pussy for him. Then, catching her clitoral ring between her thumb and forefinger, she swirled her clit in languid figure eights. Rick zoomed out again. Traci's eyes were closed as she reached up and began playing with the nipple ring on her left breast as well. Opening her eyes, she stared directly into the camera. Pulling her breast up to her mouth, she circled the dark peak with her tongue seductively.

Rick glanced toward the big bed behind him and grinned. Pushing away from the desk, he exited the room and strode up to the house to collect his sexy wife. With love, determination, and the help of five tiny golden circles, they were ringing in the season all year long.

Also by Rachel Bo

ༀ

Double Jeopardy
Symphony in Rapture

About the Author

❦

Rachel Bo began writing at a very early age. Previously published in local newspapers (general interest articles) and science fiction/fantasy magazines (fantasy fiction), Rachel was unable to devote the time necessary to completion and marketing of novel-length titles. After years of working in the science field of the private sector, creativity won out and Rachel switched to a part-time job in order to devote herself to writing. Within six months, she had made her first book sale. Though her projects to date have technically been contemporary romances, most do incorporate elements of fantasy, science fiction, or the paranormal. Rachel is also working on several full-blown fantasy stories and a menage-a-trois series.

Rachel welcomes comments from readers. You can find her website and email address on her author bio page at www.ellorascave.com.

Tell Us What You Think

We appreciate hearing reader opinions about our books. You can email us at Comments@EllorasCave.com.

THE TOYMAKER
R. Casteel

൭

Chapter One

♠

1875, Coatsville, Missouri.

The wind howled through the trees, sending the snow swirling around the corner of the house and across the porch. A sudden gust ate its way under the windowsill stirring the curtains. Samantha turned away from the scene and went back to the fireplace.

She looked down at the still, sleeping bundles of her two children and sank her heavy girth wearily beside them. Christmas was only a few days away and despair weighed heavy on her shoulders.

"I've been a fool to stay on here." She smoothed a wisp of hair from her daughter's face. "But it was the only thing your pa left us, and now, it looks like even what little we have will be taken away."

Bitter resentment welled up inside her breast at the thought of the worthless bastard. He had only done two things right in his life and both of those were sleeping within arms reach.

There were days when she could have killed the man for leaving them with nothing and running off with his lover. The fact that she was ten years younger and a hundred pounds lighter didn't help her self-esteem. His cleaning out their meager savings and riding off on their only horse had sunk her emotions even lower.

Samantha had thought things couldn't get any worse. Time had proved her wrong with the whisperings and sly looks of the other women in town. No matter what *they* thought, it wasn't her fault he left.

"I always hoped your pa would come to his senses and come home." She pulled the blankets closer around her son and stared with longing into the crackling flames.

A man from Coatsville had ridden three miles to deliver the news. She could still remember the words of the telegram ending those feeble hopes.

Sorry to inform you your husband has been shot and killed. Stop. Personal possessions will be sent to you along with any monies after funeral expense paid. Stop

Nothing had been sent, and she doubted it ever would.

Coatsville wasn't much of a town. A clapboard building housed the dry goods store, post office and telegraph. A saloon, livery, hotel and scattered houses made up the rest of the small Missouri settlement. Everything centered on and around the coal mine, even the need for the coloreds who stripped the black ore from the ground.

Samantha lifted her head. "What the...?" She was hearing things. There was no way anyone would be out on a night like this. Hearing the muffled tinkle of bells again, she climbed to her feet and hurried to the window.

In the dim glow of light shining out through the window, she saw a horse standing in the shadows. On its back, a man's head appeared out of a large wrap of some sort.

Throwing a blanket around her worn flannel nightgown, Samantha hurried to the door. Bracing herself, she stepped out onto the porch and into the face of the battering wind. The cold bit through the blanket and swirled underneath her gown, sending their icy fingers up her leg.

"Ma'am, can I trouble you for shelter?" He moved closer to the porch.

What she had thought was a horse was in fact a large pony. "Put your horse in the barn, there's not much hay but you're welcome to what you need." She motioned to the dark shadow of the small barn. "Come into the house when you finish, sir. You must be nearly frozen."

"Thank you kindly, ma'am." The stranger turned the horse and headed for the barn.

"My word, what can the man be thinking of, riding out on such a horrible night." Samantha opened the door and ducked back inside. She was so cold, she was afraid she wouldn't be able to pee without first thawing out her puss.

Samantha added more wood from her dwindling supply to the fire. Things had been difficult enough with a husband. She had done the best she could by herself but was forced to realize it hadn't been enough.

Dropping the blanket, she looked down at her worn, threadbare gown. It hung off her like a feed sack. All her clothes did. How much weight she had lost, she had no way of knowing, but she had dropped at least two dress sizes. Ensuring the children had food had been paramount, even to the giving up of her own.

She wished she had a robe but that had gone to make warm pajamas for the children. Samantha grabbed a dress as the door opened and the stranger stepped in. Clutching the material to her breast, she tried to hide her near nakedness from him. By the amused and somewhat embarrassed expression, she knew she had failed.

"Ah, thank you for your hospitality. I hope it's not a burden on you," he glanced down at the floor, "or your family."

She had to look down at him. Her nearly six-foot frame towered over him by at least two feet. Back east, she had seen midgets at the circus, but having one in her house gave her a moment of pause.

"Is your husband home?" He pulled off a heavy fur coat and unwrapped a long scarf from his head.

"I have no husband. He died sometime back."

She tried not to stare at the man, but found it near impossible. He had a full head of long flowing white hair, his matching beard nearly obscured his face, and his black-as-coal eyes twinkled back at her.

"Allow me to introduce myself, good lady." He bowed at the waist. "I'm Claudius Elfenstine. I was on my way to the North Country when I became lost. Sadly, I will not make my destination by Christmas."

"I'm Samantha Woodall, and these," she swept her hand towards the fireplace, "are my two children, Rachel and Jake Jr."

"I must say," Claudius stepped closer to the fire and held out his hands to the warmth, "your lighted window was a pleasant and welcome surprise. Even more so is this marvelous fire."

"You are welcome to stay until the storm breaks." For some reason that she couldn't quite fathom, she felt relaxed with this stranger so near. Slowly, Samantha lowered her arms and placed her wrinkled dress back on the shelf.

"We don't have much, but we'll be glad to share with you. Provided you aren't too picky on the fare."

"I am forever in your debt, Mrs. Woodall. It would be an honor, and please, call me Claudius."

"Only if you drop the Mrs. and call me Samantha. If you will excuse me I will get some bedding and place it here near the fire." She hurried to her cedar hope chest and dug out the last remaining blankets.

Claudius backed away from the fire as she knelt beside her son. As she made his bed, she looked up at him. His eyes were riveted on her and she suddenly remembered the fire behind her and the thinness of her gown.

Embarrassed all over again, she felt the heat rising from her breasts and up her neck. She started to turn her face away when she noticed the bulge of his groin. That he was becoming sexually turned on was obvious, and given the situation, understandably normal. It was the size of his erection that kept her eyes on his crotch.

He made no move to turn away or shield himself from

her and she watched as his swelling cock reached to mid-thigh. "I'll...ah, be just a minute."

"Take your time, Samantha, I find I'm in no hurry to lie down."

It was getting hot in the room and it had nothing to do with the fire. Averting her eyes, she tried to shake out a second blanket but found her fingers unwilling to cooperate.

"What is your business that takes you out so close to Christmas?" It was really none of her business, but she needed some time to regain her composure.

"I'm a toymaker by trade. I delivered some toys for Christmas and was on my way home."

"That's a shame, I'm sure your family will be disappointed." Samantha finally got his bed made and stepped back. "I hope this will be sufficient, Claudius."

"I...have no real family." He pulled off his black knee-high boots. "And it will more than do. Thank you."

Samantha crossed to the other side of her sleeping daughter and lay beside her. Partially closing her eyes, she felt a pang of guilt at watching Claudius prepare for bed. He looked at her for a moment, turned his back to her, and removed his red plaid shirt and homespun trousers. His shoulders were surprisingly broad for such a small man and his muscles rippled with each movement.

He wore farmer johns like every other man in the territory, but the similarities ended there. As he sat down and stretched out on the blanket the front of his underwear stuck out like a tent. Even in the dim light of the fire, the large head of his cock was plainly outlined against the material. Claudius pulled the other blanket over him.

Her mouth went dry and for the first time in more months than she wanted to count, she felt the wetness of desire between her legs.

"Good night, Samantha."

His voice seemed strained, almost painful. Licking her

lips and taking a deep breath, she replied, "Night, Claudius."

Turning on her side, she pulled the blanket back over her daughter. He turned towards her, watching her every move with eyes that seemed to penetrate her soul and discern her most secret thoughts.

Are you still hard? The question charged through her mind with the swiftness of a stampede. She lowered her gaze to hide the need she felt.

"She has her mother's beauty." His soft words drifted across the short distance.

"Claudius, I fear the cold has affected your eyesight," she whispered. "This body is tired, worn, and any beauty I may have had, soon fled under the harshness of the land."

"Ahh, my dear lady. That is where you are wrong. I see beauty in the touch of your hand as you protect your children from the cold. It's in your eyes as you look upon their faces and are fearful for their plight. I am a stranger and you took me in, offered food for my horse, and provided a bed beside your fire."

"Please, Claudius," she begged. "Enough of your blarney. I did what was right and decent."

"No, Sam," he said the word almost reverently. "Only a woman of great beauty and courage would do what you have done. I will not soon forget your kindness."

He smiled at her, closed his eyes, and was just as quickly asleep. His words, simple as they were, warmed her heart and lifted her spirits. It had been a long time since anyone had called her beautiful.

The sound of running water roused her. Peeping through sleep-encrusted lashes, she noticed the fire had been freshly tended. Lifting her head from the pillow of her arm, she looked to find the source of the noise that had awakened her.

A startled gasp escaped her lips. Claudius was using the chamber pot and his exposed cock was even larger than she could have imagined. He turned away from her, but even that couldn't hide the length hanging between his legs.

It was the first adult cock she had seen in many a moon. Samantha knew she should avert her eyes, but was unable to do so. Her heart began to race beneath her breast at the thought of taking his full length inside her. If she even could.

"My apologies, Samantha. The need was so great, I never thought about you waking up."

"Understandable, Claudius." The words sounded like mush to her ears, and she wondered what he must think.

For the second time tonight, she was wet. Only this time, she could smell the strong musky scent of her own need seeping out from under the covers. Can he smell it too? What am I going to do?

He shook himself off and stuffed his cock back inside his farmer johns. Claudius lay on the bed facing her, and his eyes gave her a slow, searching, questioning gaze as they traveled over the length of her blanket-clad body. She felt naked before him. Her breasts ached as the rise and fall of her chest rubbed her nipples against the fabric of her gown.

He knows! I can see it in his eyes.

With one last, hot penetrating look, he turned over and faced away from her.

The return to sleep wasn't that easy for her. Samantha tossed and turned upon her bed with visions of his cock, dancing in her head.

"Mommy! Mommy! There's a strange little man outside splitting our firewood."

The excited voice of her five-year-old daughter pulled her out of a sensual dream. The steady ring of an axe disrupted the stillness of the small cabin. A fire blazed fresh in the hearth and the aroma of fresh coffee filled the air.

Coffee was one item she considered a luxury and had refused to buy any more when so many other things were needed worse. She breathed in the strong fragrance with relish.

Steam rose from the heating tank of the kitchen stove. With Claudius chopping wood, it gave her time to clean herself up and try to make herself a little more presentable.

Ten-year-old Jake stood at the window, raptly watching the scene outside. "Children, that is Mr. Elfenstine. He got lost in the storm last night and will be spending a day or two with us. Jake, finish getting dressed and help him stack the wood please."

Jake hurriedly put on his coat and ran out the door. It was only then that she realized the extra weight on her. Claudius's heavy fur wrap lay over her. Running her fingers through the thick white fur, she wondered about it. Pictures from her childhood flashed through her mind of huge polar bears.

Samantha got up, and with excitement welling up inside her, went to the stove. Taking a quick peek outside, she debated taking a hurried sponge bath. Privacy in a small cabin was almost non-existent, but it wasn't her son she was anxious about.

Pouring a cup of strong black coffee, she took a sip and sighed. "Mmm, that's good." Drawing water from the tank, Samantha took her last bar of lye soap and stripped off her gown.

In her haste to rinse, she took her eyes off of Claudius for a moment. As she reached for a somewhat wrinkled but clean dress, the door swung open. The small piece of cloth she used to dry with did nothing to hide her nakedness from his eyes. Time seemed to stand still.

"Excuse me," he stammered.

As quickly as the door had opened, it swung shut. Embarrassed, flustered and with her hands shaking, Samantha pulled the material over her head.

Chapter Two

∞

Claudius picked up the axe, swung it in a wide arc over his shoulder and sent wood chips flying several feet away. No matter how hard or how fast he drove the blade into the wood, he couldn't shake the image of Samantha standing naked only a few feet from him.

He felt the unmistakable tightening of his trousers as his cock hardened. There was only one problem. Unlike other men, he couldn't shift it to a more comfortable position. There just wasn't room.

The frontier required sturdy women and Sam was defiantly that. At least six feet tall, with wide shoulders and a supple amount of flesh, she heated his blood far more effectively than any physical labor ever had. What would it be like to lay his head on the pillow of her breast?

Last night, the silhouette of her against the light of the fire had done little to prepare him for seeing her in the flesh. Her breasts were large, full, and had very little sag. The dark pink nubs of her nipples were easily the size around of his little finger and stuck out invitingly, as if pleading to be touched and suckled.

He looked at the stack of cut wood and quickly realized that although it would look impressive to some, it would in fact last only a short time with the long, dark days of winter still remaining. And there was no more to be split.

With a sudden insight born from years of service, he knew getting lost in the storm had not been an accident. He had been carefully manipulated and guided every step of the way. Thinking of Samantha and how she heated his blood, this was one time he didn't mind a bit.

"Run along to the house, Jake. I can smell breakfast cooking." He patted the boy on the shoulder. "Thanks for your help."

"You're welcome." With his nose glowing like Rudolf, Jake looked up with a big, wide-toothed grin. "Mom's a good cook."

Claudius walked to the house with his arm around Jake. "I'm sure she is good at everything she does." Setting the axe back behind the woodpile, he entered the cabin behind Jake.

"Claude done split all the wood, Ma." Jake's eager young voice filled the room.

"Wasn't that nice of him to do?"

Her eyes bored into his with such a fierce intensity that his heart started to race within his chest. The tension within the cabin elevated with each passing second. Even though she wore a long blue flower print dress, he pictured her in all her natural womanly beauty.

Claudius held eye contact with her longer than propriety allowed. A soft pink began to flush her skin and creep up her neck.

Samantha dropped her gaze. Her blush deepened. The tip of her tongue wetted her lips, and she began to fidget nervously. Ever the protective mother, her eyes darted from the children to him, pleading for patience and understanding. Her mouth silently formed the word, "Tonight."

Even with the shortened winter days, nightfall and the children's bedtime seemed like a lifetime away.

"Thank you, Claudius." His name oozed like honey from her lips. "I haven't had any coffee grounds in the house since their Pa left us." She poured him a cup.

He was quick to notice the subtle change of the word died to left.

"Sit down, children, breakfast is ready." Sam took a ladle, put a portion of grits on the plates and added a small egg to three of them.

Claudius edged around the table to pick up his cup. Giving a quick glance into the pot, he noticed it was empty and there was barely any food on her plate. The situation here was worse than he first imagined.

Thank God I arrived when I did.

The children sat with their backs to the stove. Sam stepped between him and the table. Her eyes went blatantly to his trousers and the hard shaft of his cock now jutting firmly down his leg. She lifted her face to his, and he saw the hunger in her eyes. With a nervous glance over her shoulder, she reached for him.

Her hand shook like the coiled tail of a rattler.

Samantha touched his crotch and lightly trailed her fingers down his ridged length. His hand tightened around the battered tin cup. Claudius clamped his jaw shut to keep from groaning out loud.

"Mommy, we're done."

He saw the regret in her eyes as she snatched her hand back and whirled around to her children. "Jake, you have chores to do. Make sure you look real good this morning. You know how Red likes to hide her eggs."

"Maybe Rachel would like to go too and help feed my horse?"

"Could I? Please!" She flung her arms up and down in excitement.

"It's may I, and yes, you may. Just don't get too close," she warned.

"Don't worry, Samantha, Rachel will be perfectly safe. Penelope is as docile as a lamb around children." Claude reached into his pocket, pulled out a sugar cube and handed it to her. "Give her this, and she will follow you around like a little puppy."

Sam's eyes wistfully followed the sugar cube, and she licked her lips.

Within minutes, both children had donned their jackets, scarves, and mittens and were headed out the door. As it closed behind them, she turned and sat on the thick wooden bench they had just vacated.

Her hand lifted, reaching out to him. Claude held up another sugar cube, and she stopped with her arm suspended in mid-air. Her eyes narrowed as he brought the sweet confection closer to her mouth. He placed the small white square between her parted lips.

Sam's eyes drifted shut in delight as the sweetness bathed her tongue. A soft moan of shear pleasure floated from her lips as she savored what he suspected was now a rare and all-but-forgotten treat.

She captured his fingers and brought them back to her mouth. "It's been a long time." With long slow strokes of her tongue, she licked his thumb and forefinger for any lingering grains of sweetness.

"Long time for what…sugar or sex?" His cock throbbed with anticipation as she sucked on his finger.

The heat of passion lit up her face. "Both." Lifting her other arm from her lap, her fingers closed around his swollen cock. She took the fingers she had been sucking on and placed them over a breast.

"I want you, Claude," her voice shook. "Tell me, is there a wife waiting for you at home?"

"No, not anymore." A shudder racked his body as her fingers toyed with the head of his shaft.

Placing a hand behind her head, he leaned closer and placed a soft kiss on her lips. Claude broke contact but didn't pull away. "I want you too, but I'm afraid we haven't time this morning."

"I know." Her voice echoed his regret.

With his second kiss, he allowed more of his desire to be known, just in case his erection wasn't proof enough. Her lips parted with only the slightest pressure of his tongue, and he tasted the sweetness of her mouth.

Samantha's free hand moved up his side and curled around his neck. Her fingers threaded their way through his hair and tightened on his long white locks. Claude captured her tongue and sucked on it, drawing it fully into his mouth. Her breasts pressed against his chest, and he longed to touch and fondle them.

She used the pause to loosen a button. "Touch me. Please."

Slipping his right hand in the opening of her dress, he found her flesh hot to the touch. At the center of her generous breast he found her nipple already swollen and he rubbed it between his thumb and forefinger.

"Oh! Claudius." She swayed towards him.

He moved his left hand along her leg, gripped the hem of her dress, and pulled it up over her knee. His fingers glided across her bare leg, dipped under the material, and up along the soft tender flesh of her inner thigh.

Muscles quivered beneath his fingers and she spread her legs farther apart. He reached the apex of her thighs and the thick mound of hair between them. The hunger in her eyes flared, and she whimpered. She was damp with need.

Claudius dragged a finger down the long cleft in her flesh. Her head fell back on her shoulders, and her breath came in short, open-mouthed gasps. Samantha rocked her hips against his hand, sending first one finger, and then a second one into her hot wetness.

Her eyes grew large and her breasts heaved as he inserted yet another finger into her. "I have small hands, Samantha. I'll be gentle."

The sound of children's laughter stopped him just short of having his whole hand inside her pussy. With deep regret, Claude stepped back and watched a flustered Samantha arrange her dress.

"Mommy! Mommy!" The door flew open with a bang.

"Penelope ate the sugar and let me sit on her and gave me a ride inside the barn."

"That's great, Rachel."

Neither child seemed to notice Samantha's flushed skin and heavy breathing, or the fact that she wasn't looking at them but stared in awe at his hand. Claudius lifted his wet fingers to his mouth and slowly licked away her musk.

She made an effort to regain her composure and turned to her son. "Jake, did you collect all the eggs, feed the chickens and the geese?"

"Yes, Mother."

"I don't see the milk pail. You know how important it is to keep ole Betsy milked twice a day. Last night you barely brought enough back for supper."

Jake looked nervous and glanced around the room. "I tried to milk her, honest. She didn't have any to give."

"Maybe she sprung a leak," Rachel suggested.

In spite of the seriousness of the news, Samantha smiled and gave her daughter a hug. "Cows don't leak, hon." She closed her eyes but not before he saw the pain and sorrow flash across them. "They go dry."

"But she might have."

"Rachel, why don't you take me out to see Betsy? Maybe she's sick or something." Claudius held out his hand.

"Could I give Betsy a sugar cube?" She latched onto his fingers and pulled him towards the door. "I know it would make her feel better."

"I'm sure it would. Now, why didn't I think of that?" Claude paused for his jacket and followed Rachel out the door.

Out in the barn, Claudius produced another sugar cube from his pocket and watched as Rachel eagerly fed it to the family milk cow. From the back corner of the building, he heard the squawking of the geese.

With the young girl holding his hand and skipping along beside him, Claudius went to investigate. In a pen, he found seven snow-white geese. He propped his foot on the lower board of the pen and stared at them.

"Do you eat them?" he questioned out loud.

"Sometimes." Her little face saddened. "But I don't like to." Then in child-like wisdom she added, "It's okay to eat their babies, but not these. They're pets!"

"Oh!"

"Yes! We raise the baby goosies during the summer and barter them off in the fall for winter supplies. Only this year a bad fox got in and killed all the babies."

"I see." With a plan forming in his mind, he took Rachel's hand and led her back to the house.

Chapter Three

๙

Samantha sat trembling from the encounter with Claude. Her response to him frightened her, while at the same time she wanted more.

"Ma, are you feeling okay?" Jake asked with worry written across his face.

"Yes, son. I'm fine." Standing, she patted him on the shoulder. "I guess I got overheated standing so close to the stove."

He glanced at the empty frying pan on the stove. "You really need to eat more, Ma."

"I will, Jake." Samantha pulled him into her arms and gave him a hug. "I promise." *Just as soon as one of those geese lays a golden egg.*

Gathering up the dishes, she carried them to the washtub and added hot water from the stove. The door opened and Claudius and Rachel shook the snow off their boots and entered.

"Rider coming, Sam." Claudius glanced out the window. "Doesn't look like a drifter."

Wiping her hands dry, she went to the door, wrapped her shawl around her and stepped out on the porch.

He was a tall man, with a waxed handlebar mustache, black topcoat and hat. The white silk scarf wrapped around his neck seemed out of place on a cold winter day. His horse halted in front of the porch.

"Mrs. Woodall." He doffed his hat and then stepped out of the saddle. "I'm William James, I own the coal mine near here. Sorry to hear about your husband. The Missus sent this over." He lifted a large string-tied sack from the pommel and handed it to her. "She thought you might could use a few things."

"The children and I appreciate your kindness, Mr. James. Please, tell your wife thank you for me. Won't you come in?"

"Thank you for your offer, but I need to be going." Mr. James stepped into the saddle, briefly touched the brim of his hat and rode back the way he came.

Reentering the cabin, the children clamored around her.

"What's in the bag, Mommy?"

"Ma, who was that man?" Jake asked in a grown-up attitude.

"The owner of the mine. His wife sent these over." Untying the string, she pulled out a five-pound sack of flour, one of salt, and a slab of home cured bacon. In the bottom of the bag there was a jar of apple jelly, blackberry preserves, and a package of horehound stick candy.

Samantha took one stick, broke it in half, and gave a piece to each child. Their eyes lit up and big smiles spread across their faces. She wiped futilely at her tears and looked up at Claude. With a twinkle in his eye, he leaned against the stone fireplace.

"Do *you* know anything about this?"

"Me?" He shrugged his shoulders. "Never seen the *man* before today."

Thinking of the candy for the children, Samantha remembered the sugar cube that Claude had promised for Betsy. She could have sworn the pocket was empty when she had brushed her hand across it earlier. But then, her mind *had* been on something else inside his trousers.

"May we go outside and play, Ma?" Jake asked.

"Bundle up first and watch your sister...and stay away from the river bank. You know the ice on the Chariton isn't to be trusted." Samantha sat on the bench-seat near the stove.

"Yes, Mother," Jake frowned. "I know that. I'm not a baby like Rachel."

"I am not a baby!" Little Rachel huffed and put her hands on her hips. "Am I, Claude?"

"No, Rachel." He laughed at her antics. "But you're too little to be playing near the river without an adult."

The door closed behind the children and she turned to Claudius. "I swore I'd never stoop to begging again, but you've reduced me to it." She started unbuttoning the top of her dress. "I don't want to wait until the children go to bed. Please, Claude." She knew she must sound pathetic, but she didn't care.

The distance between them closed until he stood in front of her and stepped between her spread legs. Samantha pulled the top of her dress open, raised the hem up to her waist, and offered herself to him.

He lifted his hands to her nipples. Strong work-calloused fingers stroked and twisted them to her exquisite delight. He lifted her heavy breasts, pulled and squeezed them, and then lowered his mouth to suckle at her throbbing flesh.

Samantha's fingers fumbled with the buttons of his trousers. Unhooking the last button, she pulled his pants down to his knees.

Claudius's teeth raked her nipple and she lowered her face into his hair as the sensation sent a hot flush over her skin.

Reaching inside his farmer johns, her fingers wrapped around the massive shaft of his cock and wrestled it from the confining cloth. "Oh! My!" Her thumb and forefinger barely touched.

Claude's heated breath bathed her breast as he chuckled.

She slid her hand up his long shaft and her fingers flowed over the bulbous wet tip. His hips jerked, and his teeth closed hard on a nipple. Claudius instantly laved it with his tongue and kissed her marked flesh.

Guiding him with her hand, Samantha rocked her hips to receive him. She jerked her head back as he slid past the outer lips of her pussy.

"Oh! Oh, Claude!" She was suffocating, being ripped apart, and falling all at the same time. Her body stiffened in climax and she leaned on him, trembling with release.

"I'm…sorry." Samantha whimpered into his hair.

Claude lifted his head and kissed her. "For what, being a woman who needs passion in her life?" With a twinkle in his eye and a funny little twitching of his eyebrows, he continued sliding deeper inside her. He paused, allowing her body a chance to adjust to the massive size of his cock.

He started moving inside her, slowly pulling out and then easing his throbbing cock back inside her. Samantha floated on a sensuous cloud of contentment. It was nothing like she had ever experienced in her life.

Hot, hungry lips captured hers. His tongue delved into her mouth to touch and tease hers. Samantha captured his tongue, sucking on it, and swallowing his soft animal-like groans.

Claude's hands roamed over her breasts and tweaked her nipples, sending sensuous jolts of pleasure to the fleshly wall surrounding his cock.

Her fingers curled around long tendrils of his hair, holding him in place as she ravaged his mouth. Through the sensuous haze building around her, Samantha sensed something…different. His hips drove hard against her thighs, and she pushed it aside. Whatever it was, she would deal with it later. For now, all she cared about, all that mattered, was the feeling of Claude inside her.

Leaning her back against the table, she rocked her hips, meeting his every thrust. His wild eyes bore into hers. Low guttural moans and harsh breathing filled the air.

She climbed with him up passion's spiraling staircase. Reaching the top, she grasped the table as her hips lifted from the bench in a wrenching climax.

Claude's hands grasped the cheeks of her ass and with one last, hard driving thrust of his cock, she felt him explode inside her. His heat filled her, washed over her, and left her shaking in the aftermath of contented desire.

He sagged against her breasts, resting his snowy head on their fullness. Claude placed a tender kiss on a nipple.

"The children are coming." His eyes held regret as he pulled out of her, stuffed his wet cock back inside his farmer johns and pulled up his pants.

Samantha gathered the material of her dress together, buttoned it and tugged the hem down over her knees.

He leaned close, kissed her cheek and whispered in her ear. "Tonight, after they are asleep?"

"Yes!" she answered almost breathlessly. Even with the proof of his climax slowly running down her leg, anticipation of their next time bubbled up inside her.

The door opened and she pulled herself out of her fantasy world as reality came bolting through the door, scattering snow across the floor. With a sigh, Samantha got up and began preparations for their noon meal.

"I noticed this morning that you need more wood." Claude took his coat from the rack by the door. "I'll take Penelope down to the river and see if I can find some to drag back."

She saw the "no argument, you can't talk me out of it," look in his eyes and in the set of his jaw. "Thanks, Claudius. I...*we*, appreciate your help."

He left, and she watched him trudge through the snow towards the barn. A few minutes later, mounted on his small but sturdy pony, Claudius rode towards the nearby line of trees marking the bank of the Chariton River.

Samantha busied herself around the kitchen. The soreness between her legs was welcome after the many months of forced abstinence. Her one and only regret, Claudius would soon be leaving.

Sleigh bells attached to Penelope's bridle announced his return. She stared in amazement at the two large logs being pulled behind the animal. Its muscles bulged and strained against the load. Snow flew from its hoofs with every step.

With an axe across his shoulder and his other hand resting gently on Penelope's neck, Claude whistled as he walked beside the animal.

A heavy sigh escaped her lips. Fresh bread baked in the oven and a small pot of beans sat cooking on the stove. *I suppose I should be thankful. If it weren't for Mr. James's visit...* She let the painful thought trail off unfinished.

The door opened and Claudius walked in carrying three fat rabbits. "I hope you don't mind, but I invited these to come for dinner."

She felt like crying. She wanted to run, throw her arms around him and give him a big kiss. Samantha took them from his hand. "Thank, you, Claude. There's always room at the table for guests who hop in. Course, they will have to change and get washed up first.

"Jake, you know what to do with these." She handed them to her son.

In the afternoon, she stood across from Claudius as they pulled and pushed the large two-man bucksaw through the logs. He never seemed to tire but always conscious of her needs, he called several welcome breaks during the long, hard grueling work.

That evening, after supper, Claudius picked up his heavy fur wrap. "I'll be in the barn if you need me."

With the children fast asleep in their beds, Samantha wrapped her shawl around her and headed for the barn.

Curious as to what he had been doing, she slipped silently inside.

The soft glow of the lantern cast a halo of light around him. Woodchips flew from the knife in his hand. On a wooden plank in front of him, sat a beautiful wooden flute and the block of wood he whittled on had the beginning shape of a doll.

Samantha bit her upper lip to keep from making a sound as his thoughtfulness brought tears to her eyes. As she watched his strong skillful fingers bring the doll to life, he laid the knife down and ran his hand through his hair. Her startled gasp sounded loud in the quiet stillness of the barn.

"Oh! There you are." He turned his head towards her and a broad smile spread across his face. "I'm making these for Jake and Rachel. Christmas is only a couple days away."

"I know." On shaky, unstable legs, she crossed the hard-packed floor to stand beside him. "They're beautiful. The children will love them."

Her fingers trembled as she reached down, brushed aside his hair and uncovered his ears. "You're an..." She couldn't bring herself to say the word. It was impossible. *They don't exist.*

"Elf," Claudius finished for her. He looked up at her with a twinkle in his eye. "I suppose you don't believe in the *Magic of Christmas* either."

Chapter Four

ᶒ

"Magic, I'm not even sure I believe in Christmas anymore." Samantha shivered, backed up several paces and crossed her arms over her breasts.

"You're freezing." He held his large bearskin wrap open and saw the hesitancy in her eyes as they shifted to the door and back again. "Please."

Her feet seemed to move her closer against her will. She glanced from his ears to the woodcarvings lying in front of him. Claudius gave her a reassuring smile.

"You're a real *Elf.*"

"Yes, Samantha. I'm a real, live Elf. Now, would you *please* sit down before we both catch our death." He patted the space beside him.

A new wave of shaking sent her teeth to chattering and she sat beside him. Claudius gently wrapped the fur around them. Samantha picked up the wooden flute, turned it over and around in her fingers, and set it down. She did the same with the doll, lightly skimming the tip of her index finger over the small delicate features of the face.

"Thank you, Claude." She handed the doll to him.

Their fingers briefly touched and he ached to hold her. "It's my pleasure. They're great kids, and I think their mother is pretty wonderful, too."

She sat there for several minutes while the doubts and fear mounted inside him. Samantha turned her head, slowly lifted her hand and once again brushed the hair from over his ears.

"Sam." Her eyes shifted to meet his. "They're real, I'm real, and our making love this morning was most assuredly real."

Her hand lowered, brushed the side of his coat, and lingered for a moment before moving away.

Reaching into the same pocket, he pulled out a sugar cube and held it to her lips. "Is this what you were looking for, Sam?"

Her lips parted, her tongue crept out to wet her lips, and then as quick disappeared. "Take it."

Trance-like, Sam opened her mouth, and he placed the cube between her lips. "It's as real as this is, Sam." He took her hand and placed it over the hard shaft of his cock.

Her eyes brightened with passion. "Is that part of the magic?"

It was like she was asking if he was real, or just an illusion. He could sense her need, as great or greater than his own, struggling with her new discovery.

"It was magic this morning, at least it was for me." Although her lips were close, Claudius held back.

"For me, too," she whispered. Her warm breath caressed his cheek.

With the light squeeze of her fingers around his cock, his willpower evaporated like the white vapor of their mingled breath. He wasn't sure who moved first, but it didn't matter. Her warm luscious lips covered his and the coldness of the night withdrew, driven away by her heat.

Her fingers pulled and tugged, undoing the buttons of his trousers and farmer johns as they moved to the nearby hay. Claudius lay back on the soft fragrant bed of clover and lifted his hips. Hungry hands pulled at his clothes, and he was soon naked beside her.

Samantha lifted her dress, pulled it over her head and knelt beside him. Her hand went to his crotch, and her fingers fluttered over the swollen head of his cock. His body stiffened in response and a low groan of pleasure rumbled in his chest.

She lowered her head, her tongue replaced her fingers as she licked and covered his aching shaft with wet kisses.

Claudius ran his hands over her generous full figure, cupped her breasts and rolled her nipples between his thumb and forefinger. The expelled breath of her sigh bathed his balls in heat.

He grasped her hair and pulled her face up to his. His lips sealed over hers, and his tongue delved into the warm recesses of her mouth. With reluctance, he let her break the kiss.

"I've been wet all afternoon with thinking about you," she whispered against his ear. Samantha brushed his hair away from his ear, her fingers traced the flared, slightly pointed tip, and then she placed a lingering kiss on it.

She moved away, got on her knees and rested her head on the hay. "I need you inside me."

Claudius rose up, scooted between her legs, and slid the head of his cock between the wet lips of her pussy. Her ass wiggled as he slid slowly deeper into her, giving her time to stretch and adjust to his size.

"I like the way you fill me, Claude," she moaned.

"It's pretty amazing for me, too." He ran his hands over her wide hips and down across the cheeks of her ass. He eased out of her, testing her readiness, and then drove his hard shaft into her with more force. Her body shuddered, she gasped, and the muscles surrounding his cock tightened.

Sam's wetness surrounded his cock like a warm silk glove. With each thrust of his hips, she grew wilder and ground her flesh against him.

"*Mmmm…Ohhh!*" Her low moans filled his ears, driving him on, even as the pounding beat of his heart threatened to overcome and silence them in his mind. Through the obscuring, sensuous fog, he heard her wanton begging.

"Harder…Claude! Fuck me…harder!" She emphasized each word with a backward push of her hips forcing him to comply with her desire. He grabbed her waist and held on as she bucked and ground against him.

His body stiffened, and in one last plunge into her depths, the night exploded around him in rolling waves of molten heat. Her responding climax tightened around him, coaxing another heated flush of release.

Claudius collapsed beside her and pulled the fur back over them. She snuggled close as he gave her a kiss.

"I've decided it doesn't matter who, or what you are." She whispered in a contented sigh. "You could be Santa Claus and right now, I could not care less."

Claudius chuckled. "Mrs. Claus might object rather forcefully if I were. This time of year, he's so busy that even she complains about the lack of sex."

Samantha rose up on one elbow. "There really is a Santa Claus?"

"Yes," he kissed her nose, "if, you believe in the magic of Christmas." In the dim light of the lantern, he saw her smile.

"I'm beginning to believe." She kissed him and gave him a hug.

Her breast pressed against him and he thought how wonderful it would be to wake up as the sun came peeking through the cracks in the siding and have her beside him.

She sat up and reached for her dress. "I need to check on the children."

"Will you come back?"

"When must you leave?" She looked at him with longing.

"Soon," he sighed. "I can stay tomorrow but then, I must go."

"That doesn't leave much time, does it?" Sadness filled her eyes.

"No, it doesn't." He lifted his hand and stroked her cheek. "I wish I could promise more, but I can't."

Samantha pulled the dress over her head and wrapped

her shawl around her shoulders. "If I can...I'll be back." She stood to leave, paused, and picked up the long, slim flute. "I'll miss you when you're gone. Could you make something for me to remember you by in the long, lonely nights?"

"Name it, and it's yours."

Claudius saw the heated flush of her skin and she turned her face away. "Make me a carving of...your cock."

He was momentarily taken back by her request. "I've never made anything like that...but for you, Samantha, I will."

"Thank you." She hurried from the barn.

She couldn't believe she had actually made the request and further surprised that he had agreed. Samantha rushed through the snow, her feet already freezing in her thin worn-out boots. Knocking the snow off her feet, she eased the door open and entered the relative warmth of the cabin. Thinking the children were asleep, she crouched in front of the fire and added more wood, banking it to burn slow through the night.

"Ma," Jake's voice startled her, "does he make you happy?"

His mature question didn't really surprise her. Children grew up quick out here. Too quick really, they didn't have much opportunity for childhood happiness. She had found it pretty elusive as an adult.

"Yes," she smoothed his hair, "Claude makes me very happy."

Jake smiled up at her. "Good, I'm glad." He rolled over and closed his eyes. "Ma, Claude will be leaving soon, won't he?"

"Yes, son, he will."

"Why don't we have Christmas Dinner early while he is still here?"

"Jake, that would be nice...but what could we fix?"

She saw his face scrunch up and a tear escape from behind his tightly closed eyelids. "A goose," he whispered.

"We'll see, son. Go to sleep."

Samantha stalled for time, checked on the children and the fire one more time. She placed her hand on the door latch.

"If you're going back to the barn, Ma, you might want to take a blanket." She thought he had gone to sleep. "I'll watch over Rachel."

"When did you get to be so grown up?"

"When Pa ran off with that floozy, and I had to be the man of the house."

Samantha stepped through the door, and her tears froze on her cheeks. She entered the barn and Claudius looked up. His smile disappeared, replaced instantly with concern as he jumped to his feet, and hurried to her.

"What's wrong, Samantha?" He wrapped his arms around her. "Is something wrong with the children?"

"No, they're fine." She held his head against her breast. "I could use a little magic right now."

Claudius led her over to the hay, and she sat beside him and told him of Jake's comments. He held her in his arms without speaking, letting her empty her burdens on his broad shoulders. After all, there was nothing he could do, and it wasn't his responsibility.

Samantha looked over at the crude table. "You've finished the doll. It's lovely. I know Rachel will love it. Thank you."

Claude stuck the carvings under the hay. "Come, Samantha." Taking the blanket from her hands, he spread it over the hay. "It's getting late."

They undressed, crawled under Claude's fur, and cuddled up close. Samantha ran her hand along his face and her fingers softly combed his beard. Leaning closer, she kissed him.

"Goodnight, Claudius," she whispered.

"Goodnight, Samantha."

An inner contentment crept over her. The feeling, strange as it might be, brought mixed emotions. She knew he was leaving, and she didn't want him to go, but he was an Elf.

With his head pillowed on her breast and his hot breath bathing her nipple, Samantha sighed and drifted off to sleep.

Chapter Five

ಸಂ

Predawn light showed through the cracks in the barn turning the floor into a shifting mosaic of light and dark stripes. Samantha placed a tender kiss on Claudius's lips, crawled from under the covers, and quickly dressed.

Fresh wood chips lay on the wooden plank.

He opened his eyes, stretched, and gave her a big, wide smile.

"Morning, Claude. I didn't mean to wake you, but the children will be needing breakfast soon."

"Morning, Sam. I'm glad we had last night together. I'll cherish the memory always in my heart."

"You sound like you are leaving."

"My dear, Samantha. I don't want to go. Nothing would please me more than to wake up every morning with you beside me, but…"

"I know." She turned away. It had been only a matter of time, but her heart ached that it was so soon. "Will you stay for dinner?"

"Yes."

She hurried from the barn before she gave way to tears.

Back at the house, Samantha stomped the snow off of her feet and opened the door. Jake was tending the fire and had water heating in the stove. He took one look at her, walked over and put his arms around her.

"He's leaving."

"Yes, son." She patted his head.

"Can't you make him stay?" he asked.

"*No!* Claudius has things that he has to do." She leaned over and placed a kiss on the top of his head.

Jake dropped his arms, and Samantha stepped to the cabinet, removed the small hatchet and laid it on the table.

"I'll do it, Ma."

"Are you sure?" She watched her young son pull on his coat and boots, and pick up the hatchet.

"Yes! After all, it was my idea."

With a resolve that she was sure he was far from feeling, Jake opened the door and headed for the barn.

"Mommy, is Jake going to kill a goosie?" Rachel sat staring at the door.

"Yes, honey. It's for Claude's Christmas dinner."

Rachel jumped up and ran to her, barreling into her legs. Samantha scooped her up and sat on the bench.

"I don't want him to leave." She whimpered against her neck.

"I know, dear. I wish he didn't have to leave either." Samantha rocked her daughter.

Somehow, Claude had woven his way into the hearts of her little family. At least, she would have company in her misery when he left.

"There is a lot to do this morning. Let's get dressed and you can help in the kitchen."

* * * * *

Samantha headed for the door to call Jake and Claude for breakfast when they walked in. Claude carried the freshly plucked goose and by the frown on his face, he wasn't too happy about it.

"Breakfast is ready." She smiled in spite of the frosty stare from Claude and the, "I'm sorry, Ma," lowered eye glance from Jake.

"You want to tell me why? I appreciate the gesture, but if you think that I require this," he held up the bird, "then you are sadly mistaken."

With her lips trembling and hurt shining through misty eyes, Rachel walked over and took his hand. "It's our Christmas present to you. Don't you like it?"

Samantha watched his scowl soften at her daughter's question. He looked up at her with a pleading cry of forgiveness, sank to his knees, and wrapped his arms around Rachel.

"Yes, dear. It's a lovely present." Claude wiped at his eyes. "Thank you. It's about the nicest present...I ever received."

Rachel gave him a bear hug around the neck and Samantha knew it was going to be just that much more difficult when he left.

"Breakfast..." her voice caught on the lump in her throat, "is ready."

Samantha tried to keep the conversation light throughout the meal, but taut emotions kept the mood somber. All she could think about was how this was the last breakfast they would share, and how empty her bed would be without Claude.

"Jake, after breakfast you need to do your chores."

"Yes, Ma."

"Might want to check on Bessie," Claude suggested. "She might have changed her mind about giving milk."

Jake got down from the table, picked up the milk bucket and egg basket. "I will, but I don't see much use in it." With slow, weighted steps, he headed for the barn.

Samantha started clearing the table.

"Here," Claude took a plate from her hand, "let me do this. You have enough to do today."

She felt the contact of his fingers against hers and turned away, lest he see her desire and the hurt his leaving caused. "Thanks."

A few minutes later, the door burst open and Jake thundered into the house. "Look, Ma! A whole pail of milk." He lifted the nearly full pail to the table. "And...and there's more eggs than I could carry in the basket."

"Maybe it's *magic*." Rachel stared at the eggs.

Samantha gave Claudius a thoughtful glance. "It just might be that there is a little magic in the air. After all, it is almost Christmas."

Claudius gave her a wink and turned back to the dishes he had been washing.

Throughout the long morning, she worked around him. It seemed as if the house had shrunk in size. Time and again, Claude found excuses to be in the kitchen and each time, they just happened to touch.

She dropped the large basting spoon and sat on the bench. "I'm all thumbs today," she complained. "We'll be lucky if anything is fit to eat."

Claudius stepped between her legs, lifted her chin, and right in front of the children, gave her a long embrace. "I have no doubt that it will be fit for a king."

The children giggled.

He stepped away, and she was reminded just how lonely she had been, before Claude arrived, and how much worse it would be once he was gone.

Claude went and sat in front of the fireplace. Rachel climbed into his lap and laid her head on his shoulder.

"Do you love my mommy?"

Samantha's heart fluttered as she waited for his answer, one she had secretly wanted to know, but unlike Rachel, been afraid to ask.

He paused and Rachel took his silence as a no. "Why did you kiss, mommy?"

"People kiss for several reasons, Rachel." He turned his head and sought her face. "I kissed your mommy, because...I love her."

Her heart burst with joy over his words and just as quickly filled with sadness. Claude was still leaving.

"If you love her, why are you leaving? I don't want you to leave."

Samantha found herself standing beside them. She knelt and placed her arms around Claude and Rachel. "Honey, Claudius has to go."

"I'll be back, if I can." He wiped a tear from Rachel's cheek.

"Promise?" she sniffed.

"Don't make promises you can't keep, Claude." Samantha warned. "Dinner is ready. Get washed up." She stood and went back to the kitchen.

Dinner, what there was of it, turned out to be every bit as good as Claude predicted it would be. However, the golden bird and the few trimmings she had managed did little to lighten the somber mood around the table.

Claudius pushed his plate back. "Thank you, Samantha. It was the best Christmas dinner I've had in a long time."

He looked around the table and she saw him blink away a tear.

"If you will excuse me," he stood. "I need to get my things from the barn."

If she knew what to say to make him stay, she would beg Claude not to leave. She wanted to run after him and throw herself at his feet. *He's leaving, and there's not a damn thing I can do about it.* Samantha sat at the table, waiting for the inevitable to happen.

A few minutes later, she heard Penelope's bells and his footsteps on the porch. With a heavy heart, she stood to greet him one last time.

"You have made this a most wonderful Christmas." Claudius gathered her children to him. "I made these for you."

He pulled the doll from under the heavy fur rug draped across his shoulders.

Rachel squealed with delight and threw her arms around his neck. "Thank you, Claude. It's beautiful."

Next came the flute and he handed it to Jake. "Merry Christmas, kids."

The flute shook as Jake put it to his mouth and blew a shaky note. Tears came to his eyes and he flung his arms around Claude. "Please! Don't leave."

Claude gave each child a kiss on the cheek and stood. Samantha felt drawn towards him and dropped to her knees as his arms went around her. "I shall miss you, Samantha."

His lips sought out hers, and she responded with wild abandon as her children clung to them both.

"Your present is in the barn," he whispered in her ear, "under the hay where we slept."

Claudius gave them one last hug, picked up his gloves, and opened the door. She followed him outside and watched as he mounted Penelope. With a sad little wave, he rode off towards the north.

She stood there in the cold watching him ride away until he was swallowed up in the trees. This was worse than when her husband had left. Claudius's "I love her," trampled on the pieces of her broken heart.

"Go in the house, children." She stepped off the porch and started running through the snow towards the barn.

Inside, she knelt on the hay and remembered the passion that they had shared. Her hands dug impatiently through the hay. Her fingers came in contact with a smooth hard object and curled around it. Even without seeing what it was, she would know the shape anywhere.

Samantha pulled the wooden cock from the hay and held it to her breast. "Thank you, Claude." Lowering her head she kissed the smooth rounded head and ran her fingers over its length.

She was wet with need, and slipped it under her dress. A whimper escaped her lips as she rubbed the wooden cock against her pussy. "Claude!" She cried out loud as she slid it deep inside her.

* * * * *

Christmas morning after breakfast, Jake came running back into the house. "Ma! Ma, come quick, you have to see this."

Jake almost dragged her to the barn where she stared in amazement at her six geese, sitting protectively on nests full of eggs.

Epilogue

ɛɔ

Claudius stood before the man and looked down at his soot-blackened boots.

"I know you haven't been happy here since your wife died, Claudius. Since your return Christmas Eve, I've noticed you seem to be even more despondent. Isn't there an elf here to take as a new wife and make you happy?"

"No, sir."

"You willing to give up your elfin powers for this other woman and her children?"

"As long as I can still make toys for the children, yes, I am." Claudius held out against hope that he could still do the one thing that had meant so much to him.

"You presume to set stipulations on leaving?" There was a twinkle in his eye and his large belly shook. "That's what I love about you, Claudius. You know how to get to my soft spot. Go, my friend. Claim your woman with whom you have found happiness. Let your toys continue to bring laughter to children, and may you both find the joy of Christmas forever in your hearts."

Also by R. Casteel

❧

Cherry Hill

Ellora's Cavemen: Tales From the Temple II *(anthology)*

Forever Midnight *(anthology)*

Mistress of Table Rock

Tanieka: Daughter of the Wolf

The Crimson Rose

About the Author

⮞

Romance author R. Casteel retired from the US Navy in 1990. He enjoys the outdoors, loves to scuba dive, and is a Search and Rescue Diver. With twenty years of military service, which included experience as flight crewman, search and rescue, and four years as a Military Police Officer, it is of little wonder that his books are filled with suspense and intrigue.

As to his ability to write romance, Gloria for Best Reviews writes "I had thought Leigh Greenwood was the only man who wrote wonderful romance...I was wrong...Rod Casteel is right there too!"

Mr. Casteel lives in his hometown of Lancaster, Missouri, and would love to hear from you.

R. Casteel welcomes comments from readers. You can find his website and email address on his author bio page at www.ellorascave.com.

Tell Us What You Think

We appreciate hearing reader opinions about our books. You can email us at Comments@EllorasCave.com.

Why an electronic book?

We live in the Information Age—an exciting time in the history of human civilization, in which technology rules supreme and continues to progress in leaps and bounds every minute of every day. For a multitude of reasons, more and more avid literary fans are opting to purchase e-books instead of paper books. The question from those not yet initiated into the world of electronic reading is simply: *Why?*

1. *Price.* An electronic title at Ellora's Cave Publishing and Cerridwen Press runs anywhere from 40% to 75% less than the cover price of the exact same title in paperback format. Why? Basic mathematics and cost. It is less expensive to publish an e-book (no paper and printing, no warehousing and shipping) than it is to publish a paperback, so the savings are passed along to the consumer.

2. *Space.* Running out of room in your house for your books? That is one worry you will never have with electronic books. For a low one-time cost, you can purchase a handheld device specifically designed for e-reading. Many e-readers have large, convenient screens for viewing. Better yet, hundreds of titles can be stored within your new library—on a single microchip. There are a variety of e-readers from different manufacturers. You can also read e-books on your PC or laptop computer. (Please note that Ellora's Cave does not endorse any specific brands.

You can check our websites at www.ellorascave.com or www.cerridwenpress.com for information we make available to new consumers.)

3. *Mobility.* Because your new e-library consists of only a microchip within a small, easily transportable e-reader, your entire cache of books can be taken with you wherever you go.

4. *Personal Viewing Preferences.* Are the words you are currently reading too small? Too large? Too… ANNOYING? Paperback books cannot be modified according to personal preferences, but e-books can.

5. *Instant Gratification.* Is it the middle of the night and all the bookstores near you are closed? Are you tired of waiting days, sometimes weeks, for bookstores to ship the novels you bought? Ellora's Cave Publishing sells instantaneous downloads twenty-four hours a day, seven days a week, every day of the year. Our webstore is never closed. Our e-book delivery system is 100% automated, meaning your order is filled as soon as you pay for it.

Those are a few of the top reasons why electronic books are replacing paperbacks for many avid readers.

As always, Ellora's Cave and Cerridwen Press welcome your questions and comments. We invite you to email us at Comments@ellorascave.com or write to us directly at Ellora's Cave Publishing Inc., 1056 Home Avenue, Akron, OH 44310-3502.

COMING TO A BOOKSTORE NEAR YOU!

ELLORA'S CAVE

Bestselling Authors Tour

erridwen, the Celtic Goddess of wisdom, was the muse who brought inspiration to storytellers and those in the creative arts. Cerridwen Press encompasses the best and most innovative stories in all genres of today's fiction. Visit our site and discover the newest titles by talented authors who still get inspired - much like the ancient storytellers did, once upon a time.

Discover for yourself why readers can't get enough
of the multiple award-winning publisher

Ellora's Cave.

Whether you prefer e-books or paperbacks,
be sure to visit EC on the web at
www.ellorascave.com

for an erotic reading experience that will leave you
breathless.